Praise for *The R*

"Rich in local color."

"Barber's first novel is full of exq[illegible] New Mexico scenery."
—*Publishers Weekly*

"A strong sense of the city of Santa Fe and its environs and the appeal of the two well-developed main characters show why this mystery was the first winner of the Tony Hillerman Prize for the best debut mystery set in the Southwest." —*Booklist*

"Looking for an undiscovered gem? Christine Barber won the very first Tony Hillerman Prize . . . and now we have Barber's very good debut." —*The Globe and Mail* (Canada)

"A spellbinding mystery wrapped simultaneously in the gorgeous landscape and in the dark, hidden recesses of the Southwest. I kept turning the pages and holding my breath for what might come next. I was never disappointed. *The Replacement Child* is that good."
—Margaret Coel, author of *Blood Memory*

"Isn't it great when a new writer comes along and makes you sit up and take notice? Christine Barber does just that with *The Replacement Child.* Don't miss it."
—Michael McGarrity, author of *Nothing But Trouble*

"Smart, taut, psychologically convincing. Christine Barber has a sure hand with character and a strong sense of place. A fine choice for the first Tony Hillerman Prize."
—Susan Wittig Albert, author of *Nightshade*

"In this excellent debut, newcomer Christine Barber weaves a heartbreaking mystery with the assured hand of an old pro. *The Replacement Child* has many charms: it's a riveting procedural, a compassionate and perceptive study of human nature, and a wonderfully labyrinthine whodunit. But it's the heart of this story that is the real charmer: the fascinating landscape of northern New Mexico and the tangle of cultures, old and new, that populate it. I guarantee that if you let Christine Barber take you there once, you'll want to go back with her again."

—William Kent Krueger, author of *Thunder Bay*

"*The Replacement Child* is a gripping story set against the deceptive calm of an ancient land in modern times. In northern New Mexico, lives and events are interconnected, and Christine Barber weaves a tale where nothing is irrelevant and no one is unimportant. Barber is a wonderful storyteller and her characters invite us into their hidden places, compelling us to turn the page."

—David Sundstrand, author of *Shadow of the Raven*

"Barber writes with charm and gusto, having a special talent for depicting her main characters."

—*I Love A Mystery* (Highly Recommended)

THE REPLACEMENT CHILD

THE REPLACEMENT CHILD

Christine Barber

MINOTAUR BOOKS

A Thomas Dunne Book
New York

A THOMAS DUNNE BOOK FOR MINOTAUR BOOKS.
An imprint of St. Martin's Publishing Group.

www.thomasdunnebooks.com
www.minotaurbooks.com

The Library of Congress has cataloged the hardcover edition as follows:

Barber, Christine.
The replacement child / Christine Barber. — 1st St. Martin's Minotaur ed.
p. cm.
ISBN 978-0-312-38554-5
1. Women journalists—Fiction. 2. Elementary school teachers—Crimes against—Fiction. 3. Murder—Investigation—Fiction. 4. Santa Fe (N.M.)—Fiction. I. Title.
PS3602.A7595R47 2008
813'.6—dc22

2008023603

ISBN 978-0-312-62816-1 (trade paperback)

First Minotaur Books Paperback Edition: July 2010

10 9 8 7 6 5 4 3 2 1

To Tony Hillerman and the city of Santa Fe.
Thank you for the inspiration.

AUTHOR'S NOTE

The Spanish words used in this book reflect New Mexico's unique Spanish dialect and, as such, do not share all the characteristics of the better-known, modern-day Spanish. For instance, most Spanish-speakers today would say *"mi hijo"* when referring to their son, while Spanish-speakers from Northern New Mexico would say *"mi hito."*

Additionally in the book, the term *Hispanic* is used instead of *Latino* when referring to someone from Northern New Mexico who is of Spanish descent. While *Latino* is the term most used in the rest of the country, *Hispanic* is the preferred local term.

The moment I saw the brilliant, proud morning shine high up over the deserts of Santa Fe, something stood still in my soul, and I started to attend.

— D. H. Lawrence

CHAPTER ONE

Monday Night

Lucy Newroe hated the word *supererogation.* It was one of those ridiculous words you'd see in a *Reader's Digest* Word Power quiz. Like *quidnunc* or *sesquipedalian*—words whose only purpose was to make the user look smart and the listener feel stupid.

Lucy had no clue what *supererogation* meant, and she didn't know how to spell it. Obviously, neither did the reporter who had written the story she was editing—he had spelled it "superaregation." The spell check on Lucy's computer wanted her to change it to "super are nation," as if that made more sense.

Normally, she would have taken the word out, but it was in a direct quote: " 'The constant superaregation by the director bordered on the absurd,' said audience member Jake Plumber." There was no changing of quotes in news stories. Either she took the word out and paraphrased the quote or kept the word in and figured out how to spell it.

"Oh, hell," Lucy said to her computer. No one even turned to look. It was about 11:30 P.M. Her side of the newsroom was empty except for her and a lone reporter, while the copy-desk side was full of people working quietly. The story deadline had come and gone, but the page deadline still was an hour away. The dance-company review she was editing didn't need to be done until tomorrow. As the night city editor, she had to wait until the copy desk finished its pages before she could go home.

Lucy got up to look for a dictionary as her phone rang. She picked it up and rambled off her phone introduction without even thinking—"*Capital Tribune* newsroom. This is Lucy Newroe. How can I help you?"—as she tried to make the phone cord reach to the dictionary on the shelf.

"Is Harold there?"

Lucy recognized the voice. It was old and female. "It's just me in charge tonight," Lucy said as she grabbed the dictionary.

"How about Steve?"

Lucy smiled. Scanner Lady always wanted to talk to the male editors, never to her. "I'm it. You're stuck with me, I guess. What's going on?"

Scanner Lady hesitated. Lucy thought she was going to hang up.

"Well, I don't know," said the voice.

"Did you hear something on the police scanner?" Lucy asked, as she paged through the *S*'s in the dictionary—was it "supere" or "supera"?

"I think I did." Scanner Lady hesitated again. "I think I heard two Santa Fe police officers talking about calling in the OMI and the state police."

Lucy tossed down the dictionary and started taking notes. Calling in the Office of the Medical Investigator meant a dead body, and calling in the New Mexico State Police to investigate meant that whatever had happened, it might involve a cop. The state police automatically took over any case that concerned a law enforcement officer.

Lucy snapped her fingers at Tommy Martinez, the night cops reporter. He turned and looked at her as she pointed to her phone. He knew what it meant. He grabbed his notepad and ran over to Lucy's desk.

"So you heard the Santa Fe cops call out the OMI and state police?" She was repeating it for confirmation and so that Tommy could hear. He guessed who it was on the phone. "Thank God for Scanner Lady," he whispered, and started taking notes.

Lucy ignored him and said into the phone, "When was this?"

"Just a few minutes ago," Scanner Lady said. "I don't want to say any more. Just listen to your scanner."

But Lucy had been listening to the scanner—it sat on a shelf right above her desk—and she hadn't heard anything. It wasn't unusual for police scanners to pick up different traffic. There were two scanners in the newsroom—one on her desk and one in the photo department, twenty feet away. The one in photo picked up more calls from the city police, while hers picked up more county calls and an occasional cell-phone call.

But both scanners were quiet. The last call had been something about a truck full of teenagers skidding into an icy arroyo.

"Are you sure?" Lucy asked. "I haven't heard anything. Can you tell me anything more? What exactly did they say?"

"Just listen. I'm sure you'll hear it."

Lucy heard the finality in her voice, but she still had so many questions. Were the voices male or female? What made her think it involved the Santa Fe city police and not the Santa Fe County Sheriff's Department? Had they said whether the killing was in the line of duty or something else?

Scanner Lady always played it like this—never giving out all the information, not even her name. She called about once a week. It had become a sort of game for Lucy to figure out who she was. Scanner Lady's voice was old, raspy. Maybe a smoker? She was definitely Anglo. Once, Lucy almost got her to inadvertently mention what side of town she lived on, but Scanner Lady went into a coughing fit and hung up before revealing anything. She never mentioned having children or a husband. And she never gave her reason for calling in with her tips. Did she just need someone to talk to?

Most of the time, her calls amounted to nothing. But a few times, what she had heard had turned into a story. That was enough that Lucy never ignored her.

Lucy hung up and looked down at her notes. All she had written was:

OMI
State cops
Santa Fe
Dead body???

She looked at her watch—11:34 P.M. This was going to be tough. Tommy was already on the phone, trying to get hold of the night supervisor at the state police. He looked up at her and shook his head.

"Just give it your best shot, Tommy. We've gotten stories later than this," she said.

And they had. Just last week they'd had a stabbing at 11:45 P.M. and managed to get a ten-inch story in the paper by the 12:30 P.M. page deadline. But a story involving the possible investigation of a police officer and a dead body was something else. Getting that story during working hours was a chore; this late at night, it was next to impossible.

Lucy was too anxious to sit. She walked over to the copy-desk side of the newsroom and watched the editors design the pages for tomorrow's paper. Across the office, she heard Tommy unleashing his phone charm. He must have been talking to a female police dispatcher: he was laughing a lot—a teasing, swinging laugh. Lucy heard him say, *"A la ve . . ."* and then, *"No sé . . ."* He slipped between the local Spanish and English, busting out his best Northern New Mexico accent for the English. His vowels were twice the normal length, stretching out the words into a singsong lullaby. His English had no hard consonant edges and his Spanish was not quick-step Mexican Spanish, but the slow, taffy-pulling colonial Spanish still spoken in Santa Fe.

Tommy was a Northern New Mexico farm boy, the second youngest of nine from a family who had lived in the mountain village of Ojo Sarco for fifteen generations. His grandmother spoke no English, only the Old New Mexico Spanish, as did all his great-uncles and -aunts still on the farm. Tommy had been the first child in his family to finish college, although a sister had done time in a vocational school for paralegals. Why Tommy had decided to become a journalist, Lucy still didn't know. But he'd been born to it.

His technique for gathering news tips relied heavily on females and flirting. Tommy would tell the middle-aged female police dispatchers of his love for his mother's tamales and how he missed his sisters. He would tell the young female dispatchers about his love for country-western music and how he lived for the smell of a woman after sex. And in return, they would tell him anything.

Lucy jumped as one of the copy editors spoke.

"Lucy, you're making me nervous. Would you stop pacing?" the editor said without looking up as he typed in a headline.

She went back to her desk, sat down, and stared at the wall, trying to relax. The room was windowless, like the sensory-deprivation cells used by the KGB to break American spies. The newsroom was painted sea-foam green, with matching cubicle dividers splitting the space up into playhouse-size streets and alleys. The ceiling was low, with the obligatory fluorescent lights that occasionally strobed. The color of the walls and the artificial light gave everything an aquarium feel, right down to the wet, dank smell coming from under the receptionist's desk.

The building itself was a mishmash of old and new. Part of it was from the 1800s, the rest from the 1970s. The result was sloping tiled floors where an errant step up would meet three steps down. Walls stopped and started in random patterns. According to office legend, the *Capital Tribune* had been built on top of the graves of Spanish colonialists killed during the Pueblo Revolt, the odd bumps and angles of the floor made when the coffins were paved over. Some of the night press workers claimed that sometimes, late at night, they heard a woman crying and praying the rosary in Spanish. One of the advertising reps had once come in to work at dawn and supposedly seen a man gliding down a hallway dressed in the brown robes of a mission priest. Lucy wondered if you could use "saw a ghostly vision" as an excuse to take a sick day.

Lucy glanced over at Tommy as he hung up the phone, flipped through his Rolodex, and quickly dialed another number.

She heard him say, "This is Tommy Martinez, from the *Capital Tribune*. Who is this?" The person on the other end said something and Tommy smiled, saying, "Beth Ann? I don't think we've met. What's your last name?" Lucy shook her head. Poor Beth Ann, she didn't stand a chance. By the end of the conversation she would be telling Tommy everything, including when they would be getting together for drinks.

Tommy paused on the phone, waiting for Beth Ann's answer. "You're a Garcia? Are you related to Tony Garcia who works at Pep Boys? . . . No? . . . How about Sarah Garcia at the state land office? . . . No? . . . Of course, oh yeah, I know your sister. . . . Me? I'm from Ojo Sarco." Tommy started to laugh. "Yeah, the hillbilly Martinezes . . ." They continued with the expected Northern New Mexico greeting: determining if they were related or had mutual friends.

The Martinezes, Garcias, Vigils, Trujillos—all the native Hispanic families in Santa Fe—were related somehow, their blood intermingling through marriage for more than four hundred years. The Spanish conquistadores came to Santa Fe in the early 1600s, and the settlers followed soon after. A Garden of Eden, with a handful of Spanish Adams and Eves. The other Spanish colonies in America didn't survive the eventual flood of immigrants. But in Santa Fe, protected by high-desert sands and a wreath of surrounding mountains, there was no flood. The colonists planted apple orchards and built adobe churches, all the while keeping the Old Ways. They were not Mexican. Not truly Spanish. They were colonial Spanish. Castilian.

Lucy waited until Tommy hung up the phone. She walked over to him and he told her what she had expected to hear: He had called the state cops, the Santa Fe police, the hospitals, the Santa Fe County sheriff, and even the city of Española police. Nothing.

"Tommy, you're heading out to the police station tomorrow morning to do your cop checks, right? Maybe we can look into it more then," Lucy said.

Twice a day reporters went to the Santa Fe police station to look over the incident reports to see if anything warranted a story. In the hot sheets last week, there had been a small item about a man setting fire to his house and running around it naked while singing "Amazing Grace." It had made an amusing story and had been picked up by the national news services.

"Actually, the Gomez trial gets started tomorrow, remember?" Tommy said.

Lucy hadn't remembered. Sam Gomez had allegedly shot into a crowd of people during the Christmastime performance of *Las Posadas* two years ago, wounding the woman who played the Virgin Mary. The trial was attracting statewide attention and had to be covered.

She thought for a second. "I'll do it. I'll go to the police station tomorrow morning before I come into work."

Tommy looked surprised. According to newspaper etiquette, editors didn't do grunt work. She should have assigned it to a different reporter instead of going herself.

"I have to get up early anyway," she added.

Tommy looked doubtful but said nothing. He wished her good night as he left.

Lucy looked down at her desk. The dictionary stared back up at her, still opened to *S.* Lucy sat down and pulled the dictionary to her.

She found it right after *superduper. Supererogation,* with one *o* and two *e*'s." It meant "the act of doing more than what is required or expected."

She smiled to herself. She really did have to get up early—sort of.

Patsy Burke sat in her easy chair, flipping channels. It was almost one A.M. She stopped when she reached *Law & Order,* her husband's favorite. It was a rerun, but she didn't mind. Her memory being what it was, it would seem new to her. She smiled at her joke.

A detergent commercial came on, but the announcer's voice was too high for her hearing aid, so she muted the sound. As she watched a voiceless laughing woman get stains out of her skirt, Patsy thought about the conversation she'd had with her granddaughter three days ago.

"Grandma, what would you have been if you could have been something?" Brittany had asked. Brittany was doing a school project on choosing a career. *As if babies her age should be thinking about such things,* Patsy thought. *They should be making zoo animals out of straws or pasting oak leaves onto construction paper.*

But in the end, Patsy had played along.

"An astronaut," she said, thinking that it would please her. Brittany loved Justin Timberlake and—since the family had gone on vacation to Cape Canaveral last summer—space exploration.

"No, Grandma, you hate flying. Now really think this time."

So Patsy thought.

She'd been born during the Depression and had grown up practical. What was that Doris Day song? "Que Sera, Sera"? Patsy had never been to college. She and John had married straight out of high school. The day after their honeymoon to Kansas City was over, she moved out of her parents' farmhouse and into John's parents' home. But she had dreamed of college, even though her mother had always said, "Don't live beyond your means, or dream beyond your dreams." One of the town girls Patsy went to high school with had gone to college, but the girl had dropped out after only four months to get married. Not that the girl would have had much of a choice. In their day, proper women picked from only two careers—nurse or teacher.

Now her granddaughter was asking her to make the choice she'd never had. Patsy said the first thing that came into her head.

"A newspaper reporter."

Brittany seemed pleased.

Since then, Patsy had played the game by herself, changing her chosen profession from day to hour. So far she had been a police officer, a beekeeper, a nurse, a florist, a professional traveler, and a TV news anchor. Today it was a talk-show host for the geriatric set, an Oprah in her eighties. "Okay, audience, today our topic is dentures." Patsy smiled, thinking she would tell her next-door neighbor Claire that one.

The show came back on and she turned up the sound. It was about a small boy who had been killed. As they showed the boy's body, she realized that he looked like George. Patsy quickly turned the channel. She flipped stations until she was sure that the shot of the dead boy was over, then settled back down to watch.

At least the tears hadn't come this time. She hadn't thought of George in months. She wondered if that meant she was forgetting him. She closed her eyes and leaned back, trying to remember the last time she had thought of him. But she couldn't. She got up slowly, her bad hip giving her a twinge. She tried to do the yoga breathing that Claire was teaching her. Something about breathing into the pain. But after a few puffs of breath in and out, she gave up and walked stiffly to her bedroom. She pulled open the drawer of her nightstand, rattling a few prescription bottles on top of the table. She opened the the cover of her white-covered Bible and pulled out four photographs. The top one was in black-and-white. George smiling back at her.

He was only a year old in the picture. George hadn't cried at all when the flashbulbs went off, making that loud pop. He'd hammed it up, smiling even more. The photographer had called him "a natural." John hadn't wanted her to spend the money at the photo studio, saying that they should wait until the family Christmas picture. But there had been no more family Christmas pictures. Four months after the photo was taken, George was trying to catch pollywogs in the creek by their farm, with John nearby putting up fence posts. George was blue when they found him in the water.

That had been more than forty years ago. They had never discussed it. She and John had packed up the farmhouse and moved to Wichita within a week. For two years they lived in a small apartment with only one room and rusty pipes. She was never able to scrub out the rust stains from the porcelain sink. The floorboards creaked so badly that Patsy barely moved while she stayed at home all day, finding ways to silently iron, cook, and clean. As if any noise might remind her that George was dead.

Patsy pulled out the picture underneath the one of George. It was of her and her sons John Junior and Harold running in a sprinkler in front of a ranch-style home. On the back in her writing was: "Home. 1961. John Jr., 8. Harold, 6." They had bought the house and moved out of the apartment as soon as she got pregnant with John Junior. The house had been built in a new subdivision. All the homes looked alike and had big grass yards. John fenced their yard in as soon as John Junior could walk. When the boys started elementary school, they wanted to take swimming lessons at the high-school pool with their friends, but John said that they couldn't afford it. Patsy didn't ask him about it. Instead, she and the boys spent the summer days running and jumping in the sprinkler.

The next photo was of John in his long-sleeved police uniform. She turned the photo over. It said, "Wichita, Fourth of July Parade, 1963," in her handwriting. John had been on the force almost twelve years by then. He looked tired in his navy wool dress uniform. He had just made sergeant a few months earlier and the extra pay went into their mortgage.

The last photo had been taken just a year ago, during a family reunion at John Junior's house in Albuquerque. Patsy sat in the middle. Her two sons on either side with their wives, her six grandchildren, and two great-grandchildren. Seven-year-old Brittany was her youngest grandchild. John Junior's young second wife had wanted more children. Patsy took off her glasses and looked at the picture more closely, the photo almost touching her nose. She smiled. She looked pretty good for an eighty-two-year-old great-grandma. But she looked odd standing with her family without John next to her.

She and John had retired to New Mexico six years ago to be near John Junior. They had searched for homes in Albuquerque but finally settled in Santa Fe, where the homes were more expensive but the higher altitude was better for John's health. Within three years, he died of a stroke. Her friend Claire said that retirement had killed John. And Patsy thought that might be true. He had wandered around the house all day, thinking up projects to do and then not finishing them. Out in the garage, there were still some bookshelves he had been making.

She heard a noise out in the living room and limped out

of her bedroom, once again trying Claire's yoga breathing. It still didn't work. The squealing was coming from the police scanner next to the easy chair, momentarily hurting Patsy's hearing aid. She muted the volume on the TV and turned up the scanner.

"Medic One, 1225 San Francisco Street, elderly woman with chest pains." Patsy wrote down the call in her journal and said a quick prayer for the woman.

Lucy drove around the block a few times before she found a parking space in the dim light. It was just after 11:30 P.M., but the streets around the Cowgirl bar were still filled with cars. She sat in the front seat, prepping herself in the rearview mirror; she reapplied her lipstick, brushed her hair, and tried to do something creative with her black eyeliner, managing only to poke herself in the eye. She wiped the eyeliner away, but now it looked like she had a case of pink eye. Very attractive. Oh well, at least the red made her eyes look more blue. Accentuate the positive, right? She bent over in her seat and adjusted her breasts in her bra—a burlesque move she had been doing since she was fourteen. When she sat back up, she had cleavage.

She got out of the car and headed through a wrought-iron gate that was almost off its hinges, past a cobblestone courtyard, and into the crouching adobe building. The Cowgirl was packed. She scanned the tables for the copy editors she was supposed to meet. The adobe-brick walls were painted a sickly salmon color and covered in 1950s photos of cowgirls in short fringed skirts and red lipstick. The chandeliers were made of the antlers of deer and steers. Behind the copper-tin bar was a brass wall hanging of a naked cowgirl lounging seductively on a saddle. It made Lucy think of chafing.

The crowd was a mix of locals taking advantage of dollar-beer night, tourists in town for the ski season, and convention-goers with their name tags still on. A woman named Lisa Smiley—if her name tag was to be believed—walked by with four beers.

Lucy stood on the bottom rung of an empty bar stool to get a look over the crowd. The French had made up a word for someone her size: *petite.* And for that she was eternally grateful. She would have hated shopping in the "lady dwarf" section at Sears.

Lucy spotted the copy editors at a table in the corner. She made her way through the crowd and was about to sit down when she realized that the *Capital Tribune* copy editors weren't alone—they were sitting with a group of reporters from the competing *Santa Fe Times.* Hell. Damn. She looked around to make sure Del wasn't there. He wasn't. Thank God. The table was split in half—women on one end and men on the other. She wiggled her way down toward the men.

In grade school, some students always sat in the front of the class and some always sat in the back; she always sat with the boys. Not because she was interested in them romantically—that became an issue only after she'd hit puberty—but because women made her uncomfortable. She could never figure out the social nuances. The female social system was too complex and required a set of emotional skills that she didn't understand. And she was never very good at "girl things"—she hated shopping for clothes—and she loved action movies. Whenever she met a woman for the first time, Lucy always felt like she was skipping steps two through four in a required dance.

Men were easier. They made sense. She was never worried whether they were smarter than she or more clever—when it came to competing with men, she knew she would always win. With women she might not be the smartest or the prettiest; she might be average. She might be blah.

She was the middle child—sandwiched between two boys, a year apart on either side. She was neither the youngest nor the oldest. Stuck in limbo. To get noticed, she became the toughest, smartest, and funniest of the boys. She simply ignored the fact that she wasn't a boy.

When Lucy was twelve, her mother took her to the Clinique counter at Macy's to get a makeover. When Lucy wore her new makeup to school the next day, the boys made fun of her and gave her the once-over, but it was the girls' reaction that was more interesting—they talked to her. They asked her about shades of eye shadow and how to apply mascara. That's when she got it—look like a girl, act like a boy. Last week she had spent sixty dollars on a haircut—not to attract men but to impress women. Two girls at work had asked her who her hairstylist was; they'd talked for twenty minutes about hair dye and wondered out loud if Lucy should get highlights in her dark blond hair. Still, at best, all Lucy could manage to strike up was a casual acquaintanceship with a woman.

As Lucy approached the table, she made one of the male copy editors scoot his chair over when she sat down. The two male reporters on either side of her moved over as well. The women eyed her from the other end of the table. Lucy hoped it was a friendly look. The waitress came over and Lucy ordered a Sprite, not wanting to fall into another Monday-night drinking bout. Last Monday, she hadn't gotten home until six A.M. and had to throw up for an hour before the bathroom stopped spinning. She'd felt like an idiot. Drinking that heavily in college was expected; when you're twenty-eight, it's bordering on alcoholism.

She listened to the *Santa Fe Times* reporters debate whether cheerleading was a sport while the waitress set the Sprite in front of her. She felt a hand reach under her hair to touch the back of her neck. Del Matteucci. She turned around. He was holding a beer and giving her that crooked smile that she loved. Damn.

"Where's your woman?" she asked, her voice colder than she'd intended. Was she still that angry?

"She's working late," was all he said as he slipped into a

chair next to her, left vacant by a copy editor heading off to the bathroom.

Lucy nodded and turned back to her Sprite, not able to think of anything else to say. They hadn't really spoken that much since they broke up six months ago. They had seen each other. Said hi. The usual. But talk about the breakup? Never.

"You aren't drinking?" he asked. She could smell the beer on him. She looked down at her Sprite.

"Actually, I'm just getting started." She leaned over and draped her arm across the back of the sports reporter next to her, asking "What's your favorite color?"

"Green," he said and pulled her closer.

"Green it is." She motioned to the waitress as Del watched her curiously.

"I want a green drink," she told the waitress. Lucy smiled brightly as she turned back to the sports reporter. She knew what she was doing. Exacting her own sort of revenge. Flirt with all the boys and make Del watch. It was petty, but it would do. She needed alcohol for courage. She asked the sports reporter if she could use his shoulder as a pillow as the waitress showed up with something called a green iguana. It smelled of tequila and sweet-and-sour mix. She took a gulp. It didn't make her throw up, so she took another.

An hour and three more colors later—red, orange, and blue—Lucy felt Del's hand on her knee. It stopped her cold. She resisted the urge to move his hand higher up her thigh. She got up silently and went to the bathroom. Alone. She wished for a second that she had some version of a female friend, so that they could gab to each other about boys while they peed. She would have to manage this on her own.

Her boyfriend—she never quite remembered to put the "ex" in front of that—was hitting on her. Del was hitting on her. She had daydreamed of something like this. Of course, her fantasy involved him begging and crying. And beating on his chest in agony at her indifference. Make it very *All My Children.*

Two top-heavy blondes with Texas hair came tripping into the bathroom. They had tiny purses that matched their completely inappropriate sundresses. Had these women never heard of January? They jiggled their way into the bathroom stalls, talking about someone named Tracy.

Lucy stared back at herself the mirror, concentrating not on her face but on the weird reflection made by the salmon-colored walls. She had moved to Santa Fe a year ago for Del. He had wanted to come; she had wanted to stay in Florida. But she was in love. So they moved. She became night city editor at the *Capital Tribune* and he took a photography job at the *Santa Fe Times*. Six months later, they split up.

She washed her hands in the bathroom sink without thinking and crumpled a paper towel into the wastebasket. She crushed a few more paper towels into balls for good measure, resisting the urge to stomp them into the floor. She was too drunk to make sense of her feelings. And the blondes sounded like they were about to leave their stalls, so she took a deep breath and walked back to the table, stumbling a bit from the alcohol. She sat back down—next to Del, out of habit. He said, "Hey, baby," in the sloppy language of drunks and leaned over to massage her shoulder with one hand, his other holding a Heineken. Something in Lucy quickened, not with pleasure but with rage. Fury. Wrath. All those good Old Testament words but with a tinge of heartbreak. How dare he? How dare he think that she would get drunk and go back to him as if nothing had happened? How dare he destroy her, unmake her, unmold her, and then come back for seconds?

Lucy had the Wonder Twins power that most women possess: the ability to flirt outrageously with a repulsive man. Or a despised man. There are various reasons women do it: It's a power trip for the pretty, and it can be turned into a fast-acting man-bug repellent. Lucy always used it for the latter reason. The flirt-and-destroy combination had served her well in college. A man who assumes that women must kneel in worship when faced with his magnetism can be tortured into a bloody, humble pulp with charm and the right words. The girl starts with normal flirting, whispered tones, and a soft smile. Make him think he stands a chance. The amateurs will quickly begin to lick their lips and excessively toss their hair. The pros move right into an accidental brush-of-hand-against-back and a few well-placed out-of-corner-of-eye looks. If the girl is enjoying herself, she can continue; but Lucy usually stopped it at that point, using one swift word or phrase to cut the man. Not deep, but fatally. If the girl is very good, she can do all this within a matter of minutes. Lucy liked to think she was that good.

She grabbed Del's bottle of beer out of his hand and took a sip of it while he watched. She fondled the long neck of the bottle as suggestively as she could. She frowned. She was a little too drunk to be convincing. Her timing was off. She put the bottle down and almost spilled it. She started to laugh. Maybe she wasn't as good at this as she'd thought.

Del touched her hand on the table and said, "I've always loved your laugh." He turned her palm up and traced her lifeline with his index finger, the touch giving her a shiver. "And I've always loved your hands," he said.

"That's not the only body part of mine that you've loved," she said with an out-of-the-corner-of-her-eye glance.

"But it's the only part I can love in public unless you want people to stare."

"There's a lot of fun things we can do in public with our hands. We just need to get imaginative."

"Like what?"

Lucy switched her voice to that of a scolding schoolmarm. "Well, I can't believe that you spilled your drink all over yourself." She picked up a napkin and pretended to wipe off his shirt, her fingertips tracing a slow swirl across his neck, then slipping lower down on his chest, sneaking toward the waist of his pants, all the while saying "tsk, tsk," in her schoolteacher tone. And all the while smiling.

He grabbed her wrist just as she was nearing his belt. "If you go any lower I'll be spilling more than my drink."

"Really? I'd like to be around for that." Del's face changed when she said that. What had been a boyish smile was replaced by the hard edge of lust.

"We can go back to my place," he said in a low tone.

"Cockroaches are scared to go to your place," she said back softly. They had always had this teasing tension. It was part of their sexual combat.

"You can come over and help me clean. Remember the time we spent all night dusting off the kitchen table?" He squeezed her hand—their fingers interlaced, their legs touching under the table. Lucy put her head on Del's chest and took a deep breath. He smelled of cigarettes and sweet sweat.

She had him. She could crush him. Destroy him like he had destroyed her. All she had to do was go home with him, feed him a few more beers, and bring him to the edge. Slowly kiss his clothes off, but keep her own on. Then, as he stood there naked, anticipating, she could say, "Oh that's right, we broke up," and leave.

It was then that she realized what she wanted more than to destroy him: She wanted to get back together. That thought alone saved her.

She smiled up at him and pushed him away, saying, "How about instead I find you a ride home, and then tomorrow morning you call your girlfriend and buy her flowers for no reason."

CHAPTER TWO

Tuesday Morning

Detective Sergeant Gilbert Montoya of the Special Investigations Team shifted in his desk chair, his .45-caliber Smith & Wesson digging into his side. He pushed his gun belt lower on his waist and wished that he still had his .357-caliber revolver. Six months ago the Santa Fe Police Department had switched to standardized weapons. Administration said that the stainless-steel Smith & Wesson, with its fixed sight and nine-shot magazine, was the weapon "best suited for the police mission"—at least according to the memo. The officers were still complaining about having to take three full-day training sessions in order to pass the shooting qualifications.

Gil had spent most of the morning entering reports. They had just finished a fairly routine drug murder the night before, with Gil in charge of the suspect interrogation, which took only a few hours. He looked at the clock on his desk. 8:22 A.M. He kept glancing at the time every few minutes until it said 8:30. Yesterday he had called fifteen minutes late and he could tell that she had been worried. His picked up his phone and hit speed dial. His mother answered with a weak "Hello?"

"Hi, Mom."

"Hi, *mi hito.*" He waited for her to say more, but she didn't.

"How was church?" His mother went to morning Mass

every day, walking the quarter mile down the dirt road to the small chapel.

"Just fine." She paused a little and said, "Father Adam wants to know when you're going to go to church again."

"Mom, I go every Sunday with Susan and the girls to Santa María de la Paz. You know that." This was a familiar conversation, one they had almost once a month. He was never quite sure if his mother was becoming senile and forgot that they had talked about it, or if she disapproved of Gil's going to the newly built Santa María instead of driving the thirty miles every Sunday to their family church in Galisteo. The one his great-great-grandfather had helped build. Or at least paid to have built.

Someone across the squad room was yelling something, and Gil looked up. It was his chief, Bill Kline, saying, "Montoya, I need you in my office."

"Mom, I've got to get off the phone." He waited for her to say something. She didn't. He said, "So, I'll come over later tonight, okay?" She still didn't say anything. It was a full thirty seconds before she said weakly, "Bye, *hito.* Have a nice day." He heard her fumbling to put the receiver back into its cradle before the line went dead. *She must not be wearing her glasses. She must have lost them again.*

Gil headed to his chief's office. Standing outside the door was Sergeant Ron Baca, pacing back and forth like a pit bull.

As Gil approached, he nodded at Baca, who stopped pacing and eyed him as he walked into the chief's office. In a chair in the corner a woman sat huddled. It took Gil a moment to recognize her. Maxine Baca, Sergeant Ron Baca's mother. Her blouse had a crusty, brown stain on the sleeve. Her head was bowed, and her fingers picked at the stain. She didn't even look up as he came in.

Gil sat in the other chair. He was about to greet Mrs. Baca but thought better of it. He kept his eyes on her to see if she would look at him. She didn't.

"Mrs. Baca has had some bad news. Melissa—you know Melissa, right?" Gil nodded; Melissa was Maxine's youngest. Kline continued: "Melissa was found this morning up by Taos Gorge Bridge. It looks like she was thrown off."

Mrs. Baca, suddenly realizing that the officers were looking at her, deliberately pulled her hands from the stain on her blouse and placed them folded on her lap. She tried to sit up straighter, but the effort seemed too great and she gave up.

Gil got up and crouched next to her, pushing his gun belt down as he did so. "Mrs. Baca, how are you doing? Do you need anything?" She shook her head violently. Gil looked at her for a moment longer before going back to his chair.

"The state police have already started their investigation, but Mrs. Baca has asked us to help her by checking into it ourselves," Kline said. He motioned for Ron Baca, who was peering through the window of Kline's office door, to come in.

"Mrs. Baca," Kline said, "we'll do everything we can."

Ron Baca stood in the doorway, not quite entering the office. He looked at the floor, not meeting the chief's gaze. His shoulders were tense, as if he were ready to fight, but when he finally raised his head, Gil saw that there was no fight in him. He didn't have tears in his eyes, only emptiness—raw and painful.

"Ron, I'm very sorry for your loss," Gil said. Ron only nodded curtly, as if words were beyond him.

Ron helped Mrs. Baca gently to her feet, their heads almost touching for a moment as son supported mother.

"Now Ron is going to take you home, Mrs. Baca," Kline said.

The pair, with Maxine leaning heavily on her son's shoulder and grasping his hand tightly, shuffled out of the office.

Gil closed the door behind them.

"Now, we have no jurisdiction in this case," Kline started before Gil had a chance to ask. "The state police are handling it. But we'll do what we can to help. This family doesn't need any more tragedy. They've had enough."

Gil knew the Bacas a little through the department. Maxine's husband, a Santa Fe police officer for more than thirty years, had been killed during a drug shootout seven years earlier. Another son had died of a heroin overdose.

"Ron is one of us, for God's sake," Kline said. "If Melissa Baca was into drugs, or prostitution or whatever, I want us to be able to find out and tell the family before they have to hear it from the state police or the damn media. I want you to be a sort of liaison for the family—handle the press, talk to the state police for them."

Gil hesitated before asking, "How much leeway do I have?"

"That's up to you," Kline said. "Just try not to piss anybody off, and low-profile it. I already told the state police officer in charge of the investigation—that Lieutenant Pollack guy—that you're going to be looking around."

"How do they know it's her?" Gil asked.

"They found Melissa's purse on the bridge with her driver's license in it, and state police says the body down below matches the photo on the license. But someone, I guess Ron, will have to do a formal ID later."

"How'd they find the body?"

"Some early-morning tourist looking at the gorge spotted it and called it in."

"They don't think it's a suicide?" The bridge was popular with jumpers. Last year, a man had come all the way from Wisconsin just to commit suicide there.

"No car at the scene. Her car was found in Oñate Park in Santa Fe this morning about an hour ago. State police crime techs are checking it."

"Has anybody seen the body close-up yet?" Recovering the body would be hard. The gorge was 650 feet below the bridge and there was no path down.

"Some rescue worker has seen her but they won't tell us anything. But they're calling it a homicide."

Kline's phone rang and Gil took that as his cue to leave. He was just closing the door of the chief's office behind him when he heard Kline say to him, with his hand over the phone receiver, "By the way, Gil, nice work on that interrogation last night. I'll be sending a formal memo of congratulations out later. Oh, and Manny Cordova is going around the office doing a fairly good impression of you."

Gil just nodded and closed the door.

Lucy flipped her alarm clock right-side up; she had put it facedown on her nightstand when she went to bed. If she couldn't see the clock, that meant she didn't have to wake up, right? It read 8:45 A.M. in big green numbers. She stuck out her tongue at the clock. When she went out drinking, she could never sleep past 9 A.M. It didn't matter if she'd gone to bed at 8 A.M.; she was instantly awake an hour later. She stood up, swaying. The blue drink had been her undoing. What had it been called? Something bird. Something sexual. Moaning bird? Screaming orgasm bird? Kicking bird? No, wait—that was the chick from *Dances with Wolves,* and not a very sexy-sounding alcoholic beverage.

She went into the bathroom to get some aspirin, but all she could find was an old bottle of Pamprin. Did that work on hangovers? She popped two into her mouth and turned on the faucet, which groaned in protest and then spit out a trickle of water. She cupped her hands and took a drink to wash down the Pamprin, dribbling enough cold water down her pajama top to make her jump and curse. She quickly brushed her teeth, trying to scrape off the remnants of last's night drinking.

Going back to her bedroom, she got down on all fours in front of her closet and began tossing shoes out, trying to find a pair that matched. After two minutes of searching, and one minute of lying on the floor when the room began to sway, she ended up with black pumps with two-inch heels. She slipped those on and almost tottered over when she tried to walk. She steadied herself on her dresser. She just needed to get outside to the mailbox. She walked out into the kitchen and got a pot of coffee brewing, then pulled her long coat over her pajamas and opened the front door. A blast of cold air hit her and she pulled her coat tighter around her.

It was sunny out, of course, as always. She smelled the sweet piñon smoke coming from the Martinezes' chimney across the street. She looked over at the Sangre de Cristo Mountains just peeking over the top of her neighbors' house. The mountains were slipping in and out of the morning shadows. Santa Fe Baldy was white capped but the lower elevations still had no snow even in January.

Through her hangover, Lucy navigated her way to her mailbox across the street, her high heels clicking happily over the pavement. It was the only sound in the morning air except the rustling of the cottonwood branches and the far-off closing of a car door.

Lucy lived on Alto Street in a neighborhood that couldn't decide if it was up-and-coming rich or down-and-out poor. It was in the old part of Santa Fe. The Martinezes across the street had been living on the land since it had been given to them by the king of Spain. The tiny streets were horse-and-carriage size. The houses were squished together with no room for backyards or front lawns. In the closeness, everyone had walls or fences, to keep out the neighbors' eyes and the dust.

All the houses were flat topped and square, Santa Fe–style. And they were beige, just like every other home, office, hotel, gas station, and utility shed in Santa Fe. Lucy could write a dissertation on the color beige. Dark beige, light beige, pink beige. Beige like the desert sand. The houses in her neighborhood tended more toward the dark beige, with white trim. It was so unlike where she'd grown up in Florida, where everything was big and overdone, bright and new.

Lucy looked back at her brown/beige bungalow, with its

Spanish tile flat roof and tall elm trees around it. It had windowsills painted purple and pink and a tile mosaic of Our Lady of Guadalupe next to the front door. The mosaic was the reason why Del had wanted to rent the place. He'd said that it was a good omen. He had gotten into the habit of touching the mosaic as he entered and left the house.

From her mailbox Lucy could count three images of Our Lady of Guadalupe on walls and doors. The one across the street was painted on the side of a garage, all in earth tones. Either that or it was dusty.

Lucy opened her black mailbox and pulled out three envelopes—all bills. She sighed and clicked her heels back across the street and, without thinking, touched the mosaic next to the door with her left hand as she turned the doorknob with her right. She tossed the mail onto the coffee table, took off her coat, and poured a cup of coffee as she kicked off her pumps, which were already digging into her toes. She went into the bathroom and started the water running in her old-fashioned tub.

She was in the shower before she remembered that she hadn't flossed her teeth yet. Damn. Whenever she made a detour from her normal morning routine, she always ended up forgetting something. She said out loud, "Floss your teeth when you get out of the shower; floss your teeth when you get out of the shower."

She was already dressed and in the car a block from her house before she realized that she had not flossed her teeth. Damn.

She stopped by the newspaper to pick up her paycheck, then drove across town to the Santa Fe Police Department. The building was out toward the interstate, in brand-new Santa Fe, surrounded by very wide sidewalkless streets that smelled strongly of baking asphalt even in the weak winter sun. Unlike her cozy, old neighborhood, this was an area of empty lots and strip malls. The police station itself was a squared-off, utilitarian "facility"—that was the only word for it—that had none of the usual Santa Fe charm. No rounded corners or curved archways. You could tell that it was a government building without seeing the SFPD sign out front. The only bow to Santa Fe architecture was the beige that the building was painted, but it was washed out and seemed an afterthought, as if the builders would have preferred a steel gray.

Lucy sat in her car, peering at herself in the rearview mirror as she fixed her makeup, which she needed badly today. The sunlight was only accentuating the dark circles under her eyes. She decided on bright red lipstick in the hope that it would overpower her unfocused eyes.

Lucy got out of her car and walked up to the reception area of the police department while the officer manning the desk, a young man with acne scars on his cheeks, watched her.

"Hi. I'm with the *Capital Tribune.* I need to look over the hot sheets for today."

The acne-scarred officer slid a manila folder to her without saying anything.

She opened the folder and looked over the reports, writing down any interesting information. Two men had gotten into a knife fight last night over a bottle of Jack Daniel's, sending one to the hospital with minor wounds. That would become a brief for tomorrow's paper or a small six-inch story inside the local section, depending on how badly they needed news. The only other report that caught her eye was about a female teenager getting picked up at Santa Fe High School for drug possession.

She closed the folder. The officer was still watching her.

"Are any of the detectives around? I have a quick question."

The officer disappeared behind a closed door. When he came back, a tall officer followed him.

"I'm Detective Montoya. Can I help you?" His eyelashes were long and dark, making his eyes look like they were lined with black eyeliner. He could have been a banker in his business shirt and tie. Lucy glanced at his shoes. You can always tell a cop by their shoes. She had expected the usual cowboy boots that the Santa Fe detectives wore, but his were generic men's dress shoes. Brown. Obviously at least a few months old, but not even scuffed. He was tall, cute, dressed well, and took care of his shoes . . . and had a wedding band on his left ring finger. Damn.

"I need to ask you about some scanner traffic we picked up last night involving you guys and the OMI and the state police," Lucy said.

The acne-scarred officer said something quickly in Spanish that Lucy didn't understand.

"What makes you think she doesn't know Spanish?" Detective Montoya said to the officer, as he escorted Lucy into the squad room. Lucy smiled to herself. She had lived in Santa Fe for a year and still knew only *gracias* and *cerveza*. With that word combination all she could say was "Thanks for the beer." Which, while useful in certain situations, didn't help in most.

The detective gestured to the chair next to his desk and took his own chair.

She took her seat and looked around. The police station was designed like the newspaper office, with its fluorescent lights, endless cubicles, and windowless walls. But instead of being painted a sea-foam green it was a not-very-macho baby blue. The office was too new to be grungy, but the desks were cluttered with papers, folders, and computers. Officer Montoya's desk was one of the only clean ones, its cool gray surface clear of everything but a day planner and a filing basket. No picture of wife and kids. *Maybe he's divorced but still hanging on to the past by wearing the wedding ring?*

He was looking at her without unblinking, without curiosity. Without interest. Like she was an interruption to his day that he would tolerate politely but could really have done without. It made her want to poke him. He was neat, calm, professional, clean-cut. And she really wanted to poke him. Really.

Instead, she said, "We got a strange phone call at the newspaper last night. This elderly woman who always calls in tips to the paper said she heard two Santa Fe police officers on the scanner talking about the state police and the OMI. I was just wondering if you knew anything about it."

Several male officers at the desk next to them started laughing suddenly. At first she thought they were laughing at her question. Hastily, she looked over at them, but they were listening to a young, good-looking officer who was sitting casually on the desk.

"I'm sorry, what was your name?" she heard Detective Montoya say to her. She gave it to him as he typed away on his keyboard.

"Well, Ms. Newroe, I'm looking at the reports from last night and I don't see anything unusual. About what time was this at?"

"Right around eleven thirty P.M." She felt him trying to rush her out of the office with his tone and manners. She didn't like it.

He kept typing at his computer. After a few minutes, he said, "I'm sorry, I still don't see anything. Can you give me any more information?"

"That's all I know," Lucy said.

"Could you call the woman back and ask her about it?"

"I'd love to, but she never gives her name. We just call her Scanner Lady," Lucy said. She still felt the urge to mess with him somehow. She wanted a reaction from him. She needed one. She had never been good at feeling dismissed, ignored, tolerated. She wanted his acknowledgment. And she was going to get it.

"I'm not sure I can be of any more help, Ms. Newroe. Sorry." He started to rise from his seat to usher her out.

"So, how is your day going so far, Detective Montoya?" she asked, smiling, leaning back in her seat, making it obvious that she wasn't about to get up. Montoya stood up and sat on the edge of his desk, not retaking his seat as Lucy had expected. He looked at her, still without curiosity, considering.

"Any interesting cases pop up?" she asked, still smiling. "Maybe a dead body or some such thing? Maybe someone tossed off a bridge somewhere?"

When Lucy had stopped by the newspaper earlier in the morning to pick up her paycheck, the managing editor had told her about a body being found in the Taos Gorge. They didn't know much. A purse was found on the bridge, which probably meant that the victim was a female. No car around, so most likely not a suicide. Tommy Martinez had been pulled off the Gomez trial to cover it. He was on his way to Taos with one of the photographers.

Detective Montoya showed no surprise when she mentioned it, but maybe a hint of interest. Maybe. She said, "So, let's play a little game here, Detective. A game of 'what if.' What if that body that the police officers were talking about on the scanner last night was the one found in Taos Gorge?"

"Taos is a long way away and that body wasn't found until just this morning, but you heard this conversation last night," Detective Montoya said.

"Yeah, but what if," she smiled again, and, surprisingly, he smiled back, "there was prior knowledge of the death?"

"You mean what if one of my officers knew about the killing last night? That seems very unlikely, considering the circumstances."

"But what if they committed the murder?" she said.

"Well, it couldn't have been a Santa Fe police officer because none of us are dumb enough to talk about murdering someone over the scanner," he said, really smiling now. "Maybe try over at the state police."

Lucy started laughing at his unexpected humor. She had been trying to piss him off, but instead he'd made her laugh out loud. She pulled her business card out of her wallet and said, "Can you call me if you hear anything? I'll be at work until late tonight."

Montoya glanced down at her card. "I didn't know editors did this kind of legwork." His smile was now gone. She had a feeling that his smiles were rare. Maybe only a once-a-day event, not like her once-every-few-minutes.

"Once a cops reporter, always a cops reporter." She wished him good-bye and left, followed out by a fresh burst of laughter from the group of officers.

Gil was getting up to leave when Officer Joe Phillips stopped by his desk.

"Good job last night," Phillips said. Gil said thanks and was about to leave when Officer Manny Cordova came up.

"Gil, man, you are the man," Cordova said with a slap on Gil's back and a handshake. "I mean, you are my hero. You should have seen the look on that Mexican kid's face when you read him his rights. The kid was like, 'What the hell happened?' "

"What did happen?" Phillips asked Cordova. "All I know is that Montoya here," he poked a thumb Gil's way, "solved a murder case in two hours. Like it's some office record."

Cordova smiled and started the story before Gil could put a stop to it.

"So we get a 10-44 and I'm first on scene," Cordova says with a swagger in his voice. "It's a Mexican national. He's already way dead, I mean door nail. He was stabbed or something. Lots of blood. So Gil gets there and does his thing and finds out that the dude was arrested for drug dealing last month along with his cousin. But no one knows where the cousin is. So Gil tells the wife to have the cousin come down to the police station as soon as he shows up."

Gil glanced at his watch, wishing that Cordova would hurry

up so he could leave and get started on the Melissa Baca case, but Cordova was just warming to his story.

"So the cousin shows up here like within a half hour, wearing like jeans and a black shirt with one of those tye-dyed T-shirts underneath, and we take him to interrogation. The kid keeps whining and saying," Cordova changed his voice to a Speedy Gonzales accent, " 'I didn't do nothing.' " Phillips started to laugh, but Cordova shushed him with a wave of his hand before saying, "So Gil has me get the kid a Coke, which I'm thinking, 'Why am I getting this a-hole a Coke?' As soon as I set it down in front of the kid, Gil 'accidentally,' " Cordova made quote marks with his fingers, "spills the Coke on the kid's pants, right on the crotch, so it looks like he peed himself."

Cordova started laughing hard and had to stop to catch his breath, before continuing. "Gil starts telling the dude he's free to go but the kid won't leave interrogation because he looks like he peed all over himself. So we get him a jumpsuit to wear. The kid is changing and Gil has me put the kid's clothes in an evidence bag. Then Gil says to the kid," Cordova changed his voice, moving it down an octave and making it sound monotone, " 'Did you know that when you stabbed your cousin it left blood on your clothes?' "

Cordova started laughing again. "And I'm thinking, 'Damn, I've been staring at this kid for three hours and I didn't see any blood splatter.' "

Gil was getting restless, but Cordova was almost to the punch line. "You know that T-shirt the kid was wearing I thought was tye-dyed, no? It was blood. The dude was stupid enough to wear the shirt he killed his cousin in to the station." Phillips started to laugh, joining Cordova, who was almost doubled over.

Gil watched Cordova and thought about Melissa Baca. He knew that Ron and Cordova were friends, but clearly Cordova didn't know about Melissa or he wouldn't have been so animated. Gil decided it wasn't his place to say anything. That was up to Kline or the Bacas.

"Gil, man, you are the man," Cordova said, a few more times before Gil could duck out.

After she left the police station, Lucy took the highway north out of Santa Fe, the snow-covered Sangre de Cristo Mountains to the east and the Jemez Mountains to the west. She followed the road past Tesuque and Pojoaque pueblos and turned toward Nambé Pueblo, heading into the moonscape desert that was blinding in the morning sun. The hodoos and mesas, whittled by wind and rain, cast a puzzle of shadows on the soft hills. As she drove, Lucy did what she always did—she watched the sky.

The huge clouds impossibly hugged the curvature of the earth, the immensity of the sky dwarfing the land below it. The clouds were crisp and God-lit. She thought of adjectives for the sky as she drove—*massive, turquoise, vast.* She dismissed every word as she thought of it—too stupid, too worn, too inadequate. She wished she had been born a poet so she could find a way to describe the Northern New Mexico sky.

Her best attempts had made her sound like a community college creative-writing professor or an advertisement—"an empty canvas of light and space filled with frothy clouds and azure nothingness that is all-encompassing in its beauty." She laughed out loud—then watched the shadow of a cloud pass over a mountain, creating a moving stripe of slate across a brown hill.

Ten miles later, the wrinkled cliffs and canyons of the desert plunged into the tiny valley of Chimayó, studded by old orchards and cottonwood trees that the winter had turned a soft brown. The trees blended into the nude-crayon bluffs like an earth-toned Impressionist painting.

It was January, so there were few tourists at the Santuario de Chimayó when she pulled up.

Lucy walked through the wooden gates and curved archway and into the small courtyard crowded with gravestones, wooden crosses, and tall cedars. She stopped to study the tombstones, which bore names like Seferina Martinez, Jacinto Ortiz, and Abenicia Chavez. Old Spanish colonial names that she couldn't properly pronounce, but which made her wish her own name had a little more flair. She looked up at the church—wooden, adobe, and lopsided. She heard pigeons cooing in the twin belfries. The pitched tin roof gleamed in the sun, its silver ridges blending into the blue-white sky. A rickety ladder on the roof led to nowhere in particular. She walked though the church door and almost tripped in the near black. Her eyes adjusted to the dark, and, as unassumingly as she could, she slipped into a pew, trying to look like she belonged and hoping that no one would ask her anything Catholic. The pews were wooden, made soft over the years. The kneelers were wood as well, with no cushioning for the faithful. Old, uncomfortable Catholic furniture. Made two hundred years ago in the belief that those who seek God must suffer to find him.

She hadn't been lying to Tommy Martinez when she said she'd been planning to get up early. She had been planning on coming here.

It had become her habit to sit in the church at least once a week for a few minutes, sometimes hours. She wasn't Catholic—she wasn't anything—but the church comforted her. The once brightly colored santos and retables behind the altar were faded. The crucifix, grisly with painted blood dripping from Jesus' head and hands, was chipped and worn. Everything was shabby, ancient, and smelled of prayers and hopes and candle wax.

Someone behind her was praying the rosary in Spanish. She couldn't understand the words; the quiet mantra was a murmur. A family came down the aisle, five in all, with the youngest, who looked about twelve, supporting the grandmother. They all genuflected in front of the altar before slipping into the back room, where the dirt was.

The santuario was famous for its healing dirt. During Holy Week, thousands of Catholics from Northern New Mexico made a pilgrimage to the church. Last year, the newspaper had interviewed an eighty-four-year-old man who had walked the thirty miles from Santa Fe carrying a twenty-pound cross over his shoulder. It took him twenty-seven hours. He made the walk for his wife, who was dying of cancer. He said that if he brought her some of the healing dirt, she would survive. Before that, Lucy had never heard a good explanation of faith.

The family was quiet. She could see them through the doorway as they scooped up the dirt from a hole in the ground and put it in little plastic bags. The hole didn't magically refill itself, as some legends claimed. When the dirt got low, the priests replaced it with earth dug up from the neighboring hillside. Lucy wondered if the family knew that. Would it make them believe in the powers of the dirt any less?

Lucy never took any of the dirt. She felt that she had no right. It was a Catholic custom, and she was an intruder, an observer who watched the faithful but was not one of them. She had been to a Mass only once, with her college roommate at Easter. It was all standing, sitting, kneeling—confusing Catholic aerobics that had made her feel alien and alone.

But the little mission church was different. The faith of those who visited was plain and uncomplicated. She saw it in their faces—they simply believed.

The santuario had been her and Del's favorite place to bring visiting relatives, who always used words like *quaint* and *rustic* to describe it. They would giggle as they scooped up handfuls of the dirt. At first, she had laughed along with them, joking that they could use the dirt and some holy water to make a divine mud mask—it would tighten pores and keep Satan away. But by the time Del's dad had come to town about seven months ago, she'd had enough. She'd begged off the trip, claiming that she had to work. It had been her day off, which Del knew, but he never pointed it out.

It hadn't dawned on her until later that Del hadn't actually invited her along. That should have been a clue.

Patsy Burke sat in her jewelry-making class, trying to thread a bead onto a piece of string. Next to her, Claire Schoen was swearing up a blue streak. Patsy had never met a woman her age who swore as much as Claire did. She and Claire were taking another continuing-education course at the community college. Claire called it "classes for crones." And Pasty could see why. More than half of the class were women her age, their gray heads bent down over their worktables.

Patsy was making a necklace for Brittany. It was her third try. The first two had come out wrong, with extra beads in silly places. Claire interrupted her with a, "Here, Pat, do this." Patsy smiled and took the thread from Claire; after a few tries, she slipped the bead into place, then handed it back to Claire. Claire had insisted that they take the class despite her arthritis. "My joints might be stiff but they still work," Claire had said in her heavy New York accent. Patsy spent most of her time in class doing both her and Claire's work. But she didn't mind.

For months after John's fatal stroke, Patsy had spent long hours staring at nothing, trying to remember what it had felt like to be Mrs. John Burke. John Junior tried to get her to make plans. Did she want to move back to Kansas to be with her sisters? Did she want to move to Phoenix to be near Harold? John Junior yelled at her, thinking that her hearing aid was broken. What he didn't understand was that she didn't care. What did it matter where she was? She was lost without John. After several weeks, John Junior started to make plans to move her to Albuquerque, to live with him and his new wife. Patsy simply accepted this. She wandered around her house, thinking about packing things up into boxes but not doing it.

Claire Schoen showed up at Patsy's door with a single, loud knock one day. When Patsy opened it, she saw a woman dressed in white stretch pants, a big orange T-shirt, and a baseball cap. She had seen the woman before. She knew her name. She lived next door. They had said hi to each other over the fence, but that was it. Patsy had grown up on a farm, where you stayed out of other people's business.

"Hey, Pat," Claire said. "Let's go for a walk."

Patsy started to say no, pointing out that she had no tennis shoes. Claire glanced at the orthopedic shoes Patsy was wearing and said, "What you've got on is fine. Let's make hay while the sun shines."

Patsy didn't know what else to say, so she did as she'd been told. They walked in the warm sun, Claire pumping away loudly, saying, "Gotta keep these old bones moving," and doing most of the talking. She talked about her husband, who had died twenty years earlier, saying, "Bless his heart," and looking genuinely sad. She talked about some man named Henry from the senior center who was making moon eyes at her. As Claire talked, Patsy realized that they had things in common. Both had two sons, both had had hip replacements, both were the widows of police officers, both did their own sewing, and both played bridge.

After an hour, they were back at Patsy's front door.

Claire said, "See you tomorrow, Pat. Same time," and went huffing back to her house.

That had been three years ago. Since then, Claire had been trying to show Patsy how to "empower" herself. As Claire pointed out, in John's death, God had granted Patsy something. What was that saying? Every time a door closes, somewhere a window opens? Or, as Claire put it, "We might be old, but we ain't dead yet."

Patsy now made her meals when she wanted to, went to bed when she wanted to. She dressed in T-shirts and, once in a while, ate spicy burritos with green chile—the kind John had never liked. It gave her heartburn, but she didn't care. A little Pepcid AC and she was as good as new.

Not that she didn't still miss John. Their life had been . . . dependable. He'd been a good provider and father. John had always said that Patsy took care of the emotions in the family and he took care of the money. He had left her with a good pension and health insurance. She still drove his last car, a Buick Skylark, but she was thinking of trading it in for one of those cute SUVs everyone in town had.

Claire had even talked her into using a laundry service. "Pat," Claire had said, "in your lifetime you have hung out more sheets than the town bed wetter." So Patsy, a former Kansas farm wife, had her laundry sent out. It made her feel mischievous.

Claire had said that the next thing Patsy needed to learn was how to pay her own bills. And Patsy was thinking about getting her first job. Maybe as a cashier at Hobby Lobby. She was going to stop by and get an application tomorrow, when she and Claire went on their weekly shopping trip.

Patsy slipped another bead onto the necklace, while Claire started a whole new stream of swearing. Patsy looked at her nervously. One of the other students had complained to the teacher last week that Claire swore so loudly that it made him uncomfortable. Claire did everything loudly because she was deaf in one ear but refused to wear a hearing aid. "I'm not sticking something in my ear where it don't belong," she would say with a snort. But Patsy thought she was just being stubborn.

Claire's voice was getting louder and a student sitting in front of them turned to stare. Patsy poked Claire in the arm, saying, "Shush." Claire turned and made a face at her and the two started giggling.

Gil walked into his house, making sure to dead-bolt the door against the broad daylight. He heard the refrigerator open and found his wife making peanut butter and jelly sandwiches in the kitchen. She wasn't even startled when he said hello.

Susan had a part-time job doing accounting work for a

gravel company in town. They had talked about her going back full-time, but she wanted to be around for their two daughters, Joy and Therese.

He sat on one of the stools near the counter and listened as she told him about an afternoon field trip she was going on to Bandelier National Monument with Joy's fifth-grade class.

Bandelier was only forty-five minutes away. Gil and the girls had been there dozens of times when they were younger. They would walk around the Anasazi Indian ruins, looking for pieces of pottery in the dirt. When Joy was little she had called them Anastazi Indians, making the word sound Italian. When was the last time they had gone there? He couldn't remember.

Susan sealed the sandwich in a Ziploc bag and put it into a paper sack with an apple. He handed her the car keys as she grabbed the bag and kissed him a quick good-bye. He reached up and brushed the hair out of her eyes as she moved away, heading out the garage door to her car.

She called over her shoulder, "Don't forget to get that St. Joseph statue from your mom when you see her tonight," then closed the door behind her.

Susan wanted the statue so that she could bury it upside down in the backyard, to help sell their house. Her sister had done it and sold her home within a week. His cousins had done it and gotten five thousand dollars more than they had hoped. Everyone in Santa Fe knew someone who had quickly sold his house after burying St. Joseph in the backyard.

Gil glanced around his kitchen. They had remodeled the kitchen and bathrooms when they moved in after he was hired by the city, spending long Sunday afternoons painting and scraping. But even after they were done, Susan said that it was never "homey." It was not her dream house. Their neighborhood had been built in the 1960s and had been ranch land back when his parents were growing up. The homes had backyards and front yards. Their place wasn't very big, just three bedrooms. Susan wanted a house with breathing room, one that was new and didn't need constant repairs.

They were looking at houses in Eldorado, outside Santa Fe, where all the homes were newly built and spacious. The nearest next-door neighbor was about a block away. The property out there was desert with chamisa and piñon. It didn't have the tall trees like in Santa Fe or where Gil had grown up near the Galisteo River.

He got up and went back out the front door, bolting it again, and settled into his car. He had gone home to tell his wife about Melissa Baca, whom Susan vaguely knew, and to let her know that he wouldn't be home until late. But watching Susan ease through making lunch, he realized he couldn't tell her. He didn't know why.

He picked up his cell phone and dialed his home number. The phone rang four times and then he heard his own voice urging callers to leave a message. He would tell the answering machine instead.

CHAPTER THREE

Tuesday Afternoon

Gil drove his unmarked Crown Victoria past Oñate Park on Cerrillos Road, where Melissa's car had been found, but the crime-scene techs had already towed it away. He continued driving, noting the time and mileage. He followed the highway north out of Santa Fe, past the pueblo casinos and roadside vendors, to Española. He spent his time watching the cars as he drove, noting the beat-up Suburban that quickly did a U-turn as soon as he showed up in its rearview mirror. Other cars slowed as he neared, not sure if he was a real police officer or just a man in a dark blue Crown Victoria.

He kept just under the fifty-five-mph speed limit as the flat road slowly made its way into the canyon of the Rio Grande. He passed the apple and apricot orchards of Velarde, Embudo, and Rinconada. The highway climbed up the canyon, the walls getting steeper. Descansos marked the roadside every few miles, the crosses showing where people had died in car accidents.

On the right side of the highway were mostly tall cliffs and a few rock piles. To the left, the wide river moved along the gorge floor, flowing past cottonwood trees and rough mesas.

Gil caught sight of a man fishing the river far below, throwing a long cast and cranking the reel, pulling the lure with the current. Fishing the Rio Grande in winter was always slow, especially in the canyon stretch. Gil and his dad had fished the Rio Grande only a few times, not liking the noise of the traffic on the highway. His dad had always wanted to be in the most out-of-the-way stretches of water.

During the drive to mountain streams, they would spend long hours debating which casting grip to use or whether bright synthetic fibers were better than natural ones for fly tying. His father, always a lawyer, would never let the argument die. Once there, they would fish in silence, usually with only the bend of the river between them. When Gil was in grade school, he would get bored within an hour or two and then would try to sneak up on his dad, who seemed to spend as much time looking at the scenery as fishing. By the time Gil was in high school, he could stand all afternoon in the water, placing cast after cast with accuracy.

His dad had taught him how to make ties, showing him how to wind and twirl the fur and feathers. But the last time he and his dad had gone fishing together, almost ten years ago, his dad had changed to using premade ties, Royal Wulffs and Humpys. Their white wings made it easier for his dad, with his bad eyesight, to see. His father, who had prided himself on his fly tying, shrugged when he pulled them out of his fly box and said, "Sometimes you do what you have to do to catch fish." And then he smiled. He died of a heart attack a month later. Gil had been just twenty-three.

The highway popped out of the canyon and Gil took the road toward the town of Taos. The brown plains stretched toward the Truchas Range of the Sangre de Cristo Mountains, where the creases of the peaks were lined with snow.

He parked on the Taos plaza and went into a diner to get a green-chile burrito and a Coke. He ate it outside, sitting on a bench on the plaza, watching the tourists who were there for the ski season. The ski area had only some of its runs open. The winter had started with a good snowfall of five inches in October. But now the temperature most days was about sixty degrees. The tourists who hadn't come for the skiing loved it. The locals just wanted it to snow.

Gil finished his burrito and tossed the wrapper. He walked back to his car slowly, keeping an eye on a group of local kids as they crossed the plaza, wondering why they weren't in school. He got into his car and drove past the turnoff for the Taos Pueblo.

One of Gil's uncles claimed that they were related to Pablo Montoya, who was hanged by the American government after a rebellion at Taos Pueblo. Gil's aunts said that the story wasn't true, that Pablo was not related to them but to the Montoya family from the town of Mora. That didn't stop Gil's uncle from getting drunk at family parties and telling the children that Pablo Montoya would come get them if they didn't be quiet. His uncle's version of the story was that Pablo and his friends were mad at the Anglos who were stealing all the property from the rich Spanish, so Pablo helped lead a revolt in Santa Fe that somehow ended up in Taos. At some point, the new Anglo territorial governor was shot full of arrows and killed—which was true, according to the history books—but Gil's uncle claimed that Pablo was the one who took the governor's scalp through the streets of Taos. The Americans eventually hanged Pablo Montoya. Gil's sister, Elena, had always wanted to take a trip to Taos to look for Pablo's grave, but that was before their dad had died. Since then, she hadn't brought it up.

Gil took the highway northwest out of Taos. The hills flattened out to a plain of grasses and sage brush. The only sign of the Taos Gorge out in the prairie two miles away was a thin line of black, invisible unless you knew where to look. One story had it that a bandit being chased by locals galloped his horse right off a cliff and into the gorge, never realizing it was there.

Gil was a quarter of a mile from the gorge before he could see it—a deep canyon in the flat plain with a single bridge over it. He slowed as he approached the Taos Bridge—officially named the Rio Grande Gorge Bridge—as it was clogged with traffic and police.

After he parked his car on the roadside, Gil wrote down the time—one hour and forty minutes, minus ten minutes for the burrito—and the mileage—81.7 miles. He stood with a group of onlookers who had gathered at the side of the road to watch the crime scene. They were going to be disappointed: Melissa's body wouldn't be brought up for hours. He watched from a distance as the state police set up a winch on the bridge to pull Melissa's body up from the river. A news helicopter from one of the Albuquerque television stations flew overhead, causing dust devils in the dirt parking lot. Gil heard someone next to him say, "What a horrible way to kill yourself," before the rest was lost in the wind from the helicopter.

Gil took out his badge and showed it to the officer directing traffic. The officer nodded and Gil walked onto the bridge. It vibrated as a truck crossed. Susan had lived in Santa Fe for most of her life, but she refused to visit the bridge. He wasn't sure if it was its height or its reputation that scared her. There had been talk of setting up a permanent winch on the bridge because the police were tired of setting one up every time a car or a body was discarded. In the past three months, two people had committed suicide off it. A few years ago, a Taos teenager had been charged with involuntary manslaughter after pushing his drinking buddy alive into the gorge. Gil wondered if Melissa had been alive when she was thrown off.

Gil stopped to read a plaque. It was a Most Beautiful Steel Bridge Award, given by the American Institute of Steel Construction in 1966, a year after the bridge was completed.

He walked up to a group of police officers by the OMI van and introduced himself. Gil thought he recognized one of the OMI techs. The tech and Gil shook hands and spent a few minutes trying to figure out how they knew each other—whether they were related or knew each other professionally. The OMI tech had decided that they were third cousins when a state police officer, a lieutenant by the look of his uniform, approached Gil and led him away from the group.

"I'm Tim Pollack. Your chief said you were coming."

Gil knew of Pollack. He was the temporary public information officer for the state police, which meant that he was the liaison with the media until someone was found to replace him. Pollack had intense blue eyes and his head was shaved, a style that state police officers seemed to favor.

Gil looked over the side of the bridge; the Rio Grande was more than two football fields below. Someone had tossed a large road-construction barrel over the side. It was a tiny orange dot on the rocks below.

"Was she alive when she hit?" was Gil's first question. It was his biggest concern. It was news that he hoped he wouldn't have to tell. He thought of Maxine Baca as she'd sat in the chief's office.

"We don't think so," Pollack said. "But we haven't seen the body yet. We do know there aren't any bullet holes, but the body is so messed up from the fall that it'll be hard to say what killed her, until the OMI sees her."

"What's she dressed like?"

Pollack, snapping his gum, gave him a sidelong glance. "If you're asking if there was CSP, we don't think so. All of her clothes, including her underwear, are intact." CSP stood for criminal sexual penetration. Three big words that meant one thing—rape.

"Any evidence she was doing drugs?" Gil asked.

Pollack said carefully, "Not that we've seen."

"Do we have a time on her death?"

"Nothing scientific, just my own calculation. It snowed a little yesterday, just a dusting. It started at about ten thirty P.M. Her body still had snow on it when we found her at seven A.M., so she was here before ten thirty P.M. last night."

"Do you know when she was last seen?"

"Her mom is a mess, but from what we could get out of

her over the phone, Melissa left their house about eight P.M. last night. We plan on doing a more in-depth interview with her later today."

"Was she brought out here in her own car?"

"We don't think so. A woman who lives near Oñate Park saw Melissa's car there when she came home at exactly nine ten P.M. She remembers because she was late for some TV show she watches. Anyway, the woman remembers seeing Melissa's car. She thought maybe it belonged to a hooker or a drug dealer. You know what that park is like. Oh, and we found blood on the back bumper that we think is Melissa's."

Gil thought for a minute. "Her body must have been already cold when she was dumped, or the snow on top of her would have completely melted. She was probably killed in Oñate Park around eight thirty P.M. and brought up here in another car." He watched a sedan full of gawkers slowly roll by.

She hadn't been alive when she fell. He felt no relief.

It was only one P.M. when Lucy started back to Santa Fe from the santuario. She toyed with the idea of stopping at one of the pueblo casinos, just to see what they were like inside, but she didn't have enough nerve to play blackjack or enough quarters to play slots. She contented herself with driving too fast and singing along with a 1980s radio station. She was well into an old Journey song when she crested the top of Opera Hill and saw the city of Santa Fe sprawled out below her. There were no high-rises to block the view, only earth-hugging houses that flowed into the curves of the hills. Not obstructing the landscape but being a part of it. None of the usual "we must dominate the world with our massive structures" city-building mentality.

Santa Fe was set up like an amphitheater, with the Plaza as its stage and the Sangre de Cristo Mountains as its backdrop. Throughout the years, the city had been built in semicircles around the Plaza, with the older houses closest to it and the newest subdivisions out in the cheap seats. The Plaza, built as the center of the conquistadores' fort, was still the center of everything Santa Fe.

Lucy drove into town and made her way through traffic. She had two hours to kill before she had to be at work. She decided to get some errands out of the way. She went to the bank to deposit her paycheck and then over to Wal-Mart.

A half hour later, she was on her way to the checkout line to pay for her merchandise—Clearasil and Lysol—when she saw Gerald Trujillo walk in. Lucy dodged into the greeting-card aisle and peeked around the corner. She watched him select a grocery cart.

Gerald was someone she liked, someone she respected. He was also someone she would rather not see. When she and Del had first broken up, she'd done the usual five stages of grief, although in her case it was twenty stages, with most being variations on anger and denial. Her mother had suggested that Lucy keep herself busy—take classes, explore Santa Fe. Like all things in Lucy's life, she overdid it. She signed up for yoga, rock climbing, gardening, and Spanish. She also signed up for a week-long emergency-medic class. Her main reason for taking the class was purely lust-driven: The man teaching it—Gerald Trujillo—was beautiful. She had met him—and ogled quite a bit—when he dropped off a press release at the newspaper announcing the class.

But she had a secondary reason for taking the class: it was held the week she and Del were supposed to have taken a fun-filled trip to L.A. She thought that spending her vacation flirting with her teacher would be better than sitting at home crying over her failed relationship.

But things didn't go as she'd planned. Somehow, she managed to get herself signed up as a first-responder medic for the Piñon Volunteer Fire Department, where Gerald was a paramedic. Then she found out that Gerald was very married.

Gerald glanced Lucy's way, and she ducked down the aisle, pretending to be very interested in the sympathy-card selection. She was absentmindedly reading a belated-birthday card when she noticed a boxed Barbie doll perched in the get-well-soon section.

It was a Tropical Scent Barbie, with the smell of exotic flowers built right into her skin. Lucy had the sudden urge to throw a rope around the Barbie's neck and hang her from a rearview mirror. It could be a new marketing ploy—Tropical Scent Barbie: She's fun to play with and makes a stylish air freshener!

Lucy picked up the Barbie, tucked it under her arm, and went off in search of the toy section.

She had started returning mis-shelved store items a few months ago. The first time, she saw a carton of milk sitting next to the feminine pads. Her only thought was that the milk would go bad if she didn't get it back to the refrigerated section. The next time, she found a head of lettuce next to some Oreos; she reasoned that if the milk deserved to go back to its home, so did the lettuce. Last week, she had spent ten minutes trying to figure out where they shelved the lemon juice at Albertsons.

Lucy strolled around—keeping an eye out for Gerald—until she found an aisle of pink boxes from floor to ceiling. There were hundreds of Barbies—even a Pioneer Barbie next to a Native American Barbie. What were the little girls supposed to do with those—reenact the fun of Manifest Destiny?

She was about to put Tropical Scent Barbie on her shelf when she saw Gerald Trujillo turn his shopping cart down the aisle.

"Hi, I thought that was you," he said. God, he looked great. Bright hazel eyes against dark brown hair. His wife was a lucky woman.

"Hi," she mumbled back.

"Still playing with dolls?" he said, smiling as he looked at the Barbie box in her hand.

Lucy felt her face color. She had no explanation for what she was doing, so she lied.

"I'm thinking of getting my godchild this."

He nodded. She steeled herself against the next question, which she knew was coming.

"We haven't seen you around the fire station lately," he said, without as much accusation as she would have expected. "What have you been up to?"

"Do you want the truth or a lie?" she asked.

He laughed, enough so that his eyes crinkled up. "Well, I think I already know the truth, so tell me a lie, but make it creative."

"I think I used the abducted-by-aliens lie last time so this time I'll go with being in jail."

"What were the charges?" His smile got wider, showing teeth.

"I didn't get arrested. I just really wanted a prison tattoo."

"Look, Lucy," he said, the smile almost gone, "I know you're busy, we all are, but you made a commitment to the station. If you plan on volunteering with us, you really need to make time for it in your life. Make it a priority. We haven't seen you in weeks."

"I know, I know, I suck."

"I'm not trying to make you feel bad, but if you want to keep your skills as a medic, you need to use them."

Lucy just nodded, her eyes on the floor. God, she hated feeling guilty.

"How about this," Gerald said. "I'll be at the station tomorrow at about eight in the morning. Why don't you stop by and we can go over some training?"

"If you make it ten instead, I'll be there." She had never been a morning person.

They murmured their good-byes and Lucy watched him turn down the aisle. She put Tropical Scent Barbie back where she belonged and started to the front of the store.

She was an aisle or two away when she heard exclamations of acknowledgment. She glanced down an aisle. Gerald was hugging a red-headed woman with a small child in her arms. Lucy felt, rather than heard, them giving each other the ritual Northern New Mexico inquiries: asking after each other's families. Maybe they had been high school sweethearts or their fathers had bowled together. Lucy felt a pang of . . . something. Envy? She turned back around and headed to the checkout line, clutching her Lysol closer to her chest as it started to slip. As she stood in line, she noticed that someone had put several packs of gum back in the wrong places. She carefully placed them back where they belonged as she waited in line.

In the parking lot, she unlocked her Toyota Camry and tossed her shopping bag onto the seat. Then she drove to work, not even caring that she was an hour early.

Gil headed back from Taos to Santa Fe, but instead of again following the road that ran along the Rio Grande, he took the highway that went up into the mountains. He noted the mileage and time again, although he already knew that taking the High Road added about ten miles to the trip. Of the two roads leading from Santa Fe to Taos, the High Road is the more famous. When Gil was a uniformed officer working on the Plaza during the summer, he was always giving tourists directions to the High Road, each carload stocked up on cameras and extra film to capture the sweeping views. The road went mostly through Carson National Forest and mountain towns like Placita and Chamisal.

Gil kept a watch out for black ice as the highway climbed, quickly leaving the desert and making its way into ponderosa pine forest. Signs along the road warned drivers to put on tire chains and watch for snow plows. It hadn't snowed for more than a month, but because of the high elevation, he could see some ice in the shadows on the forest floor. Keeping an eye out for elk, Gil thought about Melissa Baca. Why had the killer driven more than an hour away to get rid of her body? Was he trying to cover up evidence? The damage to the body from a 650-foot fall would make it hard to determine which injuries had been made postmortem and which had been made premortem. But it had been cold last night, which would have helped preserve the body. He would have to check to see what the temperature had been. That would help the OMI determine what time rigor mortis and lividity had set in.

He thought about Oñate Park, where Melissa's car had been found. The neighbors had finally gotten tired of the drug dealing there and started a high-profile neighborhood watch a few months ago, but it hadn't stopped the problems. He thought about the drug connection. The Taos Gorge Bridge had been the site of a few drug-related killings. A few years ago two men had thrown an eighteen-year-old boy alive off the bridge because they wanted to steal his car to pay for Christmas presents and drugs. Gil knew that Ron and Melissa had a brother who had died of a heroin overdose and that addictions ran in the family. But Pollack had said that no drugs had been found on Melissa.

The time frame was what bothered him most. Melissa had left home at 8 P.M. It would have taken her about twenty minutes to get from her house to Oñate Park. She was probably dead by 8:30 P.M. She had to have been at the bottom of the Taos Gorge before 10:30 P.M., when it had started snowing. It was a very tight schedule. It didn't leave much room for error or second-guessing. Either the killer was a fast thinker or he had planned ahead.

Gil drove into Peñasco, where blue smoke from wood-burning stoves hung in the air. The shadows of the late afternoon made it harder to see the highway.

Down the road a few miles was the turnoff to a small stream that fed Santa Cruz Lake. It was one of his dad's favorite fishing spots. They would hike in a half mile and make a day of it, casting from one small pool to another. His sister Elena would occasionally come with them, but she would get impatient quickly with all the standing around and being quiet. She would eventually start to climb up the canyon sides and disappear in search of some new path. Once, when Gil was ten, his mother had come with them. Elena, who must have been eight at the time, stayed close to their mother instead of wandering off. They ate leftover empanaditas and drank cold Cokes for lunch. His mother did her embroidery while sitting in her skirt on a boulder. Gil thought that maybe Susan and the girls would like to go there sometime.

His cell phone rang and he pulled over to the side of the road before answering it. It was against the law in the city of Santa Fe to talk on a cell phone while driving. It was still thirty miles to Santa Fe, but rules were rules. He answered, saying, "Hello, this is Detective Montoya."

"Gil, man, it's Manny Cordova. I just heard about Melissa Baca. My mom just called and told me. What the hell is going on?" Officer Cordova sounded hollow. His swear words had no strength.

"Manny, I don't really know anything. The state police are handling it." Gil hesitated before asking, "Did you know her?"

"We went to high school together and dated a few years ago. Her mom and my mom are, like, best friends. They play bridge together every week. Ron is like my brother. I just can't believe . . ."

"What was Melissa like?" Gil asked.

"I don't know. She was . . . she was a teacher over at some private school. She lived with her mom and was dating some gringo, some teacher at the school. . . . I just saw her a few days ago and she was all smiles. I can't freaking believe this. . . . You must know something. What are the state cops saying?"

"Manny . . ."

"Melissa would never commit suicide. Do you think it's a suicide?" Cordova sounded desperate.

"Manny," Gil said gently, "I don't know anything."

"What does Melissa look like? I mean, can you tell it's her?"

"I didn't see the body. But it's her."

Gil heard Manny swear softly before he said, "Just call me if you find out anything else. I'm going to call Ron to make sure he and his mom are okay." They hung up, and Gil got back on the road.

As he crested the hill into Truchas, the sun was setting over the Jemez Mountains. He looked to the east, where the Sangre de Cristos were a deep shade of pink. The Española Valley below was cut by the headlights of cars following the highway out of Santa Fe along the valley floor. By the time Gil reached Santa Fe, it was full dark.

CHAPTER FOUR

Tuesday Night

Maxine Baca sat in the easy chair that her husband, Ernesto, had bought her. It had blue upholstery with white dots and fancy skirt ruffle. Its back was too high, making it uncomfortable to sit in. The armrests were dirty. She smoothed them, hoping it would make them look better. She wanted to vacuum the chair but knew that if she walked to the utility closet she would be stopped by well-wishers—was that what they were called? The living room around her was crowded with people. She heard children's laughter coming from the kitchen. It was quickly quieted.

She wanted them all gone. She wanted to be locked in her house alone and not let out. She had heard people on television say that having a child die was the worst thing that could happen to you. What was it supposed to feel like when you lost two children and a husband?

She stood up and made it to her bedroom, ignoring everyone who put out a hand to stop her. She slumped in front of her shrine to Daniel and struggled to stay on her knees. Someone was behind her in the doorway, saying something. She ignored him until he went away.

She picked up the picture of Daniel, her oldest. It had been taken at his high-school graduation, a year before he died. She touched the photo. Daniel had borrowed Ernesto's best tie and they had gone to Dillard's to get him a new shirt with a collar. She carefully placed the picture back at the feet of the statue of Our Lady. She touched the corners of Daniel's First Communion picture, which was leaning against a statue of St. Anthony, her patron saint. He had been only six and had been too scared to smile at the camera. Above Daniel's shrine hung a crucifix. Maxine had dressed Our Lord Jesus in a robe of blue satin, with lace on the sleeves she had sewn by hand. The robe had been her gift to Our Lord for Daniel.

On the table next to two votive candles was a piece of coral. She picked it up. It was pink and jagged. Not much bigger than a pumpkin seed. Her mother had brought the coral when Daniel was born. To ward off *mal de ojo.* Maxine had put the coral in Daniel's crib to protect him from the jealous people who would say he was beautiful but give him the devil's eye.

Ernesto didn't want the coral in Daniel's crib, fearing that he might choke on it. But Ernesto didn't understand. His family was from town and went to the doctor when they were sick. Maxine's family still lived in the mountains and saw the *curandera.* The coral had come from the *curandera.* And Maxine knew that it would protect Daniel.

Maxine, still kneeling, braced herself against the shrine, holding the coral tightly in her hand until she felt it poking into her skin. She heard the people out in the living room talking softly.

The day after Maxine had taken Daniel home from the hospital, Maxine's mother brought the priest to the house to bless Daniel's nursery and the piece of coral. The priest had held the coral in his hand, saying something that was hard to understand in Spanish. Or maybe Latin. While the priest prayed, her mother made the sign of the cross with an egg over Daniel three times. Then her mother cracked the egg in a jar. Her mother smiled when she saw that the egg had two yolks. It was a good sign. When the priest was finished, Maxine had made him a meal of enchiladas and green-chile stew. Maxine's mother warned her not to eat the food, saying that she had to obey the *dieta,* the time after a woman gives birth when she must not eat chile or tortillas. But Maxine ignored her and ate the food anyway, thinking that it would be rude not to join the priest.

The coral had been the only thing protecting Daniel until he was baptized. He had been born the day after Ash Wednesday, during Lent. There would be no baptisms until after Easter. Maxine's mother warned her to keep Daniel nearby in case something came for him, because he wouldn't be protected by Our Lord until after the baptism.

At first, Maxine kept Daniel's crib in her and Ernesto's room. She would lie awake, staring at the crib, until she heard Ernesto snoring next to her. After she was sure that Ernesto was asleep, she would get out of bed and quietly take Daniel from his crib. She would lay him down next to her in bed with her arms around him and watch him until morning.

But Ernesto found out what she was doing one night when he reached for her. The next night, she moved both herself and Daniel into the nursery. Daniel never slept in the crib again. Instead, she would rock and nurse him all night in the blue easy chair Ernesto had bought her when he found out that she was pregnant. She eventually had a small bed moved into the room after Daniel got too big for her to hold all night. She didn't stop nursing him until he was three and a half, when she got pregnant with Ron.

Maxine's mother had nursed Maxine's oldest brother until he was five, even after her mother had given birth to Maxine's sister. There hadn't been enough milk for both children, so her sister had been weaned after four months. Her brother stopped nursing only after her mother's milk had dried up when Maxine was born. Her mother had been angry at Maxine and hadn't put any coral in her crib. The same reason Maxine hadn't put any coral in Ron's crib.

But she had put it in Melissa's.

Maxine set the piece of coral back down on the shrine and picked up Daniel's baby picture. He was smiling in the picture, his dark eyes almost covered up by his baby fat. It had been taken on his first birthday. For his first-birthday party she had made him a two-layer chocolate cake. She and Ernesto sang as Daniel, with his fat hands flying around, bounced in his high chair and watched the candle burning on the cake. Maxine had been ready to slap Daniel's hand away from the candle, but he ignored it and instead threw his face into the cake, covering his cheeks and nose with chocolate frosting.

Ron had grabbed for the candle on his first birthday, but Daniel had gone for the cake. Had that been a sign from God? Something she should have paid attention to? Maybe if she had, Daniel would still be alive.

She hadn't even known that Daniel was taking drugs. She got a phone call one day from the auto shop where Daniel worked. They asked, "Where is he?" Ernesto went looking for him and found Daniel in his mobile home, the needle still in his arm.

It was over just like that. She never had to beg Daniel to stop the drugs or to visit him in a drug center. She hadn't made any trips to the emergency room to be by his side. She never had to take him to the *curandera* to be healed or a priest for a blessing.

Everything had been normal. Daniel had come home every night for dinner and called her every morning. She went to his mobile home once a week and cleaned it. She did his laundry every Sunday. She had seen Daniel the day before he died. He'd talked about going into the army. He'd smiled and teased her about the tomatoes she was trying to grow and had mentioned his girlfriend.

They buried Daniel in the family cemetery. She turned forty a month later. She would kneel three times a day in front of the shrine she had to Daniel in her bedroom, praying the rosary for him. She spent the rest of her time at home in her housecoat, cutting out every article she could find about drug abuse. She looked at newspapers only for stories about drugs, throwing them to the floor if there were none. Ernesto would clean up the papers when he got home from work. If Ron came home, he would step on them or kick them into the corner. When she found an article, she would sit at the dining-room table and highlight phrases—*distances self from family* and *seems uninterested in normal routine.* But Daniel had been fine. Everything had been fine.

She kept the articles in a shoebox on the dining-room table and would spend hours rereading them. Looking for something she should have noticed so that she could have known, could have saved him. There must have been a sign.

Two years after Daniel died, she woke up one morning with the flu. She couldn't move when the doctor told her she was pregnant. She sat in his office chair not breathing, until Ernesto whispered in her ear, "A gift from God."

Melissa Esperanza Baca was born at six pounds four ounces, a month before Maxine's forty-second birthday.

At her first-birthday party, Melissa threw her face into the cake and ignored the candle.

Maxine was still kneeling in front of the shrine, listening to the people in the living room talk. She picked up the coral again and held it in her hand, turning it over several times, before throwing it as hard as she could against the wall, barely missing the crucifix above her head. The coral shattered and a few splinters flew back at her face.

Lucy sat in the afternoon news meeting with the other editors, not listening. They were crowded into a conference room, with the overflow of people trailing out the door. The assortment of city editors, photos editors, copy editors, graphics editors, and Web editors either sat or stood according to who got to the meeting on time. John Lopez, the managing editor, always sat at the head of the table, whether he was late or not. Dad's chair.

Lucy was bored and was using her red pen to fill in all the hollow letters in the words *Capital Tribune* printed at the top of her news budget.

They had already discussed how they were going to handle the Gomez trial—a below-the-fold story on the front page with a single photo. The trial was continuing tomorrow, so it didn't deserve better play yet. When the verdict was announced in a few days, they'd banner it.

Now they were talking about the bigger story—the woman who had been thrown off the Taos Gorge Bridge. They had found out that her name was Melissa Baca. One of their photographers had a picture of the cops pulling the girl's body off the bridge. The frame showed her covered body on the stretcher with a hand visible. The assistant photo editor wanted to use the shot.

Lucy knew they would never use a dead-body photo. Northern New Mexico is one big small town. Many of their readers would know Melissa or her family. It would be bad PR for the paper to use the photo. The assistant photo editor argued that the picture represented the scene on the bridge. Besides, he said, it wasn't any worse than what you saw every night on CNN.

Lucy was surprised that Lopez was even listening. She would have shut up the photo editor long ago. They had run a body shot only once during her three years at the paper. It was of a car crash that had killed a city councillor. The car, with the body in it, had been in the background, with cops cleaning up the accident scene in the foreground. They had thought the body wasn't that noticeable. The next day, they were besieged by phone calls from outraged readers.

Lopez nodded as the photo editor went on, as if he were really listening. They had been talking about this for five minutes. Lucy was having a hard time hiding her impatience. Why discuss something that was never going to happen?

She interrupted. "So, are we going to have a graphic, maybe a map of where the bridge is? I mean everyone knows where the bridge is, but copy desk might need another design element for the page. Who's designing page one?"

A copy editor across the room yelled, "Yo," in an exaggerated Sly Stallone Rambo voice.

"Do you have room for a graphic? How do pages look?" The copy editor handed her the page layout dummies. There was plenty of room on the inside front pages, but the local section was going to be tight.

Lopez said nothing, just looked at her intently. Lucy hoped that she hadn't just gotten herself in trouble. Not that Lopez would ever say anything. He wasn't that kind of manager. He was more like Beaver Cleaver's dad. He didn't get mad, only deeply disappointed, but his disappointment was something she didn't want.

"What's the story with the Baca killing? What do we have?" Lucy asked.

Her boss, City Editor Harold Richards, looked at Lopez, who nodded.

"Melissa Baca was killed sometime yesterday," Richards said. "She was from Santa Fe. I sent Tommy Martinez to talk to the family. He called an hour ago. He got a little info from some of his sources. Looks like she was twenty-three years old and a seventh-grade teacher at that private school, the Burroway Academy. Her father was a cop. He was one of the officers killed during that shootout seven years ago." A few of the heads around the table nodded. They remembered. Richards went on, but Lucy stopped listening. She wondered if it meant something that Melissa Baca's father had been a cop.

Gil drove up to the cinder-block house. Its white paint contrasted with the adobe-brown houses that surrounded it. The neighborhood was middle-class and had few crime problems.

Only a minor break-in every few months. The Baca house had a neat mesh-wire fence around it that was covered in ivy turned brown in the winter weather. There had been an attempt at grass in the front yard, but the dirt was taking over. There were cars everywhere. He would have suspected a party if he'd been just a neighbor passing by.

He knocked on the door. It was answered by a woman he didn't know. He asked for Ron Baca first, but the woman said Ron wasn't there, adding that she thought he was at work. Gil knew that Kline had given Ron some time off, but Ron might have picked up a shift. It was what Gil would have done. Get out of the house and get your mind on something—anything—else. Next he asked for Mrs. Baca. He had to show the woman his badge before he was let in. The house was crowded. Children sat on the floor watching *Sesame Street* on television. The letter of the day was *M*. Adults sat on couches and chairs along the walls. No one noticed him.

He heard voices in a back bedroom. All the lights in the room were on, even the closet light. Mrs. Baca sat on the bed and she wasn't alone.

Gil recognized the woman with her—Veronica Cordova, Officer Manny Cordova's mother. Manny had said that the two women were friends. Their husbands, both police officers, had died in the same shootout seven years ago. Their sons had grown up together and had been in the police academy together. Ron was now Manny's sergeant.

Mrs. Baca and Mrs. Cordova sat on the bed, holding some blue cloth between them. Gil stepped into the room and they looked up, guiltily. He saw that the cloth was a bath towel.

Veronica Cordova dropped her edge of the towel and spoke first. "We were just looking at Melissa's things. We found this on the bathroom floor. I thought . . . I thought if Maxine could just feel something . . . something that was one of the last things that Melissa used, it would . . ."

Gil said nothing. Grief made people do strange things.

Mrs. Baca was still wearing the same stained blouse. She gripped her half of the towel, wringing it.

Gil sat down next to her on the bed.

"I just came to see how you are. I haven't learned anything yet," he said.

Maxine nodded.

He went on. "What can you tell me about . . ." He was about to say Melissa's name but had the sudden thought that if he did so, Mrs. Baca would break down. "What can you tell me about Monday night?"

He leaned closer as she started quietly. "She came home from school about five o'clock. She stayed in her room until dinner. We had cold pizza, leftovers from Pizza Hut. She left right after eight o'clock. I thought she was going to see Jonathan." Gil assumed that Jonathan was Melissa's "gringo" boyfriend that Manny Cordova had mentioned.

"But you actually didn't know where she was going?" Gil asked. Maxine shook her head.

"Do you have a guess? Did she say anything during dinner that might have given an indication of where she was going?" He winced inwardly at his words. He sounded too much like a police officer. Again she shook her head.

"Who are some of her friends, someone she may have confided in?" he asked.

"Her best friend, Judy Maes, works for the city." Maxine startled herself as she said Judy Maes's name, and she shifted sharply on the bed, almost losing her balance. "Veronica, did someone call Judy? I forgot to tell Judy."

Mrs. Cordova patted Maxine's arm. "I called her. Don't worry."

Mrs. Baca slumped back down on the bed, her burst of energy lost.

"Did she get any phone calls while she was home last night? Anything?" Gil continued.

"No."

"Have you noticed anyone strange hanging around? Any strange phone calls?"

"No."

"What did you talk about at dinner?"

"I'm not sure. . . . I don't . . ." She stopped.

"How did she seem at dinner? Happy? Sad? Upset?" Gil asked gently.

"She was fine. Everything was fine." Maxine seemed to sag inwardly. She was swaying as she sat.

"I guess that's all I need to know for now. I know the state police called earlier. They're planning to come by later on tonight to ask you the same types of questions." Mrs. Baca nodded. Gil had told Pollack that Maxine's husband had been killed in the line of duty in the hope that they would go easy on her during the questioning. Gil continued. "Do you want me to be here?"

"No. If Veronica would be here, that would help."

Mrs. Cordova murmured, "Of course," as she got Maxine to her feet.

"Would you mind if I looked around Melissa's room?" he asked. Maxine nodded.

"Another thing." The women paused at the door as he spoke. "The newspapers and TV stations will be calling."

"They already have," Mrs. Cordova said. "I talked to them. They were very nice."

"I'd be happy to talk to them from now on," he said before Mrs. Cordova interrupted.

"It's not a problem," she said with a wave of a hand.

The two women stood in the doorway looking at him. When his daughter Joy was four, she would cry for her stuffed animals whenever they left the house, her "left-behinds," she called them. Veronica and Maxine were a pair of left-behinds.

Patsy Burke sat at her kitchen table reading "Bridge Play of the Day" in the newspaper and sipping chamomile tea. Claire had told that her she should put some bourbon in her tea to help with her cough that she still had from her bronchitis. But Patsy had never been a drinker.

She looked at the clock, thinking she should go to bed soon. They were going to Hobby Lobby tomorrow morning to get the application. They had already picked out Patsy's outfit—navy pants and a white blouse. Claire wanted her to wear a scarf for a touch of color and to show them "that you still got style." Patsy hadn't decided on the scarf yet. She needed to find the pearl earrings that John had given her as an anniversary present and try to remember where she had put the iron.

She took a sip of tea. She had to admit that she was nervous. She had gone over what she was going to say during the interview in her head. Claire had written up a list of questions they might ask her. A few of the questions stumped her. Like: What's your favorite book? Patsy hadn't really read any intellectual books. Claire had told her just to say, "I haven't had time for a lot of reading lately because I like to stay active." Patsy had written that down and tried to memorize it. She kept tripping over the words. It just didn't sound like her. It sounded so confident.

The police scanner on the table made a buzzing noise as one of the fire departments got paged out. John had first gotten her a scanner when he was in the police department so that she could hear what was going on. She hadn't really wanted it. But he knew that other police wives listened to them, so he got Patsy one for her birthday. She thought it was because he couldn't think of any other present to get her. She had gotten used to the noise over the years and found that now she couldn't sleep without it on.

One night, twenty years ago back in Wichita, there had been a bad summer thunderstorm and the electricity went out at their house. The scanner went dead just as they were reporting that a police officer had been shot. Patsy and the boys had been sitting down for dinner. The boys were teenagers then, but she saw that still they were scared for their father. John Junior persuaded her to call up the newspaper to see if they knew anything. She had the courage to do it only because her sons were so worried. The man who answered the phone was nice. He said that the newspaper still had electricity and he was listening to the police-officer-down call. He stayed on the phone with Patsy for over an hour, telling her exactly what the scanner was saying. And delivering the awful news that the police officer who had been shot was dead. And that it wasn't John. They said the Lord's Prayer together for the dead police officer and for John. The next day, Patsy baked the editor some cookies and brought them by the newspaper. After that, she would call him whenever she heard something bad over the police scanner and they would talk to each other and pray about it. Sometimes she would hear something on the scanner that her editor friend hadn't heard. She would call to tell him about it and he would tell her that she should come work for them as an investigative reporter. She would laugh a little at that, but every time he said it, it made her feel good.

When she and John retired to Santa Fe, her editor friend suggested that she see if one of the local newspapers would hire her just to listen to the scanner. He had said that some newspapers did that with people. But she'd never had the courage to call the newspapers and ask about it. Instead, she would just call sometimes and tell them when she heard something interesting on the scanner. She liked being able to see stories she helped with in the paper. But it wasn't the same as in Wichita. The newspaper people were so busy and didn't have time to talk. They didn't have the patience to talk to an old lady.

Patsy struggled to her feet, her hip giving her the same old twinge. She went to the hall closet and started to pull out boxes, hoping she could remember where she had put her iron. And trying to think of any book she had read that might impress the people at Hobby Lobby.

Melissa's room was muted—a floral bedspread with matching curtains. It was mostly bare, as she had lived in it for only six months, since August, when she'd returned from college to start teaching. Gil saw an old photo on her nightstand, taken during the 1980s, of a smiling older man and a young Melissa. Gil peered closer at the picture of Melissa and Officer Ernesto Baca, trying to remember if he had ever met him. Gil had been a police officer for three years when Ernesto Baca was killed. They must have passed each other in a hallway at some point. But he didn't know the face.

There were only two pictures on her walls; one was an Ansel Adams photo, the other a framed poster with the caption "Friendship is a gift from God."

Her computer was on a table in the corner. He touched a key and listened as the Mac chimed on. He wandered around the room, poking in drawers as he waited for the computer to warm up

Her drawers held meticulously folded sweaters and shirts, arranged by color and season—sweaters in the bottom drawers and short-sleeved shirts in the top ones. He ran his hands along the bases of the drawers but found nothing. The bottom drawer on her dresser was stuck. He pulled harder but it didn't give. He peered under the dresser, trying to see if the drawer was broken.

"It's always been like that," Maxine Baca said from the doorway. "Ernesto was going to fix it for her."

Gil looked up at her, surprised. She said nothing more and walked away from the door.

He got up and went back to the computer. He clicked on the Internet access first, looking to see what Web sites she had bookmarked. They were mostly reference and some teaching sites.

Next he went to her e-mail. He spent the next hour reading letters to and from friends at the University of New Mexico. Her messages were short. One friend, who called herself Buttons, wrote a long letter, talking about sex, chocolate cake, and sneezing. In response, Melissa wrote just three sentences. Three male classmates also wrote; a few of the letters were fairly suggestive, but Melissa never responded to those. Her writing style was grammatically correct and not very conversational. She used words like *conjecture* and *contemplate.*

And she ended each of her letters the same way—"Take care and be safe," followed by her full name.

It was about eight P.M. as Lucy sat at her desk, trying gently to convince her county reporter that her opening paragraph on a story about trash fees was too long. But after twenty minutes of talking, Lucy's patience was wearing thin. Her phone rang and she jumped at it, grabbing it before the first ring was over. She hoped that the phone call would give her an excuse to put an end to the conversation.

"Hey, boss, I've got something interesting." It was Tommy Martinez, who was still out gathering info on the Melissa Baca story.

"Hang on just a second, Tommy." Lucy covered the mouthpiece with her hand and, as politely as she could, got rid of the county reporter.

"Okay. Go ahead," she said to Tommy.

"Listen to this. I got it from three sources that Melissa Baca was doing heroin."

"Sources from where?"

She heard him hesitate before he said cautiously, "Law enforcement."

She wondered if one of the sources was Detective Montoya.

"Sources we can name?" she asked.

"No way."

Lucy had expected that answer. "What did these sources tell you exactly?"

"That the state cops found heroin in her abandoned car and that she's an addict."

"And so they're saying she got killed in a drug deal gone bad?"

"Yeah, or she OD'd and someone tossed her off the bridge to make it look like a suicide," Tommy said.

"When do we expect the toxicology reports back from the OMI?"

"Not for a couple of days."

Lucy thought for a moment. The last time they'd had an anonymous tip like this, they had waited until the autopsy was done to report it, worried that if they were wrong, it would hurt the family. But the *Santa Fe Times* hadn't waited and reported it in their story the next day, scooping the *Capital Tribune.* In journalism, there's no such thing as being second. The *Capital Tribune*'s publisher had come down to have a long talk with John Lopez. Lopez had never said anything directly to Lucy, but she knew she had screwed up. And she knew not to make the same mistake again.

"And how reliable are these sources? Are they in a position to know?" she asked.

"Absolutely," Tommy said.

Whenever a new beat reporter came to the paper she gave him the same speech—she wouldn't ask reporters to reveal the names of their confidential sources unless it was absolutely necessary. Her policy wasn't a popular one. Her fellow editors didn't share it; they wanted to know exactly who the anonymous sources were before they would allow them to be quoted in a story. Lucy understood their concern—if an unnamed source said something that wasn't true, they could get sued. Using a source's name protected the paper.

But Lucy had learned the hard way to not reveal her anonymous sources. When she was at her college newspaper, a fraternity started a list that it called The Romeo Roster. On the list was the name of each sorority sister and the number of drinks it took her to pass out. After she passed out, the girl would get raped. A fraternity brother gave Lucy the list, after making her promise not to use his name. The only other person who knew the name of the frat brother was her editor. A year later—after the fraternity had been suspended and sued—her editor talked about it at a party, even mentioning the name of the frat brother who had given them the list. A week later, the frat brother ended up in the hospital from the beating his former fraternity members had given him.

She wasn't about to force her reporters into making the same mistake. She told the reporters loudly and often never to reveal their sources, not even to their bosses. She trusted her reporters to make the right decision about whether a source was believable.

It was a touchy subject in the newsroom and the editors had eventually come to a truce. Each editor would enforce his own policy when he was on duty. In her case, she wouldn't ask who the sources were unless it became necessary.

The reporters knew that they had to have three separate unnamed sources confirm the facts before she would put it in a story. That was a common newspaper rule. Tommy had the necessary three.

"Have you talked to the state cops?" she asked him.

Tommy hesitated. Maybe the source was a state police officer?

"Yeah, and their PIO, that Pollack guy, would only give me the same old 'we cannot confirm or deny' crap, but then said off-the-record that we're on the right track," he said.

Not a resounding confirmation, but for the state police, it was as close as they were going to get.

"Okay, Tommy, we go with it. When you get back we'll figure out how to word it exactly. We'll have to be careful," she said, then added, "And when you call the family to ask about it—"

"I know, I know. I'll be as gentle as possible."

She sighed. She hated this part of the job. She had done it herself when she was a cops reporter—having to ask, "Did you know your dead child was using drugs?" No matter how sympathetically you said it, it still sounded cold-blooded. Strangely enough, most parents didn't scream at her. They softly answered yes or no.

She heard the excitement in Tommy's voice as he said quickly, "Bueno. Good-bye."

Gil left the Bacas and started the drive to his mother's house. He passed ranch after ranch with newly cut roads and big wooden entrance signs. He passed Flying Eagle Ranch and Split Lightning Ranch. All had gone up in the past ten years. Before that, it had been cattle land that had belonged to his second cousins and the Anaya family. A few of the ranches supposedly belonged to celebrities like Jane Fonda and Julia Roberts.

Gil slowed as he came into Galisteo and crossed himself as he passed the Galisteo church. He went past La Tienda Montoya and the Montoya Community Center. He turned off the highway and onto Avenida de Montoya, going slowly over the dirt-and-gravel road. As he passed his cousin's unpainted small house, a horse whinnied and the gravel crunched under his tires. Next was his uncle's house. According to Hispanic tradition, the family property had been divided up among the male children of each generation. The land had been granted to the Montoya family by the king of Spain. Back then, it had covered hundreds of square miles. But after four hundred years of dividing up the land among every generation of Montoyas, there was little property left. A lot of it had been lost when the Americans came and took the land through taxes. That was what Pablo Montoya had fought against and gotten hanged for.

Gil turned again onto a smaller road and drove past the Old House, its half-standing walls reflecting the car's headlights. The flat wooden roof was mostly caved in and the adobe walls were eroded. There had been talk among the Montoyas of restoring the house, one of the few true haciendas left in New Mexico. The Garcia family hacienda, which had been lost in a poker game a hundred years ago, now was a living museum over in La Cienega. One of Gil's uncles had tried to plan family weekends when they would plaster the old walls and pull the weeds out of the dirt floor, but after Gil's father had died, no one seemed interested anymore.

He pulled into his parents' circular driveway, which was closed in by a white picket fence to keep out loose cattle. The cottonwood and aspen trees were ringed with stones and a brick path led up to the New House. The land sloped slowly down to the Galisteo River.

He turned off the car's ignition and sat for a second, staring at the house. He would have to have the flat roof tarred again in the fall, and the portal that ran run around the house needed a new coat of white paint. Maybe he would repaint the house at the same time. The beige paint was starting to fade in places. The house itself was still solid. It had been built in the 1920s with a good foundation. He got out of the car and went up the front steps, the same as he had thousands of times as a kid coming home from school. His mother was in the kitchen. He smelled the posole she was cooking and heard the clank of her spoon against the inside of the pot.

"Hi, Mom," he said with a kiss on her cheek.

"Hi, *hito,*" she said, barely turning away from the stove. She looked older to him than she had yesterday, her gray hair pulled back and getting thinner. She put a steaming bowl of posole, a plate of tortillas, and a glass of milk in front of him as he sat at the kitchen table.

Gil took a bite of posole, the steaming hominy, pork, and

onions almost burning his mouth. He took a bite of a tortilla to cool his mouth and a sip of milk.

He looked around the kitchen. He had painted the top half of the walls last year, and the paint still looked good where it met the pattern of black and blue Mexican tiles starting about halfway down. You could tell that the tiles weren't real only if you touched them. During the Depression, his grandmother had spent three months painting those tiles on the walls. His family had been fairly well off during the Depression but still hadn't been able to afford real tiles. He had touched up a little of her work where it had become faded.

Gil studied a picture on the kitchen wall above the tile. It was a photo of his parents, taken before they had even started dating. His mother had been voted the 1966 Santa Fe Fiesta Queen. The same year, his father had been elected to play Don Diego de Vargas, the man who had reconquered Santa Fe after the Pueblo Revolt in 1680. Together they had gone to schools and retirement homes to talk about the history of Santa Fe while dressed in the costumes of La Reina and the conquistador general. During the fiesta every August, they reenacted de Vargas's conquering of Santa Fe.

They also had posed for a formal picture together. It had been a black-and-white photo, but the photographer had colored in by hand the red rose in his mother's black hair and the yellow of his dad's conquistador shirt. The photographer had said to them, "You look like you are posing for your wedding photo." That's how it had started. Six months later, the photographer was taking pictures at their wedding.

His mother ladled another spoonful of posole into his bowl without asking him if he wanted more, then started doing the dishes.

"Mom, come sit down. I'll help you with those later," he said, pulling out the chair next to him for her.

"When I'm done washing the dishes, then I'll sit down." But

she was never done. Next she would sweep the floor. Then start on the cookies for Therese's school bake sale next week. That was the way it had been since he was a kid. She never rested.

"Did you check your blood sugar today?" he asked. She didn't answer. "Mom, you have to check it every day so the doctor can keep track of it." She still said nothing. She thought it wasn't proper to talk about medical conditions, especially her diabetes.

Gil sighed and ate another spoonful of posole.

"Mom, do you know a woman from town named Maxine Baca? I think her maiden name was Gonzales." His mom and Mrs. Baca were about the same age and he thought they might have gone to school together.

His mom didn't answer for a few seconds, then said, "I don't think so. Is she part of your work?" She always tried to bring his job into the conversation as some sort of penance because she disapproved of it, even though she would never have said so.

"Yeah, she lost her daughter today," he said as he pulled off a piece of tortilla.

"I'll add her name to my prayer list," she said. Gil's father was at the top of her prayer list and his mother's parents were second and third. Her grandparents were fourth and fifth. Gil and Elena were next. It was strange how his mother prayed for the dead before praying for the living. When Gil and Elena were kids, they used to fight about which one of them was first on the list of the live people.

"*Hito,*" his mother was saying, "I need a new candle for your father. I want to get one so I can get it blessed by Father Jerome at the cathedral." His mother didn't drive, so his aunts took her to the grocery store, the hairdresser, and once a week to the cathedral in Santa Fe for prayers.

"Okay, Mom. I'll get Susan to pick one up for you." His mother would light the candle every night as she said her rosary in front of the family shrine in the living room.

"You know, *hito,* I think one of your cousins married a Baca," she said as she scrubbed a heavy cast-iron pan. By "cousin" she probably meant a third or fourth cousin. He didn't ask more about it. The relative was probably only distantly related.

"Come to think of it," his mom said as she dried a cup, "the woman your dad almost married was a Baca." Gill looked up quickly. His mother didn't notice and continued, "Oh, that's right, she was a C'de Baca."

"Dad was engaged before you?"

"Hmmm, but it didn't work out."

"Why?"

"The Judge wouldn't let them get married. He didn't like her family."

The Judge. First District Court Judge Gilbert Nazario Estevan Montoya. Gil's grandfather. When his mother said The Judge didn't like the woman's family, it probably meant that they weren't Castilian enough for him. Her family was probably part Mexican. The Judge disapproved of anyone who was not from Spanish nobility.

Gil finished the last of his posole and put his dish next to the sink. His mother picked it up and started washing it, saying, "Oh, *hito,* don't forget to get the statue of St. Joseph that Susan needed."

He hadn't forgotten. "Where is it?"

"Over in the Old House in The Judge's rooms."

Gil watched his mother for a few more seconds as she rinsed his dinner plate, then he put his coat on and went across the driveway, following a small dirt path in the darkness to the Old House. As kids, he and Elena had used the ruined part of the Old House as a fort against his invading cousins. One room had been the armory and Gil had constructed a complex system of walls and moats. He'd drawn maps of the minefields and rigged booby traps out of boxes and rabbit holes. Eventually all the cousins had defected and ended up inside the fort with Gil and Elena, protecting it from invisible attacking Indians.

The Judge's rooms were in the only part of the Old House still standing. The house had actually been built as both a house and a fort. At one point, a relative had built a circular watch-tower on the east corner.

His grandfather's rooms were in the west corner over by the family chapel. Ironically, The Judge's rooms were in what had been the Navajo slave quarters. The slaves had been mostly captives from the Indian invasions or bought in Santa Fe on the auction block on the Plaza. According to local custom, the slaves had become part of the Montoya family, with the Navajo sons getting pieces of land and the daughters getting dowries when they married. So, somewhere in Gil's distant past he was probably part Navajo or some other type of Indian. The Judge always left that out of their family tree.

Gil stepped through a small doorway and flipped a switch. He looked around the living room for the statue. The room itself was still clean; his mother dusted it every week. The walls were plastered in white and had a few pictures of The Judge with various political bosses. There was one with a governor. Another with President Eisenhower. There was an old carved crucifix over the smooth kiva fireplace, with bright blood painted on Jesus' face and legs. Gil stepped through another doorway. The Judge's old law books covered the walls in the room. On one low table was a collection of saints. Gil walked over to it and picked up the one of St. Joseph. It was about a foot high, made of alabaster. St. Joseph was carrying Baby Jesus and had a lily on the top of his staff. St. Joseph and the Baby Jesus both had very pale skin. But someone had painted dripping blood on Baby Jesus' hands, feet, and head, in the tradition of the Spanish colonial santos.

Gil carefully carried St. Joseph back to the New House. His mother was kneeling in front of the family shrine, clicking off the beads on her rosary. He leaned down to kiss her cheek, saying, "Good night, Mom." She didn't answer him and he left, going back down the creaking wooden stairs.

By the time he got home, Susan and the girls were already in bed. He put the statue of St. Joseph on the kitchen counter and went to bed himself.

Lucy was attempting to unlock the front door of her apartment in the dark. She had forgotten to leave her porch light on. It took her three tries before she managed to connect the key with the lock. She clicked PLAY on her answering machine, then went around her house turning on lights.

"Lucy, you really need to change the message on your answering machine to 'We're not at home' instead of 'I'm not at home.' Make it seem like there's a man around. . . ." Her mother made it sound like Santa Fe robbers called first before stopping by. The next message was a hang-up.

Lucy turned the television on. It was almost one A.M. It had been a hard, long night at work. A copy-desk editor decided that he hated the lead of the Melissa Baca story for no particular reason—"it just sounds funny" was his only excuse. Lucy had to track down Tommy Martinez, and the two of them tried to rewrite the lead. In the end, the copy editor decided that the original lead was better. Sometimes, Lucy hated copy editors.

Lucy kicked off her shoes and changed into her sweats. She flipped channels without really noticing. The vacuum was calling her name. Her carpet was so dirty it crunched. But she was sure that the neighbors wouldn't appreciate the noise at this time of night. Her apartment was the typical Santa Fe layout—kiva fireplace, rough-hewn vigas lining the ceiling.

Lucy was used to living in rented houses. None of the commitment of buying a house. You could just pack up and leave when you wanted. Lucy had gotten really good at getting out of long leases. After Lucy's dad left them when she was eight, she and her mom and her brothers had moved to L.A., then to Atlanta, and finally to Florida. They settled in Tampa but still moved from house to house for years, depending on where her mom was working as a nurse. Lucy always kept half of her stuff in boxes to avoid the hassle of unpacking and repacking all the time. When she moved to Santa Fe, Del persuaded her to unpack all the boxes. They bought a bottle of wine, ate pizza, and burned the empty boxes in the fireplace. A symbol of commitment, he called it. Or had she called it that?

After Del moved out with all his stuff, she had to figure out how to eat using only spoons since she didn't own any forks. She also had no dresser, so she just piled her clothes on the floor. It was when Del came over one day two months later and said, "By the way, the coffeemaker is mine," that she finally decided that it was time to get some new stuff. She took a trip to Kmart and picked up forks, a coffeemaker, and a weird picture of a horse, which she hung in the bathroom. It was definitely bathroom art.

She liked to think of her decorating style as eclectic, but interior designers would probably have called it mishmash. The multicolored wooden fish from the Bahamas clashed with the Georgia O'Keeffe print on the wall next to it. Her beige furniture had been bought as a group from Goodwill for a hundred dollars.

In her bedroom were five chairs that used to match a wooden table long since tossed out. The chairs were pushed up against the wall, making her bedroom look like a waiting room. She sighed. That image was accurate. Men waiting to get into her bed, followed quickly by her waiting for them to get out.

In the corner of the living room was the chest, painted yellow and red, she'd gotten with Del more than four years ago. She had been a cops reporter and he had been a photographer, both just starting out at an Orlando paper. They had graduated from the University of Florida but somehow never met. They didn't have a first date. They went to her house after a work party and he never left. Within a week they had bought the painted chest together; it replaced her orange crates as their new coffee table.

The chest was awful, really. Gaudy without having any character. Del loved it, she hated it. When they moved to Santa Fe last year, they sold all their furniture, except the chest.

He was supposed to come by a half-dozen times in the past few months to get it, but never did. It was always, "I'll get it when I move to a bigger place."

It was now pushed into a corner and covered with a lace cloth, only a tiny part of the red-and-yellow paint visible. She put pictures of her mom and her brothers on it to chase away the Del demons. She had no pictures of her father left. Those had gone into the trash years ago. She wondered if he was still living in New York. Her mother refused to say that Dad had abandoned them; it was always, "He needed to find himself." Like he was in India on a spiritual quest instead of in New York getting remarried.

Lucy walked over to the chest and pulled off the pictures and lace cloth. The photos she put with the others on the mantel. The lace cloth went, unfolded, into a drawer in the kitchen. The yellow-and-red chest she pushed out onto the back porch. Maybe some passing teenager would steal it. Maybe it would finally snow and ruin the paint. She could only hope.

Lucy turned off all the lights and fell asleep on the couch, with *Three's Company* as her background noise and night-light.

CHAPTER FIVE

Wednesday Morning

When Gil walked into the kitchen just after waking up at six thirty, Susan silently handed him the *Capital Tribune.* He read the first three paragraphs of the Melissa Baca article before he saw the word *drugs.* He left the house without taking a shower or saying good morning to the girls, who were still sleeping.

The newspaper article had used the phrase *sources close to the investigation.* He wondered who the state police's leak was. And he wondered why the state police, who had been acting so cooperatively, hadn't told him about finding drugs in Melissa's car.

Gil used his cell phone to dial Chief Kline. Kline answered groggily. Gil read to him from the article's third paragraph: " 'Baca's car was found in Oñate Park, which Santa Fe Police Chief Bill Kline called "a haven for drug dealers" during an interview last month. Sources close to the investigation said heroin and a syringe were found on the front seat of Baca's car. The sources also said Baca was a frequent drug user.' "

All Kline said was, "I'll get back to you."

Next, Gil called Lieutenant Pollack, who answered his phone with a "yo." Before Gil could say anything, Pollack started. "I bet you're calling about the newspaper article." Pollack sighed and said, "Look, if it had been up to me, I would have told you that we found heroin and a syringe in Melissa's car, but my hands were tied by my bosses. You know, all that need-to-know crap. The good news is you're pretty much the only one I can trust right now because I know you're not the leak since you didn't know about it." Gil thought this reasoning was pretty flimsy but didn't say anything. Pollack continued. "Things hit the fan here this morning. I'll have to get back to you." Pollack hung up.

Gil pulled up in front of Maxine Baca's house just before seven A.M. She opened the door and walked away without inviting him in. The house was cold—colder than the morning air outside. As he followed her into the kitchen, he wondered where all the family and friends were from last night.

She sat at the table, a shoe box full of magazine clippings in front of her. He stared at her for a second as she rifled through the box. She took out an article with the headline NEW STUDY SHOWS DRUG USE MORE FREQUENT IN MIDDLE CHILDREN. She was still wearing the same blouse as she had the day before but with different pants. Without a word, he started making coffee. As it was brewing, he went in search of the heater and relit the pilot light, which must have gone out during the night. He found some bread that was starting to turn stale and put it into the toaster. Maxine jumped when the toast popped but didn't look up. He put the toast and coffee in front of her.

He touched her hand. It was as cold as the air in the house.

"Where's Ron and Mrs. Cordova and everyone else?" he asked.

"I sent them away."

"But you need someone to look after you."

"No," was all she said. She took another clipping out of the box. He could only read part of the headline—DRUGS: THE KILLERS IN . . .

He said, as gently as he could, "You could have told me the newspaper asked you about Melissa using drugs. I would have taken care of it."

"They called so late. It was close to nine P.M. Your children must have already been in bed. I didn't want the phone to wake them." She picked up the toast and put it back down without taking a bite.

"The story in the *Capital Tribune* says you denied she ever used drugs. Did you say anything else to them?"

When she spoke, she didn't answer his question. "The state police last night asked about drugs, but I thought they just always ask that."

Gil looked at her carefully. He said softly, "Mrs. Baca, I'm going to have to ask you the same question the state police did, but this time I really want you to think about it. Take your time. Looking back, did anything seem out of the ordinary, anything that would make you think Melissa might have been using drugs?"

She collapsed onto the hard tile floor before Gil could catch her.

Mrs. Baca woke up a few minutes later. Gil had called an ambulance, but she didn't want to go to the hospital. The paramedics checked her out and said that she was fine. He called Ron but got his voice mail. In the end, Mrs. Cordova came and took Mrs. Baca off to bed.

Gil was outside, about to call his mom, when Kline called back. The state police were launching an internal investigation into the leak to the media. Kline had somehow used the problem to get Gil added as a limited member of the investigation team. He would be required to submit a daily written report and call Pollack twice a day to update him on any progress. In return, the state police would decide on a case-by-case basis what information they would release to him.

The situation felt, as The Judge used to say, hinky. It was strictly a state-police investigation, and Gil was wondering why they had agreed to have him as part of the team.

After hanging up with Kline, Gil called Pollack back to get

his assignment and see if there was anything else the state police hadn't told him.

Pollack answered by saying, "Gil, man, we're going to partner. Cool. I guess that's the upside of this whole leak thing." Pollack sounded like a middle-school kid who had finally found someone to share his adolescent secrets with.

"Anyway," Pollack continued, "we sent the syringe and the drugs to be tested at the crime lab, but we won't have those results back anytime soon. We also interviewed her family last night. The mom and brother are in the clear. I guess they were together when the girl got popped." Pollack stopped for a second, then said, "Sorry, dude, I shouldn't have said it that way. That was really cold. I forgot you knew the family." Pollack went on to say that Ron Baca had asked for permission to go to a cabin in Pecos for a while, which the state police and Chief Kline had granted.

"I guess he's really broke up about his sister and wanted to be by himself out in the woods," Pollack said. "You know how it is. It's what I'd do. I talked to him a little bit. He wants us to call as soon as we get anything."

"He's leaving his mother by herself?" Gil asked, surprised. "She really isn't doing very well."

"Seriously?" Pollack asked. "She sounded fine last night. I'll call and tell him to check on her."

Before he hung up, Pollack told Gil to go to Melissa's school. Gil's job was to reinterview the boyfriend, a fellow teacher named Jonathan Hammond, whom the state police had already talked to, and find out where Melissa had been the day she died, from four P.M., when she was seen leaving school, to five P.M., when she came home. The state police were focusing on what had happened after she left home at eight P.M. Gil's assignment was less juicy—for all they knew, she'd spent the hour getting food at McDonald's—but he didn't mind. He was doing necessary police work but staying out of the state police's way.

Gil had to make one more phone call—to his mom—before

he could get on the road. She answered after the fifth ring. She sounded tired.

"Mom, did you check your blood sugar today?" he asked. As always, she didn't answer. He tried something different: "What did you have for breakfast?"

"Oh, just coffee."

"Mom, you really need to eat more than that."

"I'm not hungry, *hito.*"

He gave up and said good-bye. It was nine A.M. before he got to the Burroway Academy. The school had several square, flat-topped buildings connected by covered walkways. Gil stopped and checked in at the front desk, then wandered the hallways of the school, walking past drug-awareness banners and posters urging abstinence. No hand-drawn pictures of ponies and rabbits like at his daughter's elementary school. A few students were in the halls, opening lockers plastered with pictures of Beyoncé as well as other entertainers he didn't recognize.

Jonathan Hammond was teaching a history class. From the hallway, Gil listened to him lecture on the Civil War battle of Glorieta Pass.

Hammond's voice was almost a monotone as he spoke. "In 1862, a group of Texans invaded New Mexico with the idea of raiding Union forts and recruiting the locals. By March 13, the Confederate flag flew over Santa Fe. The Texans pushed north, camping in Apache Canyon near Glorieta, not knowing that a Union camp was just nine miles away." It sounded like Hammond was reading a speech, but as far as Gil could tell, it was all off-the-cuff.

Only a few students were taking notes. Most were staring off into space. Hammond continued. "The two groups battled off and on for two days. On the third day—March 28—the Texans claimed victory, but it wasn't without a price. While the battle was raging, a group of Union soldiers snuck behind the Confederate line and destroyed all their supply wagons. The

Texans had no choice but to retreat back to Santa Fe and eventually Texas. The great Confederate plan to conquer the West ended in Glorieta, New Mexico."

Family history had it that a great-great-great-uncle of Gil's had fought in the battle. Major José Montoya. He had been the commander of the troops that destroyed the Confederate supply wagons. But Elena had never been able to find any record of him. Or of any other Montoya during the Civil War.

The bell rang and the students started to move. Gil went into Hammond's classroom and introduced himself. Hammond looked tired, his blond hair carefully combed but his wire-rimmed glasses slightly askew.

"I don't know what else I can tell you," Hammond said. "I already told the state police everything."

"When was the last time you spoke to Melissa?" Gil asked.

"I talked to her Monday when we were leaving school at four o'clock. We just said good-bye and I told her I'd see her the next day."

"That's it?"

"That was it."

"Doesn't sound like a very intimate conversation for a boyfriend and girlfriend."

"She was tired, I was tired. And we'd been dating for six months, so that banging-like-rabbits phase was long over," Hammond said. The vulgarity was out of place, but Hammond seemed not to notice. "Look, Officer. I know what you're going to ask: Did we have a fight recently? No. Did she have any enemies? No. Did she do drugs? No. Do I do drugs? No. Have I noticed anyone strange hanging around lately? No. Does that about cover it? Oh yeah, you want to know where I was Monday night, since the boyfriend is always the prime suspect. I was directing a dress rehearsal of *'night, Mother* in the gym from six to ten that night. I'm also the drama teacher."

"That's a pretty intense play for a bunch of twelve-year-olds," Gil said.

"I'm surprised, Officer. I thought all you cops read was Tom Clancy and Dr. Seuss."

Obscenities and insults. Gil wondered if this was normal behavior for Hammond or a result of his grief.

"Mrs. Baca thought Melissa was on her way to see you at your house when she was killed," Gil said.

"Well, she's wrong. I was directing the play. Why would Melissa come see me at home if I wasn't there?"

"Do you know where she was going?"

"I haven't a clue."

Hammond pushed his glasses back on his nose, but they were still slightly askew. Gil realized that the lopsidedness wasn't from Hammond's carelessness in putting them on, as he'd first thought—one earpiece was crooked, as if they had been sat on.

"She wasn't having any trouble here with her job or any of the students?" Gil asked.

"No. Everything was fine. Who said otherwise?"

Gil didn't answer and instead looked around. The classroom was almost full again, but the students were ignoring him and Hammond.

Hammond, now clearly annoyed, said in an exaggeratedly irritated tone, "If you will excuse me . . ."

Gil handed him his business card and was leaving the classroom when he heard Hammond begin: "In 1862, the Civil War came to New Mexico. . . ."

Lucy showed up at the Piñon fire station at ten thirty A.M.; she was late because she'd had to go back into her apartment twice—once to take her vitamin, the second time to floss her teeth. By the time she got to the station, Gerald Trujillo was waiting for her. The beige building—of course it was beige—was made of a flimsy metal, like a warehouse with huge garage doors. If it had been built in Florida, the first hurricane to hit would have swept it away. The ambulance bay smelled of gasoline and plastic. Its rooms were cluttered with old bunker gear and handheld radios stripped of their parts.

She and Gerald got into the ambulance, where Gerald proceeded to show her where the medical equipment was kept. In theory, she was supposed to know how to use it all, but in actuality, she had very little idea. For most of the week-long first-responder class she had paid little attention—she'd been too busy drooling over Gerald or not crying over Del.

She and Gerald hopped out of the ambulance and headed over to the fire engine, where Gerald opened a compartment filled with axes, saws, and what looked like really painful sex toys.

She tried to concentrate as Gerald talked. She liked the idea of being a volunteer medic, but somehow she couldn't see herself doing it. Honestly, she wasn't really the selfless type. Just being at the station made her feel inadequate. All the other volunteers had other jobs but were firefighters or EMTs in their spare time. Hell, she couldn't even manage to take a Spanish class in her spare time; these people went out and saved lives on their way home from the grocery store. The worst part was, they did it for free, out of the goodness of their hearts. It intimidated Lucy. She felt like she had no right to walk among these gods. Was that a line from a poem or was she getting high off the fire engine's diesel fumes?

Gerald was explaining how a halogen bar worked when his pager went off, making Lucy jump.

He turned up the volume on the pager as a dispatcher said, "Piñon; Highway 102, MVA; vehicle versus semi."

"Want to go on a call?" he asked.

Lucy nodded and smiled, not sure what else to do. They got into the ambulance as Gerald said into the radio, "Dispatch, Piñon Medic One responding; one paramedic, one first responder onboard."

She listened to the radio as other Piñon volunteers came up. She had been on a total of only three calls in the six months she had been with Piñon, including one other car accident. It had been a little fender-bender and all five patients hadn't needed to go to the hospital. She had tried to take one patient's blood pressure—something she had supposedly learned how to do in class—but couldn't find the pulse at the brachial artery in the crook of the arm. A brisk EMT from another department gave her a scathing look and did it instead. That was the last call she had run, almost two months ago. She had her own pager like Gerald's, but it was in the glove compartment of her car under old Taco Bell napkins and a burned-out flashlight.

Gerald took a turn too fast and Lucy braced herself against the door. A minute later, he pulled the ambulance up to the scene. Two cars pulled up behind them, the other firefighters coming POV. When Lucy first joined the fire department, she'd had no clue that POV stood for Privately Owned Vehicle. At first she'd thought it referred to some complicated firefighting device. Positive Oxygen Ventilation. Partially Obscure Velocity. Gerald had set her straight without laughing.

In the middle of an intersection sat a semi-trailer and an old Honda Civic. Or at least it looked like a Civic. Lucy was bad with cars, plus this one was barely recognizable as a car.

She saw the driver of the semi gesturing wildly as he talked to a deputy. The man looked unhurt.

As Lucy hopped out of the ambulance, Gerald told her to put on two sets of latex gloves. She had no idea why, but she didn't question him. Gerald handed her the oxygen bag and the medical pack from the ambulance. As she followed close behind Gerald, she silently reminded herself to keep her mouth shut and just listen, something she'd never been good at.

The front of the semi was slightly dented, but the entire driver's side of the Civic was crushed in more than two feet. The car had been spun around by the impact of the crash. A sheriff's deputy was directing traffic away from the scene. Broken glass and plastic crunched under her feet, and somewhere in the distance she heard more sirens.

Gerald got into the passenger seat of the Civic and motioned her into the backseat. She climbed in with a sheriff's deputy who was trying to keep the driver—a man in his forties—talking. Lucy glanced at the damage to the car's interior. The metal from the driver's-side door was crushed over the man's legs. He would need to be cut out of the car. What did the firefighters call it? Extrication? It was obvious from his injuries that he hadn't been wearing a seat belt, and the car was too old to have an airbag.

Gerald calmly said, "Hold his neck." Lucy squeezed past the deputy in the backseat and held the driver's head and neck in place from behind—keeping his head straight to maintain C-spine, the only thing she remembered from class. Gerald checked the man's breathing and heart rate.

The man was bleeding heavily from his head. Lucy was glad that Gerald had made her put on two sets of gloves—her first pair was now covered in blood.

The deputy was occasionally calling out, "Sir, sir? How are you doing, sir?" The man let out a groan.

"Do you know what his name is?" Lucy asked the deputy.

"No. He was talking just a minute ago."

Gerald used a stethoscope to listen to the man's lungs, as Lucy tried to calm her own breathing.

A firefighter appeared at the back door with a backboard and a C-collar—a medieval-looking contraption that was supposed to fit around the man's neck. And she was the one who was supposed to know how to work it. She looked around. She had no idea what she was doing. This man needed experienced emergency medical help, not some stupid girl who had taken a medic class just to get over her boyfriend. She felt the panic rise in her stomach and move up her throat.

Gil waited outside the principal's office. The chair he sat on felt like it was going to fall apart if he moved. He adjusted himself slowly. Principal Ken Strunk's secretary had said that he would be right out. That had been fifteen minutes ago.

Strunk appeared about five minutes later. He was about five feet eleven inches and trim, his brown hair graying at the temples. Gil guessed he was about forty-five. His shirtsleeves were carefully rolled up to just below his elbows and his tie was slightly loose. Gil thought that the casual image seemed very practiced.

They went into Strunk's office. It was nothing like the metal cabinets and linoleum of public schools. Abstract paintings hung on the paneled walls and the rest was done in tones of brown, with the carpeting and drapes in a deep shade of peach. It wasn't pink but peach. Gil knew the difference. When he and his wife were remodeling their house, she'd made him go to paint stores as far away as Albuquerque looking for the right shade. Twice he'd brought home colors that his wife frowned over—saying that they were light pink, not peach. Gil started to wonder if he was color blind. They'd ended up with a shade called peach-kissed that looked the same as every other shade. Gil wondered whether Strunk or his wife had decorated his office.

Gil sat in one of the fake antique chairs and Strunk sat at his desk.

"It's a tragedy, what happened to Miss Baca. She was a fine teacher who cared for her students," Strunk said, looking grave.

Gil wondered if Strunk had prepared that speech during the twenty minutes he had been waiting. "What can you tell me about her, Mr. Strunk?"

"Not much. Just as I said, Miss Baca was a fine teacher."

"How long had she worked here?"

"About six months. It was her first job after graduating from college in August. She was a dean's-list student at the University of New Mexico. Her teachers recommended her highly."

"She came to work on time? Didn't have a lot of sick days?"

"Miss Baca was very punctual and reliable. She never had a sick day."

"Do you know that for sure? You don't want to look it up?" Gil was still wondering what Strunk had been doing during that twenty minutes.

"Actually, I do know that for certain. I checked her records before you came in."

"What else do her records say?"

"Nothing more."

"Can I see them?

"No. They are confidential. I believe that since you're not the official investigating officer, you have no reason to look at them." Strunk smiled kindly after he'd said it. "I don't mean to be rude, Detective. I must be very careful in a situation like this to not involve the school in any lawsuits. I hope you understand."

"Mr. Strunk, I understand completely. You have been very helpful so far," Gil said as he watched Strunk, who loosened his tie more.

"Oh, I wish you hadn't said that," Strunk said with another small smile and a feminine wave of his hand. "I might as well be honest. In those few minutes I made you wait, I called our attorney and he told me exactly what to say. I even wrote the first part of my little speech down." Strunk held up a sheet of school stationery that was covered with very precise—almost draftmanslike—writing. "But it feels strange not to help the police fully. I guess I can still hear my mother saying to me when I was little, 'Kenneth, if you ever get lost, go find a police officer.' So, maybe we can try this again, and I'll be a little more forthcoming. What other questions do you have?"

Gil studied him for a second before he asked, "Do you allow relationships between teachers?"

"You mean between Melissa and Hammond?" Gil noticed that Strunk called Melissa by her first name and Hammond by his last. "I don't encourage teachers' dating."

"Did you discourage Melissa and Hammond, Mr. Strunk?" Gil asked.

"No. They were professional about it. I would have . . ." Strunk searched for the word, "prompted them to end the relationship if they had public fights or obvious signs of affection, that sort of thing."

"As far as you know, they got along fine?"

"Yes. Not that I actually would know." He smiled again. "The boss is always the last to find out."

"What did you think about Melissa personally?"

"I thought very highly of her. She was an excellent teacher who cared about her students very much. . . . Lord, that sounded rehearsed again, but it's the truth."

"What do you think about Hammond?"

Strunk considered the question for a moment before he answered carefully, "He is very studious."

Gil waited for more but nothing came. "Mr. Strunk, I thought you were trying to be more helpful?"

Strunk stared at the abstract painting on the wall behind Gil before he answered. "The truth is, Mr. Hammond has a hard time guiding his students. He doesn't have Melissa's natural abilities. When they started dating, I had hoped Melissa could communicate to him a little more about what it means to be a teacher, that it's not all about studying. Students need emotional guidance as well."

"Did Mr. Hammond ever do anything inappropriate in the classroom?"

"Oh, no, nothing like that. He just thinks we should give the students free rein. Melissa believed in very traditional mores. For instance, one of the younger girls came to class with quite a bit of makeup on and Melissa made her go wash it off and then sent her to my office. And I sent her to the school counselor."

"How old was the girl?"

"She was eight. Melissa realized, and rightly so, that it was dangerous for a girl that young to be putting too much emphasis on her looks. At our teachers' meeting later that day, Mr. Hammond said he thought we had overreacted. He said if the girl had chosen to wear makeup to school, who were we to tell her that it was wrong?"

Gil wondered what else Hammond let the students get away with.

"Did Melissa ever have any problems with students or parents?" Gil asked.

"Just the usual. Nothing untoward." Gil smiled to himself. That wasn't a word he heard every day in his line of work.

"How was Melissa the past few days?" Gil asked.

"She seemed normal, very dedicated as always," Strunk said, as he picked a pen up off his desk and started to play with it. Without looking at Gil, he added, "What you're really asking is did she seem like she was on drugs. I read the article in the newspaper this morning. I've already had three phone calls from parents. They all said things like, 'How could you let a woman like that work here.' And the TV stations have started calling. Our attorney told me to say 'no comment.' The truth is, she was fine. I didn't notice anything."

Maxine Baca was kneeling in front of Daniel's shrine, just starting on the second Sorrowful Mystery of the rosary. The Scourging at the Pillar. In her mind, she recited what she'd been taught in grade school: *Jesus is bound to a pillar and cruelly scourged until his whole body is covered with deep wounds.* Maxine's eyes were closed and she held her blue-beaded rosary tightly. She imagined herself at the pillar, being scourged. She thought of a leather whip. Then a stick like the one her mother had used. She bowed and crossed herself as she said, "Pray for us sinners, now and at the hour of our death. Amen."

She finished the tenth Hail Mary and then the Glory Be to the Father before opening her eyes. She shifted on her knees in front of Daniel's shrine and stared at his graduation picture before closing her eyes again and starting the next Mystery. The Crowning with Thorns. She said the Our Father while she imagined a Roman solider in front of her, pushing the crown of thorns down on her head. She imagined the blood running down her face. She started the Hail Marys again.

She finished her last Hail Mary and immediately started on the Carrying of the Cross. She didn't like this mystery. She imagined herself carrying the heavy cross down a dusty street. When the Roman soldiers told Simon of Cyrene to take the cross from her, she pushed him out of the way and continued up the hill. She recited the tenth Hail Mary in a rush, excited to get to the last Sorrowful Mystery, the one she liked the best. The Crucifixion.

She closed her eyes tighter and straightened her back as she knelt. She said the Our Father and thought of herself being nailed to the cross. She imagined the hand of the Roman solider touching hers as he positioned the nail and pounded it in. Sometimes when she had the visions, she would feel a sharp pain in her hands and feet. On those days, she was closest to God. Today she felt only a dull ache. She started on the first Hail Mary and imagined herself being nailed to the cross over and over. By the time she reached the last Hail Mary she was sweating. Next she was supposed to say the First Glorious Mystery, but instead Maxine said a Glory Be to the Father and a last Our Father.

She tried to stand up but had to put her hand out on her bed to pull herself up. She smoothed the bed as she stood up stiffly. It was the bed that had been in Daniel's nursery. The one she had nursed him in when he was a baby. She had slept in Daniel's room until he was almost eight. Ron had stayed in Ernesto's room in a crib until he was three. Ernesto had never complained about it. But one day, when she came back from the store, Ernesto had moved her bed back into their bedroom and pulled Ron's crib into Daniel's room. She had had insomnia since then, but hadn't moved the beds back until Melissa was born.

Maxine stood up the rest of the way and kissed the feet on the crucifix on the wall above her, crossing herself.

Veronica Cordova stood in the doorway of Maxine's bedroom, her hands folded in prayer. Maxine didn't know how long her friend had been standing there.

"I prayed a rosary for Melissa this morning, too," Veronica said. "Maybe we can pray one together for her later."

Maxine just nodded and walked past Veronica, who had been with Maxine since she'd fainted earlier that morning. The two women went into the kitchen. Veronica busied herself making coffee. Maxine stared at the cold toast and coffee, still on the table, that Detective Montoya had made her.

Her box of newspaper clippings was also on the table. She sat down and pulled it over, stopping to read a few highlighted words.

"I hope you don't mind, but I called the funeral home," Veronica was saying. "I hope that was all right. I thought you'd want to use the same one that we had for Daniel and Ernesto."

Maxine looked up at Veronica, who had finished making the coffee and was starting to clear off the table. They had met when Veronica and her husband had built a house three doors down. That had been so long ago. Almost forty years. That's how long Veronica had been coming over to her house every morning for coffee. They would talk about planting their gardens and share news about the neighbors. Ron and Manny had played on her kitchen floor together since they were babies.

Ron had called a little while ago, asking her how she was doing and wondering if he should come home. She had told him that she would be fine with Veronica.

She pulled another clipping out of the box and smoothed it on the table. This one was about a new study that promised a cure for drug addiction. She found a pen in the box and used it to underline the words *vaccine* and *dopamine.* The last line of the article was a quote from a scientist: "We are five to ten years away from a cure." Maxine started to underline the quote, but the pen poked through the paper, ripping into the words. She stopped, surprised, then pushed the pen harder, digging into the table and scribbling furiously.

At eleven thirty A.M., Lucy and Gerald were in the Piñon fire station writing their run reports. Two other EMTs had shown up to the accident within minutes. They had helped load the man into the ambulance and taken him to St. Vincent Hospital. Gerald told Lucy to sit in the front passenger seat of the ambulance—like a misbehaving child—while he and an EMT worked on the man in back. She felt completely ineffectual, sitting there staring out the window as the real medics helped the patient. She heard them moving in the back, talking to each other in low tones as equipment beeped and whirred. The EMT driving the ambulance never even looked her way. She knew what they thought of her, and they were right. She was not cut out for this.

The patient ended up having a closed-head injury, a broken leg, and possibly a ruptured spleen. Gerald had to explain to her in slow words what the injuries meant. Lucy was going to call the hospital later. She hoped he would live. His name was Earl Rivera, which they found out after his wife passed by the accident on her way to work. Lucy had first heard her screams over the buzzing extrication saw. Lucy had looked around crazily, afraid for a second that the saw was cutting into the patient. Then she saw a woman standing with a sheriff's deputy. The woman was doubled over and shrieking. The deputy patting the woman's back looked very scared and very young.

Lucy walked over to the woman without thinking and led her away from the scene. Lucy had her sit down on a running board of the fire truck, while she told a firefighter to go get Mrs. Rivera some water. Then she started asking questions about anything that might stop the woman from screaming. She found out that Mrs. Rivera worked for the state accounting office and that she and her husband had been married for twenty-one years. They had three children. The oldest, a girl named Joyce, was graduating from the University of New Mexico with a degree in engineering in May. Mrs. Rivera showed Lucy a picture of the family. Joyce looked a lot like her mother. Lucy helped Mrs. Rivera call her sister, who came to take her to the hospital.

Now, sitting in the Piñon fire station, Lucy was trying to figure out how to tell Gerald that she was quitting. She couldn't do this work. She wondered how anyone could.

When Lucy was seven, she'd run barefoot along a creek and gotten a piece of rusted metal stuck in the bottom of her foot. Her mother had frantically called an ambulance. The paramedic who had taken care of her was smiling and soothing; he'd told Lucy that she had beautiful eyes. She was enthralled. He was her savior.

Earl Rivera might think she was his savior. The thought almost made her laugh.

She watched Gerald as he scribbled on his report. He hadn't said anything since leaving the hospital.

Gerald looked up, catching her staring at him. He must have seen something in her face.

"How are you doing?" he asked, putting his pen down.

"Do you want the truth or a lie?"

He smiled. "The truth this time."

"I never want to see something like that again."

He sighed and finished off the last of the coffee in his chipped brown mug. "Did I ever tell you why I stopped being a full-time paramedic and became a volunteer?" Without waiting for her to answer, he said, "One night when I was working for the city, my partner and I got called out on a sick call. That's as much as the 911 dispatcher told us. As far as we knew, this guy had the flu. It turns out the guy felt sick because he had been shot twice. So there we were, without any police around, trying to save this guy, and the shooter shows back up. He fires off two more rounds and kills our patient."

Gerald went to get another cup of coffee, leaving Lucy waiting at the table. She watched him add cream and sugar. He stirred the cup a few times before saying, "I quit over that. I started my own construction business instead. It took five years for my wife to convince me to join up with the county as a volunteer paramedic. I still get cold feet every time I go to a sick call."

"I don't get the point," she said.

"The point is, you don't pick this profession, it picks you. I had no choice but to come back."

"You make it sound like a calling from God."

"It is."

"Well, I'm calling God back and telling him I don't want it."

She jumped as Gerald's pager sounded again, spilling some of the coffee in her mug.

CHAPTER SIX

Wednesday Afternoon

Of course it was a sick call.

Gerald rolled his eyes as he swallowed the last of his coffee and tied his boots on. He told Lucy to look up the address they were going to in the map book as they got into the ambulance.

She picked up the map book and flipped through the pages. "How do you work this thing?" she asked.

Gerald laughed. She hadn't meant it as a joke. "There's an index in the back. Just find the street there," he said.

Soon she was getting carsick as they sped down the tiny streets and flew over potholes.

"Goddammit! Gerald, would you please not go over every single bump," she said, trying to make herself act normal. And normally she would have yelled at a man she barely knew. "Take the next left," she said, checking the map.

She looked over at him. He was tapping his finger in time with the radio, some Eagles' song. A few minutes ago, she'd been quitting; now, she was running another call. How had that happened?

They pulled up to the house as Gerald picked up the radio and said, "Santa Fe, Piñon Medic One on scene." He got out of the ambulance and pulled on his latex gloves.

Lucy didn't move from the passenger seat. "You know, I think I'm just going to stay here," she said.

"I need you inside."

She took a deep breath and got out of the ambulance.

In front of a newish, adobe-colored stucco house with perfect landscaping was a woman, probably in her early seventies, dressed in red stretch pants, a long lime-green T-shirt, and a white baseball cap.

"Are you the one who called 911?" Gerald asked.

The woman nodded. "It's my friend. She didn't show up at my house this morning. We were supposed to go to Hobby Lobby."

Gerald and Lucy reached the front door. It was locked. Gerald called out, "It's the fire department," several times. The old woman reached into her pocket, pulled out a set of keys, and thrust them into Lucy's hand. "Here, take these fucking things. I lost my glasses so I can't open the door myself. That's why I called you."

Lucy found the right key on the set and unlocked the door and pushed it open. All three of them were in the foyer before a faint smell hit them. It was like a staleness in the air. Lucy glanced at Gerald. She guessed what the odor was, even though she had never smelled it before. She wanted to go back to the ambulance. Hell, she wanted to go home. Be anyplace but here.

"Ma'am, could you do us a huge favor and stay just outside the front door here. It would really help. Thanks," Gerald said.

The woman put her hands on her hips, looked Gerald up and down, and said, "Like hell I will."

"Ma'am, we really need you to stay here."

The old woman snorted as she stomped outside. Gerald started in and Lucy had no choice but to follow. The house was decorated in early grandma—pictures of smiling children and grandchildren hung on the walls. On coffee tables were lopsided vases and candy bowls made by small hands. They wandered through the dark house, which was stifling. The heat must have been set at eighty.

Gerald occasionally called out, "Ma'am? Ma'am, it's the paramedics," but they didn't get an answer. Lucy tried not to think about the reason for that.

They found her splayed over an easy chair, her head on the floor and her legs sticking up over the back of the chair. She had been dead for a while. Her skin was mottled and her eyes were rolled back. Lucy barely heard Gerald talking in the background.

"I wonder what killed her," Gerald said to himself. "We'll have to get a medical history. Maybe an MI. Stroke. Anything. Weird positioning of the body. I guess she fell that way." He walked over to the woman to feel for a pulse. Lucy wondered why, since the woman was so very obviously dead.

Lucy stood in the entrance to the living room. She had seen dead bodies when she was a cops reporter, but those had been covered with sheets. The most she had seen was the top of a head or the bottom of a foot. It was nothing like this. Lucy moved forward a few steps, involuntarily craning her neck to get a better look.

The woman's body was discolored, with the blood pooling in weird places because of how she had fallen over the chair. There was no dignity in this kind of death. No peace. One minute you're alive, and the next, strangers are in your home, staring at your varicose veins and stretch marks.

Gerald kneeled next to the body, peering at some long bruises on the woman's neck.

"Come take a look at this," he said to Lucy. Just then, a police scanner on an end table went off.

A cold wind hit Gil when he stepped out of his car downtown near City Hall. He had called Judy Maes to say that he was stopping by her office.

He found her standing over some blueprints. Her black suit didn't have a crease in it. He had been surprised to reach her at work the day after her best friend had been found dead. As he got closer, he noticed how tired she looked. She wore lipstick but most of her eye makeup had been wiped off, giving her dark circles. She took him to a break room near her office and closed the door.

"When was the last time you talked to Melissa?" Gil asked after he offered his condolences.

"The day before she died. We talked about stupid stuff—my car problems. My Jeep is always in the garage. My lack of a boyfriend. I don't think we even talked about her at all. God, doesn't that seem selfish of me?" Judy Maes put her hand up to her face and rubbed her eyes before she went on. "We talked for only a minute or two."

"How did she seem?"

"Normal."

"Had anything out of the ordinary happened in the last few weeks? Anything that seemed a little odd that Melissa told you about?"

"Nothing. She seemed fine. But it was always hard to figure out Melissa. She could have been completely freaked out and never shown it."

"What do you mean? What was Melissa like?" Gil asked.

"Studious. Nice. Dependable," she said. "The guys always loved her because she was such a mystery. They thought no girl that beautiful could be so straitlaced. They wanted to find her bad-girl side."

"What kind of people did she hang around?"

"That's the mystery thing—she seemed drawn to wild people but she was never wild herself. Like a moth to a flame. There wasn't a single weekend in college that I wasn't drunk, and Melissa was right there with me, but never had anything to drink herself. She would just be with us. Just kinda watching. And when we went home, she'd be the designated driver. She was always the one holding my hair back as I threw up in the toilet. Always taking care of us."

"Why do you think she never joined in?" he asked.

"We talked about that once. Melissa wasn't a stupid girl. She knew she was uptight. She said she thought maybe it was because of her brother, the one who died. She felt she was the replacement child—the one who wouldn't screw up. The one who did everything right."

The one who shouldn't die young, Gil thought. "And did she do everything right?"

"Too much so, sometimes. She once saw some friends cheating on a test and turned them all in. And these people were pretty good friends of hers. She was weird that way—she watched us drink ourselves stupid every night and said nothing about it, but as soon as someone did something she considered morally wrong, she would have no mercy."

"So she had no problems at all? Gambling? Debts?"

"Melissa? Never in a million." Judy shook her head. "I heard the newspaper did some story about her doing drugs. But no way. Her only real problem was dating guys who were jerks. She's dated some real losers. It was the same kinda thing—she would never be a bad girl herself but dated bad guys."

"Was anybody ever violent?"

"This one guy, she only dated him for a week or so a couple of years ago, but I can't remember his name. God, what was that asshole's name? Anyway, he slapped her for some stupid reason and that was that."

"Did she ever see the guy again?"

"You mean recently? Not that I know of. If she did, she didn't mention it."

"What about the new boyfriend—Jonathan Hammond?"

"I think they were having a little trouble . . . not that she ever said anything. With Melissa you had to watch the way she said things. Like last week I asked how things were going between them and she said, 'As well as might be expected.' In

Melissa-speak, that meant something was wrong. But she wouldn't tell me any more. My guess is that she was going to break it off."

"What do you think of her boyfriend?"

He could tell that she didn't like the question. She answered it carefully. "I think he was a step up from her usual loser."

"But still a loser?"

She hesitated again. "I think he's not a nice person."

"What do you mean?"

She sighed. "He never really thought about her. This one time he wanted her to spend the night at his place, but she had the flu. She wanted to go home. He gave her this long speech about her lack of commitment to their relationship and how she only thought of herself. He even took out this psychology book and read to her something in it about narcissistic people. She was so achy she could hardly move, and *she* was being selfish?"

"But he never threatened her? Was he the jealous type?"

"No. He was too snooty for that. Truthfully, I think he was a white boy who liked having a *morenita* girlfriend that he could show around to all his white friends."

"What makes you think so?"

"He was always saying stuff. Like whenever he had to repeat something to Melissa if she didn't hear him, he'd say, 'Maybe I should say it in Spanish so you'd understand.' He was just being condescending. He knew she didn't speak Spanish."

Gil nodded. Melissa was like many Hispanics native to Northern New Mexico: of Hispanic descent but not Spanish-speaking. Most of Gil's family didn't know Spanish, either. The Judge had made sure that Gil learned it.

Judy Maes was wiping tears from her eyes with her fingertips.

"Let's get back to the drugs," he said. "Did you ever see her do any? Pot? Anything?"

"Are you insane? She would have died first." Realizing what she had just said, Judy covered her eyes.

"Can you think of any reason why she might have had drugs in her car?"

"She wouldn't even know how to buy drugs. That person who wrote that story in the paper should be shot." Her voice turned cold. "Melissa wasn't a tecata. She wasn't an addict. She hardly drank caffeine. I smoked a joint once in college and she bought me books on the dangers of pot. She wanted me to go with her to some Narcotics Anonymous meeting. All this for taking just one hit off a joint. She said drugs were the devil."

Gil wondered what could possibly have happened to make Melissa give in to the devil. Going from no drugs to injecting heroin in just a few months was a long, hard fall. Who or what had given her that push?

Lucy watched the Santa Fe County deputies secure the dead woman's home. The first officer on scene had instructed her and Gerald not to leave. Not that she would have. They sat in the ambulance, waiting.

She had no way of knowing whether the dead woman was Scanner Lady. She had never seen Scanner Lady, never known her name, never known where she lived. All Lucy knew was her voice.

"Gerald, how many old ladies in Santa Fe do you think listen to police scanners? A few, right? At least more than one? Maybe more like six? With a population of a hundred thousand between the city and the county, maybe more like ten or twenty. How unusual is it? It can't be that weird a hobby."

She knew she was rambling. She had been for the past ten minutes. Gerald sat quietly, listening to her, not commenting. She had told him everything—about Scanner Lady's call, about talking to Detective Montoya.

She kept talking. "This is just a coincidence. Maybe the dead woman ran a meth lab in her guest bedroom and that's why she had a police scanner. Who knows? Just because a woman who owns a scanner gets killed right after I look into a phone call from a woman who owns a scanner doesn't mean the two incidents are related." She winced at her words—not only was she rambling, she wasn't making any sense.

Lucy slouched in her seat. She was just seeing a conspiracy here that didn't exist. Journalists loved conspiracy theories because in their line of work, sometimes the conspiracy theories turned out to be true. "It's not Scanner Lady. It can't be her," she muttered.

She jumped as a deputy knocked on the ambulance window. She and Gerald were escorted into the house. Deputies and fingerprint dust were everywhere. The police photographer clicked away. They were led into the back bedroom.

A big man with a round chest introduced himself as Major Ed Garcia, the investigating officer. Gerald greeted him warmly, calling him Eddie and giving him a handshake/hug. Lucy wondered how they knew each other. Cousins? Uncles?

Gerald explained how he and Lucy had come to the house and found the body. It was a quick summary, taking only a few sentences. Garcia nodded and didn't ask any questions. It was all routine. They gave Garcia their names, addresses, and phone numbers. A deputy was about to escort them out when Lucy said, "Actually, Major, I was wondering about something." She felt Gerald shift his stance next to her. He probably wanted her to shut up, but she didn't care. She needed to know.

"I work at the newspaper, and we have this woman who always calls in with tips she hears on her scanner. I was just thinking that maybe this woman might be our tipster."

Garcia looked at her intently. "You work at the newspaper? What do you do there?"

Lucy heard the edge in his voice. The innate distrust of journalists. "I'm an editor."

Garcia glanced accusingly at Gerald, then back at Lucy. She could tell that the major was getting nervous. He didn't say anything.

She made herself smile brightly. "If I could just hear her voice, maybe just hear her answering-machine message, I would know if she's our tipster and let you guys get back to work."

Garcia wasn't buying her Pollyanna act. "I'm going to have to check with my superiors," he said.

"I just need to hear her voice, that's all. I just need to be sure. I only need to listen to the answering machine. How could that hurt anything? I swear I'm not going to run out and tell the newspaper anything."

"Like I said, I need to check with my bosses. I have your name and number. I'll call you."

Lucy was about to argue but Gerald grabbed her arm and steered her out of the room. Damn police. Because she worked at a newspaper she was automatically labeled untrustworthy and willing to do anything to get a story.

As she walked through the living room, Lucy glanced furtively at the answering machine. It had been dusted for prints. If only she had listened to it before the cops showed up. But she had been trying to preserve the scene.

As they walked out into the bright sunlight, the OMI van pulled up. Lucy looked at the deputy escorting them.

"Deputy, what's the operating theory? What do you guys think happened?" Lucy asked.

"Robbery that got interrupted," he answered with no intonation.

"A robbery? Was anything taken? There were no signs of a struggle. The strangulation marks were made by a rope or something. If she had surprised a robber he would have reacted quickly and used his hands, right?"

The deputy shrugged. "Who knows?"

"The dead woman—what was her name?" Lucy asked.

The deputy hesitated. He had seen the exchange between her and Garcia.

"How can it hurt to tell me her name? I have to know so I can write my report anyway. If I don't find out from you, I'll just call dispatch for it," Lucy asked.

The deputy hesitated again before he said quietly, "Patsy Burke."

"How could God allow a man that stupid to live? Someone should have killed Garcia with a rock a long time ago," Lucy said as they climbed back into the ambulance. It took her a second to remember the half hug that Gerald had given Garcia. "Oh, sorry. I forgot you guys are related."

"We're not related. We played football together in high school, although we might be second cousins on my mother's side." Gerald smiled a little. "He's not a bad guy."

"You could have fooled me."

Gerald shook his head and said, "He's just doing his job."

"Well, if his job is to be a jerk, he's great at it."

"In his mind, you're the enemy. The newspaper has it out for the police."

"No, we don't, and I wasn't there as a member of the media, I was there as a stupid medic." She winced as she realized what she had just said. "Sorry, Gerald. I take back the 'stupid' part."

Gerald didn't answer as he turned onto the highway.

Lucy picked up her cell phone and dialed 411.

"What are you doing?" Gerald asked.

"I'm going to get Patsy Burke's phone number. I want to listen to her answering-machine message."

"That's not going to get you anywhere. The cops will just pick the phone up."

"I'll hang up."

"Ever hear of star-69?"

"Does that work on cell phones?"

"Do you really want to find out?"

"Goddammit," Lucy said as she slapped her phone shut. She tapped her knee against the door. "Gerald, turn around," she said suddenly.

"What for?" he asked without slowing down.

"I can talk to the friend, that neighbor lady, the one who called us. I bet she knows if Patsy Burke was Scanner Lady."

"It's no good," Gerald said. "They had her inside in one of the bedrooms. Didn't you see her?"

Lucy hadn't seen anything in the house; she had been so focused on Garcia and the answering machine.

She looked out at the highway, watching the Burger Kings, Albertsons, and Jiffy Lubes go by. She stared at the brown van driving in front of them. The make of the van was indeterminate; it was just old. On the back window was written KLASSY VAN in silver letters, because nothing says classy like using a K to misspell a word. As they passed the van, she looked at the driver, who was busily gesturing into his cell phone.

"Gerald," she said without looking at him, "what do you do if you think you got someone killed?"

Gil was on his way to check on Maxine Baca when he got a page. As the dispatcher put it, "There's a woman at the office who is anxious to see you." What the dispatcher meant was that the woman was being difficult.

As he pulled into the parking lot he saw the editor from the newspaper leaning against a gray Toyota Camry. What was her name again? Something Newroe. Where had he put her business card?

"Ms. Newroe, how can I help you?"

She took a deep breath, and Gil wondered if it was to calm herself or for courage.

"Detective, I need to talk to you." She ran a hand through her dark blond hair. "It's connected to what we talked about yesterday, but now it's of a personal nature, not a professional one, so I'm not here as a journalist but as a . . . Oh hell, I don't know what I'm here as. God, I'm not making any sense." She smiled, laughing at herself.

Gil realized that she was nervous. "We can go inside. . . ."

"No, no, please, let's stay out here." The suggestion had upset her.

"Okay. Well, there's a bench over there." They sat down near some bushes.

She breathed deeply again before starting. "I know this whole thing is going to sound odd, but please bear with me." She looked at him, and he nodded. He stopped himself from saying anything more. He wanted to comfort her and calm her down.

She continued. "So, okay, besides being an editor at the paper I'm sort of a volunteer medic with the county, over at Piñon—just so you know that. Just a few hours ago, we get a page out to this house where we find this dead lady named Patsy Burke. We call the sheriff and everything and they say she's been murdered." She stopped, inhaling again. "Here's the weird part that you're going to think I'm a freak for even considering: she had a scanner turned on in her house."

Gil watched her watch him. She seemed to have calmed down now that she was telling the story.

She continued without waiting for him to comment. "I know this whole thing is a long shot, but what if she is Scanner Lady? That tipster I told you about? I mean, it could be. The only way for me to know for sure is to hear her voice, but the deputies wouldn't let me. I just wanted to hear her voice on the answering machine, to rule out the possibility it's her, you know?"

"You explained all this to the deputies?" Gil asked. She

nodded. "And they wouldn't let you listen to the answering machine?" She shook her head.

"Who's in charge of the investigation?" he asked.

"Major Garcia," she said, with a hint of bitterness. He knew Garcia. He was a good investigator.

"What does he think happened?"

"A botched burglary."

"Ms. Newroe, it seems you should be talking to the sheriff's office, not with me."

"I know. I've tried. But they're being uncooperative." She emphasized the last word. "They said they'd call me, but in the meantime, the next step is to assume it's Scanner Lady. I know I'm jumping the gun a bit, but without evidence to the contrary, you stick with the illogical—isn't that what Sherlock Holmes always said?"

"Okay. We'll assume for the moment it was Scanner Lady," Gil said. "How can I help you?"

She got up from the bench and paced back and forth twice before answering. He could tell that she was trying to choose her words. She was nervous again.

"Well, here goes: if it is really Scanner Lady, she might have been killed because of what she heard on her scanner Monday night. What she told me about. The only two people in my office who knew she told me anything were myself and my reporter. I checked with him—he didn't tell anyone. The only person I told was you, in a room full of cops. So . . ."

"Wait a second. Assuming that you don't think I killed her, are you saying you think someone in the police station overheard our conversation and killed her?"

She didn't answer and kept pacing, not looking at him, like his daughter Therese did when she was telling a lie.

"Ms. Newroe, there are so many things wrong with that assumption, I don't even know where to begin. She could have been killed in a burglary, like Major Garcia said. The deputies know what they're doing. Or she could have been killed for some other reason that has nothing to do with you. That would make the most sense. And even if she was killed because of what she told you—"

Lucy interrupted him. "Believe me I know, I know. I've been through this in my head. It might not even be her, for chrissakes. But it all comes back to this for me—what Scanner Lady told me involved a crime some cop committed. I talked about it in a room full of cops. The next day she's dead. I think it would be illogical of me to think that the two things aren't connected." She was more defensive now.

"Ms. Newroe, even if all that were true, the main problem is that in our conversation yesterday, you never even said her name. You told me you didn't even know her name. How could one of my police officers have killed her if he didn't know who she was?"

"I know. I know. None of this makes any sense." Her voice sounded like she was crying, but there were no tears. "But don't you get it? I've got to know if my big mouth and her getting killed are connected. If there's even a remote chance that I got her killed, I have to know."

"Ms. Newroe, I really don't see—"

She must have heard the finality in his voice, so she interrupted him. "Listen, Detective Montoya. Scanner Lady said she heard two Santa Fe police officers discussing a dead body. Maybe they were talking about Melissa Baca's since that's the only dead body we have around currently. Doesn't it interest you that there's the slightest of possibilities that whoever killed Melissa Baca may have killed Patsy Burke?"

He didn't answer her because he didn't know what to say.

She stopped pacing and stood so still that Gil wondered if she was holding her breath. She turned to him quickly. "What about the conversation between the cops over the scanner? That has to be on tape at the dispatch center, right?" The 911 dispatch center automatically recorded all conversations on the police-radio frequencies.

Gil shook his head. "I checked on that last night. I listened to the dispatch tapes from that night myself. There was nothing." Even though he hadn't really known what he was looking for, he had spent twenty minutes checking the tapes.

"How can that be? Maybe someone erased them. You guys have had that problem before."

Four years earlier, two police officers had made the mistake of discussing over the radio how they looked at porn on the Internet while at work. When the investigators went to find the tape of that conversation, it had been "accidentally" erased by one of the dispatchers. The police officers and the dispatcher had been fired.

"I thought of that, so I asked the dispatcher working that night if she had heard anything. She hadn't. And I believe her. There is no evidence of that call." He said the next part gently: "Maybe your Scanner Lady made the whole conversation up. Maybe she's a lonely old woman who wants a little attention."

She looked him in the eye. "Thank you for your time, Detective. I'm sorry if I seemed upset. It has been a difficult day."

She turned and walked quickly away. Gil watched her get into her car and leave. He felt like he had just lost an argument with his wife.

Lucy left the police station and drove straight back to Scanner Lady's house. The yellow crime-scene tape fought against the wind. The deputy posted at the front door looked bored as he talked on his cell phone. Lucy parked down the street and walked to the house next door to Scanner Lady's. She knocked and an old face peered out the front door.

"Hi. You're Claire Schoen, right?" Lucy asked. She had called the newspaper and gotten one of the interns to look up Mrs. Schoen's name in the cross directory, where all you needed was the address or phone number and got the resident's name.

"My name's Lucy Newroe. I was one of the medics who came to help your friend Mrs. Burke." Lucy felt her name being chiseled on some gravestone in hell. An hour ago she'd been ready to tell Gerald that she was quitting the fire department, and now she was using it to con an old lady.

"Oh, yes," Claire Schoen murmured as she opened the door wider, letting Lucy into a living room designed in Southwestern Tourist Shop—pink, howling coyote bookends and a kiva. Lucy counted seven chile ristras hanging from the ceiling. A fake Navajo rug on the wall clashed with the geometric designs on the couch. Lucy thought the color of the brown carpet probably was called cinnamon mesa or chocolate petroglyph.

Mrs. Schoen blended into the scene with her cowboy boots, broom skirt, and checkered vest. An elderly Dale Evans. With a touch of alcohol on her breath and smeared, bright pink lipstick. Old-lady-colored lipstick.

They sat down on the geometric couch with Mrs. Schoen twisting a Kleenex in her hands and occasionally dabbing at her eyes. Lucy guessed her to be about seventy. Mrs. Schoen was drinking a brown liquid from a coffee cup, but Lucy was sure that it wasn't coffee.

"How are you holding up?" Lucy asked.

"Like hell," Mrs. Schoen said. "The police asked me if I heard anything last night but I didn't hear a thing. I wish I had; maybe I could have done something. I would have given that robber a piece of my mind. I just saw Patsy yesterday and she felt fine."

As if getting murdered has something to do with your health, Lucy thought.

She nodded. "So, tell me about Mrs. Burke." Lucy hadn't been a reporter in more than a year, but she asked open-ended questions out of habit.

"We were going to go to Hobby Lobby today to get her a job. And tomorrow we were supposed to get together with a bunch of blue widows and play bridge like we always do."

Lucy was nodding and saying things like, "You don't say?" at places where she thought it was appropriate.

Mrs. Schoen started crying again. "Why would someone hurt Patsy? She was just an old lady. She would have let the robber take whatever he wanted. That goddamn asshole."

Lucy tried to hide a smile. An old lady who cursed and drank. Maybe that would be Lucy in fifty years. As Mrs. Schoen continued to talk, Lucy considered how to broach the real reason why she was there. She was too tired to be truly devious, so she decided just to switch the subject. Maybe Mrs. Schoen in her grief-and-alcohol-induced haze wouldn't notice.

"When I was in Mrs. Burke's house, I noticed a police scanner."

"Oh yes, she loves to listen to that thing, bless her heart."

"Why did she have it? It's an odd thing to have around."

"She likes to have it for background noise. I never understood why she doesn't just turn on some music, but it's her business."

"You know, I have a friend who has a scanner and calls up the newspaper whenever she hears anything interesting." Which was a lie.

Mrs. Schoen jumped in excitedly. "Patsy does that, too." Lucy let out the breath she'd been holding. "She loves to call the newspaper about something she hears and see if it's in the paper the next day. She just crows and crows about it when that happens, bless her heart."

"Do you know how often Mrs. Burke would call the newspaper?"

"Oh, I don't know. Maybe once a week or so. It depends on what she hears. She doesn't talk to me about it much because she knows I think it's a damn waste of time. You've got better things to do in life than to call up the newspaper."

Lucy changed the subject again. Mrs. Schoen didn't seem to notice the jumping around.

"I didn't see any ashtrays in the house. Was Mrs. Burke a

smoker? It's just good to know for our medical files." Lie number two.

"Hell no. She hates the stuff. I think it gets her sick."

"Did she have any breathing problems? Maybe asthma?"

"She had some bronchitis last year that she was having a hard time getting rid of. And of course she has allergies." Of course. Everyone in Santa Fe had allergies. Allergies and bronchitis would account for Scanner Lady's raspy voice and occasional coughing fits.

"Mrs. Schoen, I was also wondering if you had a videotape of Mrs. Burke or maybe a tape recording? Maybe an old message she left on your answering machine? I sometimes like to hear the voices of patients I was never able to meet." This last lie was the biggest but Lucy breezed past it.

"Oh, that is so sweet." Lucy cringed. "But I don't have anything like that. Sorry."

Lucy rose from the couch and said her good-byes. At the door, Mrs. Schoen said, "Thank you for stopping by, bless your heart. I just hope they catch that asshole before I do."

Gil stayed at the station doing reports and trying to get hold of Pollack. At five P.M., he got into his car and took the interstate north, toward Eldorado and his mom's house. He triple checked his speed before he set his cruise control for five miles under the seventy-five-mile-per-hour speed limit. Twenty minutes later he got off the freeway and slowed as he drove into Eldorado, where he stopped at a Texaco to fill up. As he pumped his gas he stared across the highway at the Eldorado subdivision. He and Susan had looked at three houses in the area. She liked the elementary school, which was better than the public schools in town. Eldorado was also only ten minutes from his mother's house. They were looking at four-bedroom houses, planning ahead to when his mom came to live with them.

He turned and looked at the other cars at the gas station, checking for strange behavior or stolen cars. But this was Eldorado. The four SUVs in the parking lot showed signs of doubling as minivans. In one car, Gil saw a child's car seat correctly buckled in, and another car had a bumper sticker that read MY CHILD IS AN HONOR STUDENT AT ELDORADO ELEMENTARY.

He went inside the gas station to pay. It took him a second to realize that he was the only Hispanic in the store. There were an elderly couple, a woman and her two young kids, and a man in a business suit. Gil paid the female cashier, who had a sunny smile and wished him a nice day.

He took the highway south into the grassy Galisteo Basin, then turned to follow the train tracks past more new ranches. At some point his family had owned this land, but the deed to the property had been eaten by mice, so when the Americans came, his family couldn't prove that they owned it. Back then, one of his relatives had tried to stay on the land to protect the acequia that irrigated the family gardens and orchards. But someone had hit the man over the head with a shovel and killed him. The acequia had since grown over. Gil and Elena had gone on expeditions as kids to try to find the acequia, pretending that they were conquistadores. He had made them aluminum-foil helmets and swords and carefully made maps of their route. They found petroglyphs and an old kiva left by the Galisteo Pueblo Indians, but not the irrigation ditch.

He pulled up to his parents' house and went inside to the kitchen. His mom had made an enchilada and green-chile casserole. He kissed her cheek as she pulled the casserole out of the oven.

"Here, *hito,* I was keeping this warm for you," she said as she scooped out a spoonful and set it at his usual place at the table.

"Mom, before I eat, I'm taking your blood sugar. Where's your machine?"

She waved her hand and said, "I lent it to your aunt Sally. She thinks Uncle Benito is having a problem." His mother never used the word *diabetes.* She always called it a *problem.*

"Mom . . ." he started, ready to question her about it. But instead he said, "I'll get you a new one."

He took a few bites of the casserole, then got up to get milk out of the refrigerator. As he pulled the fridge door, the hinge Jammed. The open door settled below the outer frame and pulled the entire weight of the fridge forward.

"Mom, how long has this door been like this?"

"Oh, I don't know. A month or so."

He opened and closed the door several more times to see how the hinge was broken so that he could fix it. He also opened the freezer to check its hinges. It was fine. He was about to close the freezer door when the movement dislodged one of the packages in the freezer. It came sliding out slowly. He caught it like a football. The package was wrapped in butcher paper. He saw "10/11" written on it in his father's big handwriting. Below it was "Brown Trout. Rio Chama." He remembered when his dad had caught the fish; he had called Gil at college and told him about it, laughing as he remembered how he had slipped into the river as he reeled the fish in. Gil put the package back in its place on top of the other frozen fish. He had never asked his mother why a stack of fish Dad had caught ten years ago was still in the freezer, and he probably never would.

Gil closed the freezer door and went outside to the workshop to get the tools he needed. The workshop was a shed almost attached to the house. It was a small room with two windows. A collection of old fishing rods stood in the corner. There were a few made of hazel and some of ash. His father had believed in using a six-foot rod, saying that it gave him the precision he needed in the fast mountain streams. Gil's old rod had also been six feet. Susan and the girls had gotten him a new one for Christmas. An eight-and-a-half-foot carbon fiber rod, zero weight, with titanium line rings, a cork grip, and a light trout reel. He hadn't used it yet.

He found the Phillips screwdriver and took it and the pliers back into the kitchen, shutting off the workshop light behind him.

CHAPTER SEVEN

Wednesday Night

Maxine Baca sat in her car in the driveway, not able to remember why she was there. She had been left alone to sleep while Veronica Cordova went to pick up some groceries. As soon as Veronica closed the front door, Maxine had gotten out of bed and into the car. But she didn't know why.

She watched her breath on the windows. She thought about driving her car through the closed garage door, but there was no one left who would care if she did. She climbed out of the car and tried to pull open the garage door, remembering too late that Ron had put in an electric door last month. She got back into her car, found the door opener, and pulled her car in.

Still she didn't get out of her car. She sat in the dark garage and thought about Ernesto. He had built the garage five years after they were married. He had said that he wanted her to have a place to put her washer and dryer, but he'd really built it to have a place to put his worktable. His tools that used to hang on the walls of the garage were at Ron's mobile home. Almost everything that was Ernesto's was gone. She had made sure of that. There was only one box left on the shelf in the back of the garage. She shifted in her seat so that she could see it. In it were his awards from the police department and things from his desk at the station.

When she'd heard that Ernesto had been killed, she wanted all his things out of the house. She gave his clothes to the Salvation Army and his car to Manny Cordova. She'd thrown his favorite coffee cup in the trash. She didn't remember much of his funeral. She remembered being helped by Melissa into a wheelchair she had gotten from somewhere. Melissa had pushed her into the church for the funeral and pushed her into the cemetery for the burial. Ron might have been around somewhere, but she didn't remember. She thought she remembered Melissa putting her back into bed. The whole thing seemed like she was watching TV. The morning after the funeral, Maxine had gotten up and put on her apron. She'd cooked up some eggs and swept the front porch. Ron had shown up for breakfast in a police uniform. She hadn't cried. What did it matter? It would be better if Ron died quickly, so that they could buy the plot next to Ernesto and Daniel and bury him there. Everything was out of her hands and in God's.

That same day, a police officer had brought over the box of things from Ernesto's desk. She didn't care enough to throw the box out. Melissa had sat on the living-room floor and gone through it. Whoever had emptied out his desk had tossed everything into the box—paper clips, a half-eaten Milky Way bar, a few pens. All Maxine had been able to think about was that it was getting her living-room carpet dirty. She'd had Melissa put the box on the shelf in the garage and hadn't thought about it for seven years.

But there was something in the box that she wanted now. Something she had just remembered was in it. Ernesto's police revolver. Maxine got slowly out of her car, wondering if she could reach the box without getting out a stepladder.

Gil sat at the head of the dinner table, taking a helping of mashed potatoes. Susan sat at the other end, with their two daughters between.

"Joy, how did the Bandelier trip go yesterday?" he asked.

"Boring and stupid," she said sullenly.

Gil pretended that he hadn't heard her. "Remember when we used to go there when you were little?"

She glared at him and said to Susan, "Can I be excused?"

They had been sitting down for only a few minutes, but Susan nodded. Joy went running to her room.

Susan, who was acting as if nothing had happened, said to Gil, "When you bury St. Joseph, make sure and put a garbage bag over him. I don't want him to get dirty. . . ."

"But, Mommy," Therese interrupted. "If you put one of the black bags over St. Joseph he won't be able to see."

"That's true," Gil said. "How about I put a clear bag over him?" Therese nodded her approval.

She and Susan talked for the rest of the dinner about her classroom's newt and a friend named Zookie, whom Gil had never heard of.

He was in the kitchen, rinsing the dishes and putting them in the dishwasher, when Susan came up behind him.

"Don't take it personally, she just doesn't like any man right now," she said as she rubbed his shoulder. "The Bandelier trip didn't go well."

"Why not?" He turned to look at her, softly brushing the hair out of her eyes.

"The boy she likes completely ignored her and instead talked to Jennifer Vigil the whole time."

"What boy?" This was the first he had heard of a boy.

"I promised I wouldn't tell," was all she would say before shooing him out of the kitchen.

He changed into his sweatpants and went out into the freezing garage.

He did three sets of twenty jumping jacks to warm up. The only sound was the slapping of his tennis shoes against the concrete floor. He opened the garage door and started out at a brisk run. He jogged every Monday, Wednesday, and Friday right after dinner. He started slowly, waiting for his muscles to warm up, then took it up a notch. He checked his watch as he rounded a corner, then took it up some more.

His basketball coach had made him start running when he was fifteen. He was at St. Michael's High School and just starting to reach his eventual six feet two inches. By his senior year he'd been an all-state point guard. He'd been good enough to get a basketball scholarship to the University of New Mexico to play for the Lobos.

As he rounded a corner he slipped a little on some ice he hadn't noticed in the dark. He kept going, picking up the pace, mostly to fight off the cold.

He had never played a game for the Lobos. He had torn his rotator cuff during a practice the second week of school, when his shoulder hit the head of another player. His shoulder had never completely healed: that was why he couldn't wear a shoulder holster and had to wear a gun belt.

He'd started dating Susan his junior year. Two weeks after graduation they were married. He'd gone to UNM law school while she supported them with an accounting job at a doctor's office. Two years away from graduation, Susan had become pregnant. A week later, his father had died. He'd dropped out of law school, and they moved back to Santa Fe. And he'd gotten the only job he could take with some dignity.

He slowed as he came near a suspicious-looking car parked in the street. There was a man sitting in the driver's seat in the dark. Gil jogged slowly, making sure to stay in the driver's blind spot. As he neared the passenger-side door, the man got out of the car and walked into a house. Gil sped up again, feeling the cold starting to work on his toes.

His family disapproved of his becoming anything other than a lawyer. Supposedly, back in the 1600s, one of the first Montoyas had been appointed acalde, the colonial equivalent of a judge, but that Montoya had been thrown out of office by the locals and sent back to Spain. The Judge would pull out newspaper clippings written in Spanish about Montoya mayors and governors and articles in English about Montoya state senators and congressmen. All of them had been lawyers, just like Gil's father.

At the family fiestas, relatives would still say things to Gil like, "The Judge had such hopes for you," or, "The Judge must be turning over in his grave." Gil would just walk away.

At a fiesta last year, his father's cousin, his face red from alcohol and with tamale crumbs clinging to his black mustache, had said, "Your dad would be so disappointed in you." Gil turned slowly to look at him. Gil was about a foot taller and could see the bald spot on the back of his cousin's head. The cousin backed up quickly, almost tripping over a picnic bench. Elena was suddenly next to him, putting a hand on his arm and steering him away from the crowd. She said, "Did you know that the first Montoya to come to New Mexico with the conquistadores was out chasing ambulance carts within a day?" He didn't answer her, so she squeezed his arm and said, "There are fifteen generations of Montoyas going to a hell made especially for lawyers. I'm just glad you won't be there with them." She smiled. "Besides, I'll be there to keep them company." Elena had been in her first year at UNM's law school at the time. Now she was finishing up an internship at the state attorney's office.

He saw the lights of his house down the street and slowed to a trot.

Lucy had gotten to work late and missed the editors' meeting. Now she was at her desk, trying to concentrate. She was having a hard time of it. The photo caption she was editing seemed not to make any sense. Half the words were misspelled and no one was identified. The photo itself was great—the director of the Santa Fe ski area was looking forlornly at the ugly brown patches of dirt on his ski slopes. The photo was running tomorrow with a story about the weather. No snow was in the forecast for the next week.

Her boss, City Editor Harold Richards, was editing the article about Patsy Burke's murder. Harold didn't normally read stories. He was doing it because Lucy couldn't. It would have been a conflict of interest for Lucy to edit the story since she had been at the crime scene as a medic, not a journalist. It was one of those ethics rules that her University of Florida professors had hammered into her. She hadn't actually told Harold why he needed to edit the story instead of her. And she didn't plan on telling him. She would never have this problem again—never inadvertently run across a dead body—since she wasn't planning on staying a volunteer medic at Piñon.

As she watched Harold edit the story, she wondered what Major Garcia had said when they interviewed him. She moseyed over to the fax machine, which sat next to Richards's desk. She pretended to look over a faxed press release while she glanced at the computer screen over his shoulder: " 'A 63-year-old woman who was found dead in her home on Wednesday was murdered,' said Major Ed Garcia of the Santa Fe County Sheriff's Department. However, Garcia would not release the cause of the woman's death." That's where Lucy stopped.

She knew the cause of Patsy Burke's death—she'd been strangled. She tossed the fax into the recycling bin and went over to Tommy Martinez's desk. Tommy was on the phone, so she stood nearby, wondering how she could tell him what she knew about Patsy's death without breaking any rules. Ethically, she couldn't say a word about it. Patsy Burke had been her patient and the same patient-confidentiality laws that governed doctors also governed lowly medics like herself. She also was bound by those pesky journalism-ethics rules, although those were slightly bendable.

But telling Tommy would serve a dual purpose. The *Capital Tribune* would scoop the *Santa Fe Times* on Mrs. Burke's cause of death. (*Take that, Del.*) And if the newspaper put enough pressure on Major Garcia, he would have to look into whether Patsy Burke was Scanner Lady and if her phone call to Lucy had had something to do with her death.

The power of the press at its finest.

Lucy would have to stay vague when telling Tommy. Maybe something like, *The investigation isn't considering everything.* She wouldn't even be mentioning Patsy Burke and therefore, technically, not breaking any rules. Maybe say, *Did you ask Garcia if she was strangled?*

Hanging up, Tommy said, "What's up, boss?"

She started, then stopped. She knew that what she was doing was exactly what Garcia expected her to do: compromise the investigation by leaking what she knew to the newspaper. She would be proving him right: she was untrustworthy. If the newspaper printed Patsy Burke's cause of death, he would know that she had given it to them. And then Garcia would never seriously investigate whether Patsy was Scanner Lady.

Lucy said, "Forget it," and walked away.

Gil sat on Joy's bed reading *Little House in the Big Woods.*

They had started the book, at Joy's request, a week ago. The first night, eight-year-old Therese had developed a new habit—asking questions every other sentence. The situation so exasperated eleven-year-old Joy that she held her hands over her ears. Gil knew that Therese was doing it only to annoy her sister.

In the end, they had come to a compromise.

Therese was allowed to ask three questions per reading session. But she usually asked only one question, wanting to save up the two others in case something she genuinely didn't understand came up.

Gil read six pages and stopped when he noticed that

Therese was drifting. Joy was still wide awake. He marked the page and closed the book. He went over to Therese's bed and turned off her reading light. Putting his hand on her head, he repeated in Spanish the same blessing his father had said over him every night—"May the angels watch over you as you sleep and may God smile on you when you awake." He kissed her forehead as she smiled a little and turned on her side. Joy looked disinterestedly at the ceiling. He put his hand on her head and repeated the blessing. She kept staring straight up. He expected her to pull away as he kissed her forehead, but instead she said, "Please tell Mother I need to speak to her."

He found Susan sweeping the kitchen floor.

"I was hoping we had a few years before Joy started the teen-angst thing," he said.

Susan laughed. "She's just had a bad week."

"Our daughter would like a word with her mother."

Susan put the broom against the wall, then he heard the door close to the girls' room. Gil picked up the statue of St. Joseph, still sitting on the kitchen counter, and pulled a clear plastic bag over it. He took it out to the garage, got a shovel, and headed to the backyard. He picked a spot away from the trees so that he wouldn't hit any roots and started digging. The ground should have been frozen at this time of year, but only the top layer was hard. The lights from the house gave a glow to the backyard, enough for him to see what he was doing in the dark. He stopped for a second and looked back at the house. He needed to clean out the gutters and trim the elm tree. He had been thinking about planting an apple or apricot tree in the spring, like they had had at his house when he was a kid. But they might be living in Eldorado in the spring.

Gil put St. Joseph upside down in the ground, facing east for good luck, then filled the hole back in. He put the shovel away and went inside. Susan was still in the girls' room.

He got a beer out of the fridge and sat on the couch to watch ESPN. It was forty-five minutes before Susan came back.

"What's wrong?" he asked.

"Just girl stuff," she said and went back to her sweeping.

At ten P.M., he turned on the local news. The investigation into Melissa's death was the lead story. They had picked up the *Capital Tribune*'s article about her drug use. But they went further than the newspaper article: they mentioned her brother Daniel's drug death and had talked to the Bacas' next-door neighbor, who said into the camera with enthusiasm, "If I thought one of my kids was doing drugs, I'd kill them."

Lucy was bored. She was reading articles on the Associated Press wire on her computer when she heard a voice behind. She spun around in her chair without thinking.

And came face-to-face with Mrs. Claire Schoen. *Hell. Damn. Dear God, please make her have Alzheimer's or dementia or maybe a bad case of glaucoma so she can't see me.*

"I thought you were an EMT?" Mrs. Schoen said shrewdly.

Oh, hell.

"Um . . . I am a medic, but I just do that as a volunteer. I really work here." *Smile brightly,* Lucy thought, *smile brightly.*

"You could have told me that when we talked before. How much of what you told me was bullshit?" Mrs. Schoen's voice was cold. *Help. Change the subject.*

"So can I help you with something?" *Keep smiling brightly, Lucy.*

Mrs. Schoen watched her closely for another moment before saying, "Someone named Tommy Martinez asked me to drop off this photo of Patsy."

Lucy noticed that she was clutching a picture. She could just make out the image of a group of women who looked like they were playing cards.

"Right. I didn't know Tommy had asked you to do that," Lucy said. "Um . . . Well . . . We just need a photo of . . ." Lucy almost said "Scanner Lady." "We just need a photo of Mrs. Burke to put in the story for tomorrow's paper. That way the readers know what she looked like. We do that a lot in cases like this."

Claire Schoen just stared at her.

"Let me have you talk to the photo editor," Lucy said as she steered Mrs. Schoen to the darkroom and made the introductions.

Lucy sat back down at her desk and cursed up a holy storm, trying to remember what lies she had told Mrs. Schoen. Lucy had purposely tried to give her the impression that she was a full-time medic. Damn. This was karma coming back to bite her in the butt.

As Mrs. Schoen was leaving, Lucy stopped her. "Look, I'm sorry I didn't say anything before about working here. I'm an idiot. I wasn't trying to trick you. I'm . . . I'm very sorry about Mrs. Burke. Honestly."

Tears came to Mrs. Schoen's eyes as she said, "Thank you, bless your heart." She wiped away the tears with a Kleenex she pulled out of her bra and said, "The more you cry, the less you pee." Then she walked away.

Lucy was finished with work by eleven forty-five P.M. and by midnight she was sitting at the Cowgirl bar with a table of drunk journalists from both local papers. No wonder the public had no faith in the press. They were all alcoholics.

The letter of the night was *S*. Lucy had started with a screwdriver and a stinger. Now she was waiting for the waitress to deliver her snakebite—whatever that was—while she and the copy editors debated whether a slow comfortable screw counted as two *S*'s or one. She had wanted a tequila sunrise but a cute sports reporter from the *Santa Fe Times* had nixed that, saying that the drink had to start with an *S* to count, not end in one. Lucy could have argued the point. The game was of her creation, after all, but she decided instead to go sit on the sports reporter's lap. It seemed like a good solution.

She hadn't even considered not drinking tonight. She thought she would go insane if she kept thinking of Patsy Burke. Or kept trying not to think of her. Lucy took a sip of her snakebite and changed it to a gulp in midsip. She would give up drinking tomorrow. Maybe. If she didn't find another dead body. If she didn't get someone else killed. *Help.* Another gulp.

She tried to focus her attention on the man whose lap she was sitting on. She took his beer out of his hand and put the mug on the table. Then she took his now-free hand and wrapped it around her waist.

"I was falling off," she said, smiling. He smiled back. They talked in the slurry voices of drunks. She felt slightly sluttish at how brazen she was being. She smiled to herself. Brazen. Now there was a Harlequin-romance word. She had been having a mild flirtation with the man for months, but she didn't know him well. She knew that he was from Alabama, wasn't a very good writer, and needed to learn Associated Press style. He also didn't quite have the knack with women. His movements were always a bit off. He was the kind of guy who needed a set of sex instructions: insert tab A into slot B. But he had sweet lips. She planned to kiss him. Maybe a lot. But that was all. She needed a distraction from her messed-up life, not an addition to it.

The waitress returned with Lucy's next drink—a screaming orgasm. Lucy took a big swig out of the glass and poured the rest of her snakebite into it. She mixed the two drinks into one, slopping some liquor over the side.

The sports reporter asked what she was doing. Lucy smiled. A hard smile. "I'm making a new drink. I'm calling this one the Scanner Lady." Lucy winced at the taste as the drink hit her throat. But she tipped it back farther and kept gulping, not stopping until the dregs were running down her blouse.

CHAPTER EIGHT

Thursday Morning

The police station was freezing when Gil got there just after eight A.M. The receptionist told him that the repairmen were working on the heat. He kept his coat on as he dialed his mother's number.

She answered on the fifth ring. "Mom, I'm going to go buy a new blood-sugar machine for you today. I'll bring it over later."

"Oh, don't worry about it, *hito.* Aunt Sally is bringing mine back. I told her how upset you are about it."

"Okay. But you have to do the test as soon as you get the machine back and call me with the number." She didn't say anything and they hung up.

Next, Gil called Pollack to make his morning report. He didn't have much to tell. Pollack answered with a cheery "Good morning." Gil told him about his interviews from the day before. Pollack said little, not giving Gil even an idea of where their investigation was headed. He told Gil to stay focused on what had happened during the hour before Melissa had gotten home. Pollack was saying, "Okay, thanks, good-bye," when Gil asked, "Did you get the autopsy results?"

Pollack hesitated. "Yes, we did, but I'm afraid that information is being restricted, Gil. Sorry." The state police had agreed to release information to him, but only on a case-by-case basis.

"Can I ask why?"

"We don't want it getting into the hands of the media." That intrigued Gil. The autopsy must have turned up something. "Could you at least tell me the cause of death?"

Gil heard Pollack put his hand over the receiver and say something to someone in the background. When he got back on the phone, all he said was, "I'm afraid not."

"How about the toxicology results?"

"We don't have that yet, but when we do, the answer will probably be no. You know how it is. If it wasn't for that damn press leak, I could tell you. Sorry."

Gil hung up and called the OMI, but the clerk told him that access to the file was restricted. Gil tried getting around the clerk by calling all the medical investigators he knew. He left five messages.

He spent the next hour calling other officers at the state police, the Taos Sheriff's Department, and the Taos police. They were just as frustrated as Gil. Pollack wasn't releasing the information to anyone.

At nine thirty A.M., Lucy locked her front door and got into her car, pulling on her leather gloves in the cold.

It was a little too early for her to be out of the house, but her hangover had had her up at 7:58 A.M., and now the headache was keeping her awake. Her search under the bathroom sink had yielded only an empty bottle of Pamprin.

She remembered little of the night before, although she was fairly sure that she had done some almost-illegal things with the sports reporter in the parking lot of the bar. She hoped he wouldn't call her. Sort of. She needed to stop getting drunk. Really. She was getting pathetic.

She went to Albertsons to get some aspirin and spent five minutes reshelving two oranges and some toilet paper. On her way home, she decided to make a detour.

She parked her car across the street from Patsy Burke's house, unremarkable and adobe colored. There were old newspapers collecting in the driveway—Lucy counted two *Santa Fe Times*es. But no *Capital Tribune*s. Someone must have swiped those. It was the only newspaper worth stealing. The crime-scene tape across the door had come loose and fluttered in the wind like the tail of a yellow kite.

She waved at the man across the street who had come to watch her. The neighbors probably loved this—their own little *Cops* show.

Lucy had called Mrs. Burke's number an hour ago only to be greeted with "this number has been disconnected."

She had considered trying to break in and listen to the answering machine, assuming it would just be a matter of trying all the doors and windows. But she was too chicken and paranoid to try it.

She sat in her car just watching the house, wondering about Patsy Burke's life. Lucy had been in too much of a hurry to ask Claire Schoen about Mrs. Burke's children. Lucy wasn't even sure she had kids. The pictures in her house could just as easily have been of nieces and nephews.

The flower beds in front of the house were brown, but obviously well tended. A wreath made of pink ribbons and dried flowers hung on the front door. Lucy was sure that Mrs. Burke had made it herself. Old ladies did that type of thing, didn't they?

Lucy glanced in her rearview mirror and saw a gray sheriff's car coming down the street toward her. She quickly drove down the block and into the cul-de-sac, careful to keep her car out of sight.

She got out of her car and made a show of checking a house number against a piece of paper in her hand, which was actually a receipt from Burger King. She glanced back up the street. Major Garcia and a gray-uniformed deputy were going into the house.

She got back into her car and sighed. The only way for her to get out of the cul-de-sac was to drive past Scanner Lady's house. And Garcia might see her. And think she was nuts.

She noticed a dirt road leading from the cul-de-sac, likely a utility road or a very well-worn ATV path. Some Santa Fe neighborhoods got around the county street planners by making their own back-door roads: short dirt paths that led to major streets.

As she started down the road, her Camry made loud complaints about the ruts and grooves. Thankfully, the road was dry. Chalk up one good thing to the lack of snow. She went over a huge bump and almost walloped her head on the ceiling. Just like a roller coaster. She started scanning for a country-music station. Dirt roads called for country music. She turned up the volume on an old Tim McGraw song and tried to sing along. He was saying something about still loving a woman who had dumped him for another man. Country-music love always sounded like stalking.

The road twisted around piñon trees and dropped down into an arroyo. She'd been driving for only a few minutes when the road made a sharp curve right. She had to cut the wheel to avoid hitting the cement base of a cell-phone tower.

Gil was still at his desk at the police station when Officer Manny Cordova came over and sat heavily in the chair next to Gil's desk.

"I have two things," Cordova said with his usual smile. "The first one is that I talked to Ron, and he said to give him a call if you need any help. He's still up in the Pecos."

"When is he coming back to town?" Gil asked.

Cordova shrugged. "I don't know. He did this exact same thing when his dad died. He stayed up there for weeks. It's just his way."

"What's the second thing you had to tell me?"

"I remembered something last night," Cordova said. He kept scanning the office from side to side. "It really didn't hit me until then. I think I saw Melissa Baca at Oñate Park about four thirty P.M. the day she was killed."

Gil looked at him, considering. There was only one reason why Melissa Baca would have been there.

"Tell me about it," was all Gil said.

"Well, I was driving down Cerrillos Road going to an MVA on St. Francis and Alameda when I passed the park. I always drive slow when I go by there, you know, to check it out, no? So I drove past slow and saw a purple Dodge Reliant lowrider with New Mexico plates next to a car that looked liked Melissa's brown Chevy."

There was only one purple Dodge Reliant in town. It belonged to Hector Morales. Morales wasn't usually at the park himself—he usually had one of his runners take care of the small deals. But occasionally he would take a buy at the park to show his employees how it was done. He believed that trafficking drugs was all about the marketing and the personal relationships with his clients. It was based on some idea he'd gotten from watching a late-night infomercial when he was on cocaine. He used his MySpace page to drum up customers, but he and his clients wrote in a code that the police had never broken. Morales had had three dealing arrests in the early 1990s. Since then, he had been arrested dozens of times but always found a loophole. Morales's street nickname was Pony but the police called him Teflon.

"Anything else, Manny?" Gil asked.

"Well, I was pretty far away but it looked like the driver of the Dodge Reliant handed the driver of the Chevy something." Cordova sounded like he was testifying before a grand jury. "That's all I saw."

"Are you sure it was Morales's car?"

"Oh yeah. I've busted him plenty. I'm one hundred percent sure it was him."

"How about Melissa's car? How sure are you that it was hers?"

Cordova thought for a second. "I'd say about seventy percent. If I hadn't been going to that MVA, I would have stopped to check it out. You know that, sir, right?"

"Manny, I guess I'm concerned that you didn't bring this up before. Didn't you think it was important?"

"Sorry, Gil. I just didn't think of it. Melissa wouldn't be at a place like that. It looked like her car, but I can't be sure." Cordova looked at the floor. "And I feel bad that I didn't stop. I know I should have, or called it in. I know I broke procedure." He looked back up. "Anyway, I hope it helps."

Cordova got up and walked off before Gil could ask more about it. But Gil had finally figured out what Melissa had been doing during that hour after she'd left work but before she got home: buying drugs.

The dirt road came out onto the highway. Once she hit the pavement, Lucy drove to the Santa Fe County Sheriff's Department. She entered the glass-and-steel building and asked the front-desk clerk if she could see Major Garcia, knowing full well that he was at Scanner Lady's house. But she didn't care. The receptionist told Lucy to wait. Which she did, in a gray metal chair that rocked when she tapped her foot against the floor.

Lucy had finally figured out how no one but Scanner Lady had heard the conversation between the cops on the police scanner—blame it on the cell tower just a few blocks from her house. The officers hadn't been on the police radio; they'd been on cell phones.

Lucy couldn't believe that it had taken her so long to figure that out. Police scanners were notorious for picking up cell-phone conversations when a cell tower was close-by. The frequencies between the towers got all mixed up. Cell-phone calls sounded like normal traffic on a police scanner. Scanner Lady wouldn't have been able to tell the difference.

At the *Capital Tribune* last summer, they had heard about a house blowing up on the west side. Lucy had sent a reporter and photographer scrambling while she listened closely to the police frequencies. At ten P.M., close to deadline, Lucy was still waiting to hear from her reporter when the scanner piped up. Two police officers were talking. Lucy knew within seconds that they weren't on the police radio—they were swearing and using first names as they discussed the explosion over their cell phones and talked freely about the cause of it—a meth lab in the basement. She quickly called the reporter. The reporter, without revealing his source, got confirmation from the police that it had been a meth-lab explosion. The next day, she'd gotten an e-mail from John Lopez congratulating her on the scoop.

She planned to explain this to Garcia. If he ever showed up. After forty-five minutes, she settled on writing Garcia a note, asking him to call.

CHAPTER NINE

Thursday Afternoon

The news meeting was lasting forever. Lucy tried to hide her second yawn. Patsy Burke's death had become a brief. The story's first paragraph would be, "Santa Fe sheriff's deputies are still investigating the slaying of an elderly woman who was found dead in her home on Wednesday." Her murder went from a front-page story to a four-paragraph brief inside the local section within twenty-five hours. A new record.

Melissa Baca's death had also been moved from the front page to the local section, and it said basically the same thing as Patsy's—no new leads. Melissa's death had been more spectacular than Patsy's—a schoolteacher being tossed off a famous bridge—so it was being buried more slowly.

Lucy tried to pay attention as they talked about the front-page package—a story about how much water the new municipal golf course was using.

As they were wrapping things up, Tommy Martinez came to the door and motioned her outside.

"I think I can get a hold of a copy of the Melissa Baca autopsy," he said.

"Fabulous. When can you get it?"

"In a few hours."

"Any clue what it says?"

"Not yet."

She went back into the news meeting and told the other editors what Tommy had said. Melissa Baca's murder was back on the front page.

The office was still cold as Gil did a property search on the Internet. The station was quiet; most officers who weren't out on patrol had found a reason to go someplace warmer. He was trying different variations of the name Baca in the search engine—C de Baca, C'Baca, Cdebaca. Baca and its cousin name, Ce de Baca, were fairly common in Northern New Mexico. There were four Bacas—none related—of the 139 police officers who worked for the city of Santa Fe.

Chief Kline had asked Gil to find Ron Baca and fill him in on the investigation as a courtesy. Gil had called Ron's cell phone several times, only to be greeted with, "The number you are calling is not in service." He knew that Pollack had said Ron had an alibi for Melissa's murder. But he was curious why Ron would have gone off to the Pecos and left his mother all alone. It didn't make sense to him.

Gil was searching for any property belonging to the Baca family. He thought maybe Ron was staying at a family-owned cabin in the Pecos and was hoping to find a phone number for it. But there was nothing. The search turned up only Mrs. Baca's house, Ron's mobile home, and a mention of a trailer that had been bought by Daniel Baca in the late 1970s.

"You know, Gil, you'll go blind sitting that close to a computer screen."

He looked up to see Officer Joe Phillips blowing into a steaming cup.

"You didn't get me any coffee, Joe?" he said without smiling.

"Get off it, Montoya. You know I don't drink that stuff. This is cocoa. It even has little marshmallows in it. I thought it wasn't macho enough for you," he said, laughing. Phillips had been on the force for only a little over a year, but he had a lot of common sense.

"Actually, Joe, you can help me with something. Does Hector Morales still live in that apartment on Airport Road?" he asked.

"Nah, he moved a few months ago. Do you need to find him?"

"I was just about to go look for him."

"I'd wait until tonight. It's Thursday. He'll be at the Silver Cowboy. It'll be safer, and you won't have to worry about his girlfriends or his kids being around," he said before walking off, sipping his cocoa.

Gil was getting ready to leave when the phone rang. It was one of the medical investigators, Cindy Cornell. They'd worked on a stabbing together two years back. She told Gil the same thing everyone else had: "I don't have a copy of the Baca autopsy, and I can't get a copy." But she added, "I did hear that the report is back on the syringe they found in Melissa Baca's car. It was wiped clean of prints, which is weird."

Gil agreed. Drug addicts weren't usually so neat.

"Oh, yeah," Cornell said. "I also heard a rumor that a newspaper was leaked the autopsy."

"Which newspaper?" asked Gil.

"The one with the green name. I mean, it's written in green. Do you know which one I mean?"

He knew which one she meant—the *Capital Tribune*.

The copy editors invited Lucy on a walk to Starbucks a few blocks away, but she turned them down. She needed to be alone. The dark was just starting to settle in as she walked toward the Plaza. Piñon smoke clung to the air, warm and sweet. The haze in the air made the streetlights glow and wink softly. The setting sun was starting to hit the Sangre de Cristos, making the peaks look pink and purple. She made her way down tiny alleys and through archways leading to courtyards with now-dry fountains. The stair-step, two-story buildings were seamed together, with one giving way to the other, so that each block was made up of one huge, mismatched structure. A curved missionary arched roof flowed into the flat-topped pueblo roof of the next building, which joined the art-deco tile of the next.

The shop owners in the low adobe buildings were starting to close up. Every other store seemed to have the words *trading company* in its name. Golden Bear Trading Company. Eagle Wings Trading Co. The cheap stores sold cowboy hats from the Philippines and American Indian rugs made in China. The expensive stores sold antique photos of Georgia O'Keeffe and turquoise bracelets made on the pueblos.

She heard laughter coming from the third story of La Fonda hotel's patio just above her. The hotel was one of the most famous and tallest buildings in town, at barely five stories. Only St. Francis Cathedral was taller. By law, no building could be taller than the cathedral.

When she reached the Plaza, she watched the tourists. It was easy to spot them. They were always so much better dressed than the locals. If you could afford to vacation in Santa Fe, you could afford to dress well. A family walked past her, the kids looking like blond Stepford children in their neat white shirts, pressed khaki pants, and parkas. The father was J. Crew, the mother Ann Taylor. Clean-cut American upper class.

Down the street, a man was yelling incoherently, his voice guttural and coarse. She thought at first he had Tourette's syndrome, but as she got closer she realized that he was just German, yelling to his relatives across the street.

She made her way to the tamale vendor on the corner of the Plaza. The man nodded at her in recognition, and she ordered the usual: pork with red chile. Lucy was a firm believer in food ruts. She got stuck in them often. Two weeks ago it had been baked potatoes. Last month it had been sopaipillas with honey.

The tamale steamed as the man handed it to her, almost falling out of the corn husk it was baked in. She paid for her food and found a cold bench on the Plaza to sit on.

She watched the jewelry sellers sitting under the portal of the Palace of the Governors, which was a palace only in the New Mexico sense. It was a huge, dark-beige-adobe hacienda built in the 1600s on top of an old Indian settlement. The palace had changed hands frequently over the years: Spanish, Indian, Spanish, Mexican, American, Confederate, American. Every passing army seemed to have conquered it. The building was now a museum, but she could still make out the edges of the old fort.

Lucy always marveled at the walking encyclopedia she had become since working at the newspaper. She could have been a Santa Fe tour guide, sitting in a bus and telling vacationers from Minnesota, "And off to your right is the oldest public bathroom in the United States."

She watched one of the sellers under the portal of the Palace of the Governors polish a squash-blossom turquoise necklace laid out on a bright blanket. The woman was sitting bundled up in comforters, to fight off the cold shadows and the hard concrete. All the sellers under the portal had to be American Indian. It actually was a rule. There had been some big lawsuit in the 1990s brought by Hispanic sellers who thought they had as much right to sit under the portal as the Indians. The state supreme court had decided the issue. Only Indians. So the Hispanic sellers had been forced to sell their paintings and santos on the other side of the street, which didn't seem that bad a fate to Lucy. They got to be in the sun and away from the shade of the portal. They got to be on the Plaza.

The Plaza itself was only about a block square, with sidewalks crisscrossing its grassy areas. If it had been back East, they would have called it a park, and a small one at that. But here it was the Plaza, with a capital *P.*

The early conquistadores had built the Plaza to serve as a vegetable garden and center of the fort. It had been a place of cockfights, public floggings, Indian slave markets, and bullfights. It was the end of the Santa Fe Trail in the 1800s. Its renown had grown from that.

The real estate along it was the most expensive commercial property in Santa Fe. When the Gap opened a store on San Francisco Street across from the Plaza in the late 1990s, the newspaper wondered in its editorials what was becoming of Santa Fe. A brand-name store on the Plaza? Treason. But by the time the Starbucks opened down the street, the groans had turned into simple grumbling.

Lucy tossed her tamale wrapper into a garbage can and walked back to work, dodging a group of children and harried mothers.

Once in the newsroom, the receptionist greeted her with, "Some cop is trying to get a hold of you. He said he'd call back."

Finally. It was about time Major Garcia decided to call her back. She'd left him two more messages since getting to work.

Her phone was ringing as she sat down.

"Ms. Newroe?" It was a man, but definitely not Garcia. "This is Detective Montoya. We spoke yesterday?" Like she could forget. "I've been trying to get a hold of you. Would it be possible for me to come down there to talk to you?" *Interesting,* she thought. Most likely he wanted to ask for the names of the anonymous sources who had leaked the info about Melissa Baca's drug use.

A half hour later, Montoya and Lucy sat in the conference room at the newspaper. She had a cup of awful-tasting coffee in front of her. She was gripping the Styrofoam cup in her hand purely for composure, like a smoker feeling calmed just by holding a cigarette.

"I heard you have a copy of Melissa Baca's autopsy," Detective Montoya said. So, he was going to try to talk her out of using it.

"And?" The less she said, the better.

"I was wondering if you could do me a favor. I'm not asking you to break any rules, but I wanted to see if I could get a copy of the report."

Lucy was surprised. Definitely not what she had expected. "Don't you people have one?"

"I don't have access to the report," Detective Montoya said. Then she knew: he was being shut out by the state police. "I'm acting as the liaison for the family. I'm trying to help them through the process and be there as a spokesman for them."

She finished the thought for him: "And it would help if you knew what the autopsy said before it hit the papers tomorrow so you could coach the family on what and what not to say?"

"I wouldn't put it like that."

Lucy admired Montoya for coming to her with his hat in his hand. The relationship between the media and the police was adversarial at best. Newspapers used the police to get the crime stories that sold papers. The police used the newspapers to print the stories that showed the public they were keeping the city safe. Montoya had just stepped over a well-established invisible line. Lucy wondered why.

"I should have it around nine P.M. I don't feel comfortable faxing it to you. I can come drop it off when I get off work around eleven P.M.," Lucy said.

She wasn't actually breaking any journalistic rules by giving him the autopsy, but she was stretching a lot of unwritten ones. Most editors wouldn't even have considered it, not wanting to encourage a relationship with the police. But she had a reason: if she scratched his back, maybe he would scratch hers. She needed help with the Patsy Burke problem. And he could give it.

Not that she would get in trouble for giving Montoya the paperwork. She would be very careful. She would not reveal where they had gotten the autopsy from—not that she actually knew. Tommy hadn't told her. And Tommy was already calling the family to get their comments, so Montoya wouldn't have time to tell the relatives how to spin the details. Montoya wouldn't even see the autopsy until eleven P.M., so technically she wouldn't be leaking any information—by that time, the story would be up on the *Capital Tribune*'s Web site and accessible by the general public.

Montoya hesitated. "Actually, I'm going to be out doing some legwork."

"On the Baca killing?"

As he answered yes, she watched him. She didn't like the look he gave her. She still didn't know him well enough to be able to interpret his looks. He looked like he didn't trust her.

"Fine. Just tell me where and when to meet you. Denny's? Village Inn?"

Gil knocked hard again on the front door of Ron Baca's mobile home. No answer. It was just after five P.M. and almost fully dark. It had been in the fifties again today, but as soon as the sun went down, the cold had come in with a mission.

He walked around the mobile home looking for a window to peek in. All the blinds were down. He left his card on Ron's door with a note to call him when he got home from the cabin.

After that he drove to Mrs. Baca's. The house was full of people again. His knock was answered by Betsy Sanchez, a woman he'd briefly dated in college before he met Susan. The last time he'd seen Betsy had been after a Halloween party when he was eighteen. She had gotten mad at him about something—he couldn't remember what—and had slammed his car door as he dropped her off at home. She was Mrs. Baca's niece. They chatted without enthusiasm.

He found Mrs. Baca sitting in a blue-and-white-upholstered chair in the living room. She was hunched over, staring at her hands, a half cup of coffee on a table next to her. She had more color in her cheeks, but she jumped when he spoke to her. She was wearing different clothes, although Gil wasn't sure they were an improvement—a very loose sweater missing a middle button and a pair of green pants. She looked like Therese when she tried to dress herself for kindergarten.

She got awkwardly out of the chair and offered him some coffee. Two relatives nearby spoke up at once, saying, "Let me do that, Tia," and, "Maxine, I can get that." Betsy Sanchez gave him a cold, accusatory look, as if he should have stopped Mrs. Baca from suggesting the coffee. Now he remembered—Betsy had gotten mad at him about how much time he spent playing basketball.

Gil took Mrs. Baca's elbow and led her into the kitchen. A woman in her fifties stopped in midsentence to watch them seat themselves at the table. Gil asked the woman and her two friends to leave. They shuffled out, saying, "Maxine, we're right here if you need us."

Mrs. Baca waited until they were out of the kitchen before she said with a strange intensity, "Can't you make these people leave my house? I can't have them here."

Gil didn't know what to say, so he kept quiet. He had stopped by to ask how she was. He now realized that she had changed her clothes and drunk her coffee probably to make her relatives leave her alone. Mrs. Baca got up, rinsed a washcloth under the faucet, and started wiping down the kitchen counters.

He tried to think of kind words, something to make her feel better, feel something. But there was nothing to be said. Instead, he asked, "Have you heard from Ron?"

"He's not here."

That, Gil already knew. "When was the last time you talked to him?"

"He called today, this morning. I don't know what time."

"Did he give you a number to call him at?"

"No. He said his cell phone wouldn't work where he was."

He had avoided asking Mrs. Baca the next question for days, hoping that if he waited, she would be more up to answering. "Mrs. Baca, what did you do after Melissa left Monday night?" It was probably one of the first questions Pollack had asked her. Mrs. Baca was automatically a suspect since she had been the last person to see Melissa alive.

"I cleaned the dinner dishes, then Ron came over and worked on the washing machine. It's been broken." She kept wiping as she talked. She was now working her way across the kitchen table.

"What time did he get here?"

"Not too long after Melissa left."

"This is important, Mrs. Baca. Do you remember exactly what time he got here?"

"I hadn't finished loading the dishwasher. I said good-bye to Melissa when I was putting the glasses in. He got here when I was putting the plates in. Maybe five minutes after Melissa left."

"And how long did he stay?"

"He fixed the washing machine, however long that takes."

Gil asked gently as she wiped down the refrigerator, "When did he leave?"

"I was watching the end of Jay Leno. I wanted to go to bed, but I didn't want Ron to have to stay up alone."

"And did Ron leave at all while he was here?" Gil asked

"No. He never left."

That would have made it around eleven thirty P.M. when Ron went home. He was at his mom's house before Melissa was killed and didn't leave until after her body had been dumped.

The state police were right; it meant that Ron wasn't involved. His running off to the mountains wasn't out of guilt. It was nothing more than mourning.

Gil made it to his mother's house in twenty-five minutes. He found his mother pulling a fresh batch of *bizcochitos* out of the oven. She still made the cookies out of lard, not shortening, and put sliced almonds on top instead of the way Susan made them with the colored sprinkles.

"Oh, *hito,* I'm almost done with these," she said as she put the next dozen into the oven. "Your dinner is in the refrigerator."

He took out a plate of leftover green-chile enchilada casserole and sat at the table to eat.

"Mom, you never called and told me what your blood sugar was," he said.

"Oh, I didn't want to bother you at your work."

He shook his head. "What was the number?"

His mother didn't answer right away. She was taking the cookies one by one from the baking sheet and putting them on the cooling rack. "You know, *hito,* I don't remember. I'm sorry. I think I wrote it down but I don't know where I put the paper. . . ."

"That's okay, the machine keeps a record of it. I'll go check." He got up from the table and found the blood-glucose machine in the bathroom. He hit a few of the buttons and a list of numbers came up. The last date recorded was from two weeks ago. He carried the machine back into the kitchen and said, "Mom, you didn't check your blood."

She didn't look up as she said, "I know, *hito,* I'm sorry. I know you wanted me to."

He got the machine and the test strip ready and said, "Mom, come here." She came over to the table and sat down, giving him her left hand. He pricked the side of her finger with the lancet and let a few drops of blood fall onto the test strip. He put a Band-Aid on her finger as he waited for the machine to read the strip. She went back to work on the *bizcochitos*. The machine beeped and he looked at the number. It was a little high but within the normal range.

He ate a few of the *bizcochitos* while he called the girls to wish them a good night. But all he got was the answering machine at his house. He left his good-night message on it.

CHAPTER TEN

Thursday Night

The vinyl seat made a soft sound, like a slowly deflating whoopee cushion, when Lucy plopped into the booth opposite Detective Montoya at Denny's. She tossed a copy of Melissa's autopsy report on the table without saying anything.

Lucy summed it up for him: "There was no rape." She refused to use the cop's term—*criminal sexual penetration.* It made something inhuman sound acceptable. "She had pizza shortly before she died. Time of death was about 2030 hours. I guess that means about eight thirty P.M. on Monday." Lucy couldn't get the bitterness out of her voice. Patsy Burke deserved to have this kind of attention paid to her death, too. Garcia still hadn't called her back about the answering machine.

She continued. "Oh, and she was strangled. The OMI thinks someone used their hands, no rope or anything. They think there were some defensive wounds, like she put up a fight. She had a couple of scrapes that don't add up. But I guess everything is messed up from the fall."

"She was dead when she was tossed off the bridge," Montoya said.

Lucy nodded and asked the waitress for coffee. "The toxicology report won't be in until tomorrow, so we don't know about drugs. But the autopsy says something like 'no marks consistent with intravenous drug use.' So, shooting drugs were a fairly new thing for her. I guess she could have been doing coke or whatever."

They sat quietly for a few minutes, Montoya reading the autopsy and Lucy rat-a-tat-tating a straw on the napkin holder.

"So, can I talk to you about Scanner Lady?" Lucy asked. That was her real reason for being there.

Montoya closed the autopsy report, folded his hands on the table in front of him, and said, "Absolutely." She smiled. Good. He knew the score.

Lucy told him about talking to Claire Schoen and finding the cell tower. Montoya nodded without comment. Then she asked, "What do you think?"

"It sounds completely circumstantial." Lucy made a sour face at him, and he smiled and added, "But plausible."

That was twice she had gotten him to smile. She was hoping for a third.

"Please, Detective Montoya, let's not go overboard with enthusiasm here."

"Lucy," she raised her eyebrows; this was the first time he had called her by her first name, "you've still got a lot of problems with your theory that the killer was a police officer who overheard you and me talking at the police station. Mainly, how could the killer know you were talking about Patsy Burke when you didn't even know her name?"

"Yep, that sure is a big hole," she agreed in a fake Texas accent. "But isn't there a way to triangulate cell towers or something? I mean, I'm sure that's not what you call it, but you police-type people must have some gadget to find cell towers. The killer finds the cell tower and he finds Scanner Lady."

"That's the kind of equipment they have at the FBI and big-city departments. We just can't afford something like that," he said. "I think it's more likely that it has nothing to do with you or the cell-phone call. It was probably someone who knew her. Or a robbery. Sometimes coincidences are just coincidences."

They both thought quietly for a moment before Lucy said, "You haven't asked me who the police sources were who leaked the newspaper the info about Melissa's drug use."

"Because I knew you wouldn't tell me."

"That's right, I wouldn't, but a girl still likes to be asked."

He smiled again. His third smile. *So he likes to be teased.* She could do that.

Detective Montoya looked at his watch. Lucy wondered where he was in a rush to be at ten to midnight. He finished off the rest of his coffee and started making it's-time-to-leave movements.

"So you headed home to curl up with your gun?" she asked, flinching for a second at the sexual innuendo, which she hadn't meant.

"No. I have some things to take care of," he said.

"On the Baca case?"

He didn't answer her and said instead, "Thank you for your help, Miss Newroe. Good night."

She watched him leave, wondering what had happened to their joking ease. Was it because of her gun comment? And why had he switched back to using her formal name? She realized that it bugged her. Really bugged her. She finished her coffee and left her money on the table. She reached the parking lot just as he was pulling out in his unmarked police car—so obvious for what it was. She jumped into her car and turned onto Cerrillos Road. There was enough traffic for her to blend in. And even if he did see her, she could just as easily have been on her way home. He stopped at the light. She was four cars back. He turned into the Silver Cowboy parking lot, and she continued on her way, pretending that she was just driving past. She took the next left and made a U-turn, going back down the street. She slowed as she passed the bar. She saw him get out of his car and go inside. She wondered what he was doing. He didn't seem the bar type.

She made another U-turn and pulled into the parking lot.

She parked well away from his car, on the other side of the lot. She skirted around the quiet side of the bar and stood outside the door for a second, waiting until a big group of people headed inside. She fell in with them and made her way through the door. The bar was huge and crowded. She thanked her genes for making her short. She could hide in the forest of tall people all night. She looked around for Detective Montoya. She didn't see him at any of the tables. Maybe he was in the bathroom.

She didn't know what to do next. She wasn't even sure why she had followed him. She tapped her fingers nervously against her leg. She didn't know how to move. She needed a drink. She went to the bar and asked for a Coke, which the bartender gave to her quickly, then he moved away. She took a drink and started drumming her fingers against the plastic cup. She should have asked for a rum and Coke. Maybe she should sit down. Maybe she should go home. She turned around, and came face-to-face with Detective Montoya. Or, in her case, face-to-chest. She swore out loud before she could stop herself.

Gil took a sip of his club soda as they sat at a table near the dance floor. He had noticed her following him as soon as they had left Denny's. She hadn't even denied it when he asked her. She'd just sworn and said, "You caught me," with one of her laughs. She had agreed to leave as soon as she finished her soda.

"So is it Gilbert or Gil?" she asked him over the music. He must have looked confused, so she added, "I have to call you something. I think calling you Detective Montoya seems kinda weird." He told her, then they sat quietly for a few minutes, with Gil watching Hector Morales across the bar.

Morales was wearing a silver shirt with black jeans and black boots. He was standing at the bar with four men who seemed to be acting as unofficial bodyguards. Gil had arrested one of the men—Jesse Kurt—for heroin trafficking less than a year ago. Gil wondered what Kurt was doing out. He had been given a seven-year sentence.

Gil had gone to high school with one of the other men. They had been in an English class together, but he couldn't remember his name. Robert something.

"Why are you so interested in that guy at the bar? He doesn't look like your type," Lucy said. She was trying to get a rise out of him, as she had been since she'd first met him. He didn't answer her.

She didn't give up. "Okay, Detective. You don't have to say anything. I'll figure it out myself. The guy at the bar must be connected with the Baca case somehow. I know Melissa Baca's boyfriend is a teacher at the school and a white guy, not Mexican like this guy here. So, this isn't her boyfriend. Is this a guy she was doing on the side?"

She waited for his response. He ignored her and kept watching Morales. She saw something in his expression and said, "Okay, so she wasn't having an affair. But she was doing drugs. With that outfit, that guy has to be a drug dealer. I interviewed a million guys like that back in Orlando. So I guess he was Melissa's dealer, right?"

Now Gil looked at her and said, "I think it's time for you to go."

Then she did something completely unexpected—she laughed out loud and said, "You know, Gil, that cop face of yours was perfect and the monotone voice was right on. Beautiful."

She chuckled for a few more seconds before saying, "So, are you going to beat this guy up when you question him?" She was smiling.

He had never known someone who smiled so much. It was hard to stay annoyed with her. "I'll try to restrain myself," he said.

"If you feel any violence coming on, just let me know so I can pretend I didn't see it."

"Will do."

"So, how can I help?" she asked, finishing her soda.

"You can go home. I'll go find Morales tomorrow at some point when there are fewer people around, and he doesn't have any buddies nearby."

"Oh, okay. No problem. Let me just go to the bathroom." She flashed him a smile as she got up.

She was about five feet from Morales before Gil realized that she wasn't heading to the bathroom. She was too close to Morales for Gil to stop her. A couple of Morales's friends were already checking her out.

He watched her brush her elbow against Morales's back. Gil heard her laugh and then apologize. They turned back to the bar together, but not before Gil caught sight of Morales's face—a man who'd just gotten lucky.

Gil didn't know what to do. He didn't know what her game was. He had done everything he could to keep her out of this. Should he go up there and get her? But that might put Lucy in danger. Maybe he should take the chance. But maybe not. Gil was not used to being so uncertain. In the end, logic won. They were all in a public place and safe because of that. He would wait it out. For a little while.

He felt wooden, solid. He knew he looked too much like a cop. He got up and walked to the pool tables, making a show of watching a game between two rough-looking white men. He studied them closely for a second to make sure he hadn't arrested them before, then went back to his surveillance.

He saw Lucy and Morales walk out onto the dance floor before he lost them in the crowd. They popped back up again near the stage, where the band was playing some fast country song. Morales was spinning Lucy in circles, and she laughed as she came to rest back in his arms. Now they were on the side of the floor nearest Gil, shuffling along with the beat. Morales's back was to him as he whispered something in Lucy's ear. She laughed again—and then quickly stuck her tongue out at Gil as she caught sight of him in the crowd. Gil laughed out loud, startling himself.

Morales and Lucy spent another twenty-five minutes dancing and drinking—with Morales doing most of the drinking. Gil had been hoping that she would finish whatever she was doing and leave fairly quickly. The less contact she had with him, the less danger she was in. Gil considered pretending to arrest her. Or acting like a jealous husband. He would give it another ten minutes.

It was one fifteen A.M. and Gil was trying not to yawn when she made her move. Morales and Lucy were sitting at a table working on margaritas when Gil saw Lucy's hand slowly slip up Morales's back. She whispered in his ear.

Gil turned away to watch a couple on the dance floor do a fast two-step. Lucy was seducing Morales. If he had known that she was going to do this, he would have stopped her a half hour ago.

He looked back. Lucy's hand played on the back of Morales's neck; Morales moved closer to her and kissed her lightly on her mouth. As he did, Lucy looked over at Gil and winked. Then she turned back to Morales and smiled at him as she got up slowly. The two of them headed out the door, Morales's arm around her waist.

Gil went out the door after them, his eyes slowly adjusting to the dark night. He was just outside the door when he heard her say to Morales, "But I like it when you do that." Lucy and Morales were just disappearing around the corner of the bar when Gil caught up with them. Gil grabbed Morales by the back of his collar and pushed him up against the stone building a little too hard.

Morales started cursing. Lucy started yelling, "What the hell do you think you're doing? Let him go, you asshole." She pushed Gil. He fished his badge out of his pocket and flashed it at her.

Lucy stumbled backward. "Oh, man. You're a cop? I'm

outta here." She was overdoing it a little, but Morales seemed not to notice. She winked at Gil again and slipped around the corner. Gil could see her shadow and knew that she was listening. At least she was safely out of the way.

Gil had Morales against the wall and was frisking him with one hand while holding him with the other. "Do you know who I am?" Gil asked as he worked.

Morales looked at him over his shoulder. "Yeah, you're a damn cop."

"Right, and I have a few questions."

"Go to hell." Gil pushed him against the wall again to get his attention. He carefully pulled Morales's keys out of his pocket and tossed them onto the ground. Sometimes gang members sharpened one key on the chain into a knife for the cops to cut themselves on as they frisked. Morales had nothing else on him except his wallet.

"Let's try this again," Gil said.

"What do you want? I'm not carrying. I ain't got nothing on me. You can't bust me."

"I don't want to bust you. I want to ask you some questions."

"I'm no snitch."

"It's not about your business, Hector. It's about a dead girl. Melissa Baca."

"The girl who went over the bridge?" Hector momentarily looked confused. "I don't know nothing about that shit."

Gil let go of Morales's shirt.

"I'm not asking about who killed her. I'm asking did you ever deal to her?"

"I don't deal, man." Morales's eyes were glazed over from the alcohol. Gil had watched him drink four beers and two shots of tequila in less than two hours.

"Right. But maybe you heard about someone dealing to her."

"Hell no. She saw me on the street once, you know, and

spat at me. She spat at me. I didn't do nothing 'cause her brother had died on the stuff, and I felt bad about that. I liked Melissa, man. We went to school together, you know."

"What do you know about her boyfriend, Jonathan Hammond—was he a user?"

"Shit, I don't know. I've never seen him."

"Someone said they saw you with her the day she died, handing her something out your car window at about four thirty that afternoon at Oñate Park. You drive a purple 'eighty-six Dodge Reliant, right?"

"Yeah, that's what I drive, but they're lying. What day was that? Monday? Hell, I was in district court all day. And you can check on that shit. I was up for my DWI hearing before that lady judge—that Padilla woman—in Española."

Judge Janet Padilla's magistrate court was a half-hour drive from Santa Fe.

"And your car was with you at your hearing?"

"Hell yeah, man. With the alarm set and all that shit. My car was there, and I was there."

"How do you know no one took your car? Do you know where it was at four thirty that afternoon?"

"Yeah, I know where it was. I was in it. The court was out for a, whatddaya call it—recess?—for an hour from like three thirty to four thirty, and I went outside to smoke a cigarette, man. I smoked in the car 'cause it was cold as a bitch that day, you know? I was only going to stay outside for one smoke but the asshole parking-lot guard was watching me the whole time like I was going to steal a sign or some shit. So I sat there for the whole hour just watching him. I wasn't gonna let that asshole intimidate me, you know, man?"

It would be easy enough to check. Morales and his car were pretty hard to forget.

"What happened at your hearing?" Gil asked.

"They let me off, man," Morales said with a sly smile, " 'cause it's my first offense for drinking and driving."

"Good for you, Hector." Gil backed away, allowing Morales room to get by.

Morales started to leave but stopped after a few steps.

"Melissa didn't do that shit. Whoever said she did, you look at them. She'd of died first before doing that shit."

And maybe that's what happened, Gil thought.

Maxine Baca knew only that it was past midnight. She sat in Melissa's bedroom with the lights turned off. She was holding one of Melissa's old shirts, one she had worn in high school. Maxine had given it to her as a birthday present. It was dark red with gold buttons. Maxine had given her gold earrings and black pants to match. Maxine and Ernesto had fought about it. "You spoil her too much," he'd said. "You shouldn't get her presents that we can't afford." But Ernesto hadn't understood.

After Daniel died, Maxine knew she had to do penance for the sin that had caused Daniel's death. Her sin of gluttony. One of the seven deadly sins. She had been selfish. Her mother had warned her, but she hadn't listened. When Daniel was born, her mother had told her to follow the *dieta.* The *curandera* had warned her, too. But Maxine hadn't wanted the priest to eat alone, so she ate a whole plate of enchiladas and green-chile stew. She knew right away that she had sinned. The food had gotten her sick. But she had hoped that the coral would stop the sin. But it hadn't been enough. Maxine had been too selfish. It had been a test from God. God was trying to see if she would give up everything for her child. But she hadn't. She couldn't go even a day without eating a full meal—her child meant that little to her. And God had punished her for her selfishness by taking the thing she loved most in the world.

After Daniel died, Maxine had been worried that her sin would cause him to go to limbo, the place where God sends all the unbaptized, since she had committed the sin before he was baptized. Her sin had undone the protection of his baptism. She prayed the rosary three times a day. The only food she would eat was the host and the wine at Mass every day on her way to visit Daniel's grave. Ernesto ate mostly frozen foods and Ron didn't come home for dinner. Ron stayed at Manny Cordova's house down the street. Veronica Cordova would bring over a casserole every few days for Ernesto to eat. For two years she prayed to God the Almighty to forgive her and not to punish Daniel, but God hadn't listened. Maxine knew this because her pain over his death had never healed. She found a *curandera* to go to in Española. Most of the other *curanderas* had died because no one went to them anymore. But the one in Española told her she had the Anger Sickness over Daniel's death and sent her home with some holy water and ground-up osha root. The *curandera* told Maxine to make enchiladas and green-chile stew and bury it to the left of Daniel's grave as penance for not obeying her mother. She buried the osha root as instructed, to show her sacrifice to God, and poured the holy water at the left of the grave to prove that she was ready to accept God's will. Then she had to spend the night praying at Daniel's shrine.

Maxine had been tired after staying up all night praying and had gone to bed. When she woke up, she had felt sick. Ernesto took her to the doctor. She sat in the waiting room of her doctor's office knowing that she had the flu. Ron had brought it home from school. She had a runny nose, vomiting, and fever. She wasn't pregnant. She knew what it felt like to be pregnant. She'd had two babies, after all.

She knew exactly when she became pregnant—the moment the flu had turned into a baby inside her. She was sitting in the doctor's office with Ernesto when the room began spinning. She had to put out a hand. Her stomach hurt and, a moment later, it became warm. By the time the doctor came in, she knew that she was pregnant. Her fever and runny nose were gone. She felt the fullness of a baby in her. In that instant,

God had given her a little girl. It was a miracle from God and Our Lady. God had accepted her penance for her sin and had given her another baby to care for. God was giving her a second chance.

Maxine touched the sleeve of the soft blouse. The color had looked so good on Melissa.

She pulled a loose thread on the blouse and watched a button fall to the carpet and bounce its way over to Melissa's dresser. Maxine just stared. Melissa had used the broken bottom drawer on the dresser as a treasure chest. The drawer didn't open, but there was a hidden shelf underneath. When she was a teenager, Melissa had kept her private things there. Maxine got up slowly from the bed, bent over the bottom drawer, and pried it open.

Gil had waited until Morales had driven away before he and Lucy left. He was giving her a ride home. Lucy had argued with him, wanting to drive herself, but he had seen her drink a margarita. And this way, he could guarantee that Morales wasn't following her.

They were driving quietly in the car when Lucy said, "I find it interesting that during that entire conversation with Hector you never said one swear word."

Gil looked at her; she wasn't smiling.

"I don't see what difference it makes," Gil said.

"But it does. You just roughed up a drug dealer and never once said damn or hell. He was swearing up a storm and you did nothing."

"I didn't rough him up and still don't get what difference it makes." And he didn't. What was she getting at? He looked at her again. She still wasn't smiling.

"It's just interesting," she said.

He pulled up in front of her house and went around to the other side of the car, opening the door for her out of habit, just as he did for his wife and his mother. She smiled up at him. "Why, heavens be, Detective, you are so gallant," she said in a southern accent.

He walked her up to her front door, surveying the street as he did so, looking for any sign of Morales. As she was unlocking her door he said, "Just so we're clear, you obviously aren't going to tell anyone what you overheard tonight."

"Obviously."

"And if for any reason you think that Morales is trying to get in touch with you . . ."

"News flash, Gil. I didn't give Hector my phone number or even my real name. He thinks I'm Tina."

"Just be careful."

"Oh, you do care. Does that mean you're not mad at me for taking the Hector matter into my own hands?" She smiled coyly. "So to speak."

"Let's not get into that."

"You are mad at me. Look, I was only trying to help. You said yourself that you needed to get Hector away from other people in order to question him. I was just doing my civic duty."

"Like I said, I don't want to get into it."

"Okay, but you're missing a great opportunity for us to get into our first fight," she said as she went inside, adding "good night" over her shoulder as she closed the door. He waited until he saw the living-room light go on before he walked back to the car.

He sat in his car for another five minutes to make sure that they hadn't been followed, then he drove home. Gil pulled up to his house and got out. He took the four plates of *bizcochitos* that his mother had given him out of the trunk of his car and tried to balance them on top of one another. He opened the front door of his house quietly, then bolted it behind him, almost dropping the cookies. It was almost two A.M. He put the *bizcochitos* on the kitchen counter and walked as silently as possible to his bedroom. He reached around the corner and flicked on the closet light so that he could see as he undressed. He was down to his underwear before he realized that Susan wasn't in bed. He turned on the lights in the bedroom, in the hallway, in the girls' room, in the family room, in the kitchen—they weren't there. He sat down on a stool in the kitchen in his underwear. The answering-machine light was blinking—most likely the message he had left for the girls, wishing them a good night. Had Susan said that they were staying at her mother's tonight? He didn't remember. She must have. But he couldn't remember. He pulled his pants and shirt back on and drove the four blocks to his mother-in-law's house. Susan's car was in the driveway. He headed back home.

He realized that he hadn't bothered to think of a way to explain to his wife why he was just getting in at two A.M. It felt strangely annoying that there was no one waiting at home to ask him where he had been all night.

CHAPTER ELEVEN

Friday Morning

Officer Manny Cordova was busily erasing something when Gil stopped at his desk the next morning.

"Manny, let's go have a talk."

Manny looked up, surprised. "Sure," he said, and he followed Gil into an interrogation room.

Manny eyed the manila file folder that Gil slapped on the table as he sat down.

"What's up, Gil?" he said as he took his seat across from Gil.

"That's what I'm wondering, Manny."

Gil opened the manila folder and started. "Yesterday you told me that you saw Hector Morales's car in Oñate Park around four thirty P.M. on Monday. You said you saw a person in Morales's car hand something out the window to someone in a Chevy that resembled Melissa Baca's—is that correct, Manny?"

"What's this about, sir?"

"That's what we're getting it. Is that what you said?"

"Yeah, that's what I said."

"You know what I can't get, Manny. I can't get why you're lying to me."

Manny looked at the door as if he expected someone to walk in. In that instant, Gil knew for certain that Manny was lying. Gil hoped that Manny had just made an honest mistake. Gil watched him open his mouth to speak, then shut it again and look down.

Gil tossed a pile of papers onto the table. "Those are court records from Judge Padilla. Hector Morales was in Española at his DWI hearing from two P.M. to almost six on Monday. A guard in the parking lot remembers watching Morales sit in his car and smoke at least four cigarettes from about three forty-five P.M. until after four thirty. Morales and his car were both in Española, Manny. So, my question is, where were you at four thirty P.M.?"

"I was driving to an MVA when I passed by Oñate Park—"

"No, you weren't. According to an incident report, you were out at a gas station near the interstate checking on a drunk male. That's all the way across town." Gil sighed. "Hector Morales says he never sold drugs to Melissa Baca."

Manny finally looked up. "You're going to believe a mojado drug dealer over me?"

Gil looked at Manny until he looked down again. Then Gil waited. The tricks he used to get confessions out of suspects worked on cops, too. All he had to do was wait.

And Manny obliged. "Gil, man, what are you saying? Okay, so I wasn't there. I heard it from one of my informants, and I thought it would sound better coming from me."

"Who's the informant?"

"Hell, I don't know, just some guy. I didn't know him."

"Some guy you don't know comes up to you out of nowhere and says he saw Melissa Baca on the day she died buy drugs, and you believe him? Does this guy know Melissa by sight? Does he know Morales by sight? Come on, Manny, let's do better than that."

Manny still didn't look up.

"Manny, what are you doing? Are you trying to sink your career? Just tell me the truth." Cordova didn't move. "For God's sake, what is this?" Gil asked.

Manny stared at his hands. "Sir, can I go back to work now? I have to finish my run sheets."

Gil leaned back and sighed. "Why did you go 10-7 for twenty minutes at eight nineteen P.M. on the night Melissa died?"

Manny was still looking down. Gil had thought for sure the question would shock him enough that he would look up. He didn't answer for a few seconds.

"I went to get something to eat," Manny said.

"According to the call logs, you already ate. Two hours earlier."

"I was hungry again."

"Where did you eat?"

"I grabbed something at Burger King."

"Burger King takes five minutes. You were unavailable for twenty."

Twenty minutes was enough time for Manny to have killed Melissa but not to have transported her body to Taos. At nine P.M. Manny had been seen at an alarm-check call by another officer. "Manny, if you know anything about Melissa's murder . . ."

"I don't. I was eating," he answered dully.

Gil sighed. Pollack was outside in the hall, listening to them talk. Gil's job was to shake Manny loose. He was more likely to confess to someone he knew. Since Gil couldn't get anything out of Manny, it was Pollack's turn.

"Good luck, Manny," Gil said as Pollack came in.

Gil left and found Chief Kline in the next room, watching through the two-way mirror and listening to Pollack question Manny. Kline looked both controlled and tense, like a man on a tightrope. His gray hair was cut whisker-short, his black uniform crisp.

"What are you going to do? We don't have enough to hold him," Gil said.

"He'll be suspended until we can figure out what the hell is going on," Kline said.

"He was seen at an alarm-check call at around nine P.M. the night Melissa was killed."

"I know. Enough time to kill her but not bring her anywhere," Kline said. His light Texas accent skipped over the word *anywhere.*

Gil watched Pollack and Manny through the glass for a minute before he said, "Sir, I think maybe it's time I get off the case. Now that one of our own may be involved—"

"I think it's premature," Kline interrupted.

"Sir, I feel strongly that this is a state police investigation—"

Kline cut in again. "Lieutenant Pollack and I agree that this is not the time for you to be excused from the case."

Lucy rolled over and looked at the clock. It was 9:07 A.M. Hell. She really needed to sleep more; her night out drinking with drug dealers had given her a hangover. She tossed for two more hours, trying to get back to sleep, but finally gave up at 11 A.M. Two vitamins served as her breakfast. She called a cab and went to get her car, which was still in the parking lot at the Silver Cowboy.

A few minutes later, she was parked in front of Patsy Burke's house, the crime-scene tape hanging limply. She heard a crow making a racket somewhere nearby. She craned her neck to look up. The bird was swaying on a power line that drooped over Scanner Lady's house. Wasn't a crow an omen, a warning of impending death? *Sorry, you're too late, buddy,* she thought.

She yelped as her cell phone rang. It was Major Garcia.

"I'm sorry I haven't called you back, but things here have been dicey," he said kindly, surprising her. She wanted to be mad at him.

"Um, no problem," she said.

"I've been looking into whether or not Patsy Burke was

Scanner Lady. Her neighbor, Mrs. Schoen, confirmed Mrs. Burke was in the habit of listening to the police scanner and calling the newspaper." Garcia hesitated. "In fact, Mrs. Schoen told me that you asked her the same thing."

"Oops. Sorry. I didn't mean . . ."

"Don't worry about it. I know you were just trying to come to terms with it," he said gently. Wow. Maybe he was a nice guy. Lucy silently took back all the times she'd wished he were dead. Garcia continued. "We do have a problem, though. The answering machine won't be much help in confirming if she's your Scanner Lady. The voice on the message isn't Mrs. Burke. It's a man's voice. We called her son, and he confirmed that he made the message for her so people would think a man lived in the house. You know how it is. We've tried to find another recording of her voice, but no luck so far. We'll keep trying."

Before hanging up, Garcia promised to call her back when he found out more. She thought, *Like I believe that,* before she could help it. She rolled her eyes, reminding herself that she was supposed to like him now.

Lucy noticed that the voice-mail light on her cell phone was blinking. She called in for her messages and cringed as she heard Gerald Trujillo's voice reminding her that they were meeting at the fire station later in the day for more medic training. She quickly deleted the message.

Down the street, the crow over Patsy Burke's house had gone, but Lucy could see the top of the cell tower in the distance. If Patsy Burke had been home, she could have heard Lucy's entire cell-phone conversation with Garcia over her police scanner.

Gil was sitting at his desk, having just hung up with his mother, when he heard someone call his name. He looked up to see Maxine Baca standing with an old jewelry box in her hands. Joy had one like it that she kept her "secrets" in—old birthday cards, valentines from boys, and a small ring that Gil had given her when she was five.

Mrs. Baca hadn't slept, he was sure. Her hair was unbrushed and pushed up on one side, making her look off-kilter. She shoved the jewelry box into his hands.

"I found that under her dresser last night. I didn't know what to do with it so I . . . You can have it and people can say what they want." Gil opened the box and looked inside. He expected to find heroin and needles. Instead, he found himself staring at a stack of Polaroids.

The ice-skating rink at the Genoveva Chavez Community Center doubled as a cool-down room for Lucy. Her arms ached, and she knew that she had overdone her workout, trying to weight-lift out her stress. She hunched over on a cold metal bench and peered at the kids' feet as they skated, trying to figure out how they balanced on the blades. Lucy had grown up mostly in L.A. and Florida, where ice skating was not a popular pastime.

Before moving to New Mexico, she'd had a Clint Eastwood fantasy of the state—filled with cactus and dust and cattle. But Northern New Mexico was nothing like that. In the summertime it was green, its fields filled with wildflowers. In the fall the aspens turned bright yellow, cutting a stripe of gold across the Sangre de Cristo Mountains. In the winter the snow came.

New Mexico was now in a drought; it hadn't snowed in a month. Everyone wanted snow—they prayed for it. But Lucy had a secret: she hated snow. She liked the *idea* of snow. It was pretty, and she loved how it looked like white icing when it coated the tops of the mountains. But she had no idea how to walk in it, drive in it, or deal with it. When she met her first snowfall in Santa Fe, she wanted to call in sick to work so that she wouldn't have to figure out how to maneuver her car in it.

She'd tried to learn to like it—had even taken skiing lessons with Del last year. But her instructor had pulled her aside, saying, "You really don't have the knack for this." After that, she'd given up trying to live with the snow and decided to hate it. It was more honest than pretending. If it never snowed again, she'd be happy.

The metal bench was getting cold, so she took her towel and headed out the door. The sweat had dried, and her face felt like it was coated in dust. She glanced at the newspaper racks next to the door. A headline in the *Santa Fe Times* caught her eye: WOMAN STRANGLED, POLICE SAY. At first Lucy thought the story was about Melissa Baca, that the *Santa Fe Times* had managed to get hold of her autopsy as well. But the article was about Patsy Burke. Lucy felt a burn of guilt. If only she'd somehow been able to tell Tommy Martinez that Patsy Burke had been strangled. Damn ethics rules. Now, the *Santa Fe Times* had scooped them on the cause of death.

Lucy fished out fifty cents and pulled out a paper. The first paragraph of the article on Patsy Burke was wordy. It needed about ten words taken out. That gave Lucy some comfort. The rest of the story didn't reveal anything new.

She got into her car and threw the paper on the passenger seat before the thought struck her. What did it matter which newspaper got the story first? Strangled or not, Patsy was still dead. And Lucy was responsible.

Lucy looked at her watch. She was supposed to meet Gerald Trujillo at the fire station in a half hour. She still had time to run home and take a shower. She would only be a few minutes late.

She waited at an intersection, trying to make a left turn out of the community center. Just as the traffic broke enough for her to merge into the lane, she took a right instead of a left toward her house. The road she was on intersected with the highway and she turned onto it, the traffic becoming lighter, then turning into a trickle. She headed east, not toward the mountains but toward the plains, unrelenting in the distance.

She didn't know where she was going.

CHAPTER TWELVE

Friday Afternoon

I'm curious why you didn't mention that you and Melissa were having problems," Gil said as way of greeting Jonathan Hammond. Gil stood in the doorway to Hammond's apartment. He hadn't been invited in. He had called the school after Mrs. Baca's visit, only to be told that Hammond had the afternoon off.

"It wasn't problems," Hammond said. "It was just a rough patch."

"What do you mean 'rough patch'?"

"We had a disagreement."

"About what?"

"It was something minor."

"What was it about?"

"It really isn't something that needs to be discussed."

Gil realized that he wanted Hammond to be Melissa's killer. But twelve students and several teachers had seen Hammond directing the dress rehearsal. The state police had talked to all of them. Not a second of Hammond's time was unaccounted for the night Melissa died.

Tired of standing in the cold doorway, he walked into Hammond's apartment without being invited. It was decorated in brown and the furniture was mostly large antique pieces. The place was fairly neat, except for an overflow of books in piles on the floor and a half-finished bottle of Jose Cuervo on the coffee table.

Gil took a packet of photos from his pocket and tossed them onto the oak dining-room table, watching for Hammond's reaction. There wasn't one.

"You don't seem too surprised to see these photos. You must have seen them before?" Still no reaction. "Maybe you took them?" That barely got a rise out of him.

"No."

"Who did take them?"

"I have no idea." Hammond stared at the photos without touching them.

The pictures were of a redheaded girl who looked twelve. She was in poses that rivaled those in the Kama Sutra. There were eleven pictures in all. And in every one she only wore a string of pearls. In a few, she covered herself with a Japanese fan.

The photos were copies; Gil had given the originals to the state police. The chain of evidence on this case was going to be a nightmare if they had to go to court. The photos had passed from an unknown someone to Melissa, to her mother, to Gil, to the state police. A good defense attorney would rip that apart, if they ever got a suspect.

The pictures had been dusted for prints. Melissa's and Maxine's were on them along with about a half-dozen others that couldn't be identified. Gil already knew that one set on them was Hammond's; he had been fingerprinted three years ago after a DWI arrest, which meant that Hammond could have been the one who took them.

The photos themselves didn't offer any clues. The only thing visible in the background was the couch the girl posed on—pastel blue with dark blue swirls. The couch hadn't been sold by any of the furniture stores in town. It had been a longshot, but Gil had given it a try. "The work is either custom done or an antique," one store manager had offered. From where Gil stood now, he could see clearly into the only other room in

Hammond's apartment—the bedroom. There was no blue couch with dark swirls in sight.

Gil had had no luck in finding out who the girl was. Burroway Academy didn't have a yearbook. He had left messages at Principal Strunk's home and office. His secretary said that he was out of town and she didn't know how to reach him. The secretary was of no further help; she'd been working at the school for only a few weeks and said she barely knew who the teachers were, let alone the students. Hammond was the only one left to ID the girl.

"Who's the girl?" Gil asked Hammond, who had sat down at the table.

"One of Melissa's students."

"Her name?"

"Sandra Paine. Her father's an ob-gyn at St. Vincent." Hammond smiled to himself. "Dr. Paine. Would you want a guy named that to deliver your baby?"

"And how old is she?

"I guess about twelve. Sandra was showing the photos to some friends in class and Melissa took them from her."

"What did Melissa do about it?"

"She didn't get a chance to do anything. She was killed the same day."

"When did she show them to you?"

"During lunch on Monday." That would explain why his fingerprints were on the photos.

"She was killed eight hours after finding these photos. You didn't see any connection?"

"No."

Hammond sat very still. Gil let the silence stretch. He waited for Hammond to fill it. After a few moments, he did.

"I told Melissa I didn't see that much wrong with this," Hammond said as he waved his hands over the photos. "If the girl was doing it of her own free will, what's the problem with it?"

"Is that why you got in the fight? Melissa broke up with you, didn't she?"

"Sort of. I knew it was only a temporary breakup. She'd never actually leave me."

"She was on her way to your place when she was killed, wasn't she?" Gil asked.

"Yes. She was going to pick up her things. She had some sweaters here or something. She didn't want me around when she came by."

"You got into this fight during lunch the day she died?"

Hammond nodded.

"Do you think Melissa told anyone she was going over to your house that night?" If someone had known where she was heading, he could have been waiting for her and forced her to pull over. Or maybe have a prearranged meeting at Oñate Park?

"I doubt it," Hammond said. "Melissa wasn't like that. She didn't do that typical female thing where she had to confess everything to everyone. At most, she might have told Judy." But Judy Maes had told Gil that she didn't know where Melissa had been going that night. Gil would have to ask her again.

"There are a couple of things bothering me, Mr. Hammond. Your fingerprints are on these photos. You seem to be the only person who knew where Melissa was going when she was killed, and you had just had a fight with her."

"But I have an airtight alibi, don't I, Detective?" Hammond said with a stiff smile. There was no way to break the alibi. The state police were looking into the possibility that Hammond had hired someone. They were checking his bank accounts and going over his phone records. Pollack had wanted Gil to interview Hammond again, "to shake up the Shinola in him," in Pollack's words.

Hammond started systemically turning the photos over, facedown. "I made the mistake of telling Melissa that I once had a crush on one of my students," Hammond said without prompting. "I was just trying to get her to calm down, to get her to see she was overreacting. I was trying to make her see that it's natural for teachers, especially men, to become enamored of their students after they hit puberty. There are several books on the subject. It's all very much human nature. It can be a good thing for both parties. Attraction is a very primitive thing. Very uncontrollable."

"You're a sixth-grade teacher? That would make the student you had the crush on, what, eleven?"

"I never acted on it. But what's the harm in looking? And what's the harm in these photos if the girl was willing?"

"Mr. Hammond, this man—the man who took these photos—acted on it. Doesn't that concern you?"

"I think it was understandable."

"Understandable? How?"

"Officer, please. The girl looks like she's enjoying it, so who are we to tell her it's wrong? We don't give young adults enough credit. They are able to make their own decisions, and I think we should let them. She made the decision to have these photos taken."

Hammond turned the pictures back over and started touching them again, this time using his index finger to trace around the edges.

"Who took the pictures, Mr. Hammond?"

"Why don't you ask the girl in them? Or won't she tell you?"

Gil felt the need for brutality. He slowly started collecting the photos. He held them with the images facing the palm of his hand. He was tired of looking at them. "Who was it?" he asked quietly.

"I honestly don't know. After our fight, Melissa wouldn't tell me. She was afraid I would warn him." Hammond stared off into space.

"Do you even know if it was a man? Could it have been a boy?"

"Melissa never said, but by the way she was talking I could tell it was an older man. She kept saying things like, 'He needs to face the music,' and that sort of thing. I don't think she would have been talking that way about a twelve-year-old boy."

"But she knew who it was." Hammond nodded. "And she planned to confront him?"

"That was the idea. Bring the poor fool to justice."

Maybe confront him at Oñate Park, give the man a chance to turn himself in? That sounded like something Melissa would do.

Gil got up from the table, wanting to be as far from Hammond as possible. He leaned up against the far wall and folded his arms, forcing Hammond to look up at him.

"Melissa didn't give you any indication if she had talked to him yet?"

"No. She wouldn't tell me anything at all."

"Who are Sandra's friends at school?"

"I have no earthly idea. Melissa would have known; but I've never had Sandra in any of my classes."

Gil walked out without saying anything more. Hammond might not have killed Melissa Baca, but Gil would make sure that Principal Strunk fired him.

Gil rang the doorbell at the Paines' house and glanced around the enclosed courtyard that he was standing in. A now-dry pond fed what was usually a tiny stream that twisted through brown flower beds. It was an excessive use of water in the desert. The door was opened by a man in his late thirties or early forties, with dark hair and eyes. He was wearing pressed jeans, loafers, and a crisp blue cotton shirt. Gil introduced himself, and Dr. Michael Paine led him inside. The story-high windows in the living room gave a broad view of the Santa Fe Valley. The leather couch Gil sat on was soft.

"Dr. Paine," Gil started. "Your daughter, Sandra, is a seventh-grader at Burroway Academy, is that right?"

Dr. Paine said yes and added, "Her teacher was that dead woman, Miss Baca. Is that why you're here?"

"In a way. I'm just checking into a few things," Gil said noncommittally.

Dr. Paine seated himself on the couch across from Gil, pulling up his pant leg so as to not lose the crease in his jeans.

"Dr. Paine, has your daughter been in trouble at school lately?" Gil asked.

"I assume you already know she has been or you wouldn't be here. What did her teachers tell you?" the doctor asked, looking unconcerned.

"I just have reason to believe that she has been . . ." Gil hesitated; he didn't want to use the wrong word, "involved in things that may be inappropriate for a girl her age."

"You can be more candid than that, Officer."

"Had Melissa Baca called you or your wife recently to express concern about Sandra's welfare?" It would have been very much like Melissa to call the parents, Gil thought.

"We've never spoken to or met Miss Baca."

Strange, Gil thought. He knew all of Therese and Joy's teachers.

Gil pulled a picture out of his pocket. He had had Sandra's face blown up on one of the Polaroids. He wasn't about to show Paine the actual pictures. Sandra's father didn't need to see how fast his daughter had grown up. Gil showed the blowup to Paine. "Is this Sandra?"

Paine didn't even take the photo and barely glanced at it. "And if it is?"

Gil finally got it—Dr. Paine knew about the photos. Maybe had even seen them. Maybe even taken them?

"Dr. Paine, what is your relationship like with your daughter?"

"Let me save us both a lot of trouble, Officer," Paine said smoothly. "My wife and I know about the photos, which is where I assume you got that snapshot you're holding. We don't approve of Sandra's actions and are punishing her appropriately for it. We will not be filing any charges against the man who took them, and if you file any charges on her behalf, we will not cooperate."

"May I ask what the punishment was?"

"No. That is a matter for my family." The doctor casually rested his arms along the back of the sofa and smiled slightly. "I hope you understand."

"Who was the man who took them?"

"I have no idea. We didn't ask her for a name."

Gil shook his head. Paine seemed completely at ease discussing his daughter's sexual relationships. He was almost too unconcerned. Gil simply did not understand the man.

"I think Melissa Baca was going to confront whoever took the photos," Gil said. "We want to find that man and question him."

"I'm sorry, I can't help you."

"Do you even know if Sandra was forced into making these photos?" Paine didn't answer, so Gil tried again. "Dr. Paine, your daughter was exploited by this man. I think it's strange that you don't want him punished."

"Wouldn't it hurt Sandra more to see her name on the ten o'clock news?"

"We don't release the names of any victims. . . ."

"Officer, please," Paine said, smiling weakly, "You know as well as I do that these things are always leaked to the press. Honestly, my wife and I discussed this at length. We simply feel that this a family matter for us to handle. It's in Sandra's best interest. We have decided it is not a concern of the police."

"I think a sexual predator is most definitely a police concern," Gil said. Paine stared at him impassively. "Dr. Paine, can you understand how it looks that you're being so uncooperative?"

"I assume you're implying that it was me," Paine said, frowning a little at Gil's question. "If you want to continue with that line of questioning, you can contact my wife's attorney."

Gil tried a different tact. "Can I talk to Sandra?"

"I'm sorry, that's not possible. She's been sent to Denver to stay with her aunt."

Conveniently gone so that the police couldn't question her, Gil thought. But at least if she was out of town, she was also safe from the man who had taken the photos.

Paine eased back in his seat. "Besides," he said, "it wouldn't do you any good to talk to Sandra. She is very stubborn. She would never tell you anything, and she'd just call you a million nasty names. She gets it from her mother. And believe me, Sandra wasn't forced into taking the photos. She did it willingly. She'll try anything."

Gil was having a hard time finding his way through this interview. Dr. Paine wasn't reacting correctly to any of the questions. He had had no emotional outbursts and didn't even seemed concerned about his daughter. He looked like a man engaged in boring dinner conversation. Gil wondered why that was.

"Where is your wife?" Gil asked. Mrs. Paine might be more willing to help her daughter and give him the names of friends Sandra might have confided in. At the very least, Gil might be better able to judge her reactions to his questions.

"She's out right now, but I will tell her that you stopped by."

"May I ask where you were on Monday night?" Gil asked.

Dr. Paine looked at him calmly. "Once again, I must remind you that any further questions in this area must be directed to our family attorney. However, I don't want to seem difficult. I was in surgery until nine P.M.."

"And your wife?"

"Here at home with Sandra," he said.

Gil glanced around the huge room. "Can I see any other couches you have in the house?"

"There are only these two." Paine sat quietly, looking at Gil. The man was too calm. Was he on medication? Had he been drinking? Or was he telling the truth? Was he so used to Sandra's misbehaving that it no longer interested him? Gil had seen the families of drug addicts act unconcerned because they had seen it all before. They were tired of the drama. But this was a twelve-year-old girl. How much drama could she have caused?

Gil got up, gave Paine his business card, and asked him to give it to his wife. He was opening the front door when Paine said, "It seems to me you should be looking at Miss Baca's drugged-out friends. That's what she gets for leading that kind of life."

Sandra Paine watched the tall Hispanic detective through the upstairs window as he left. The back of his head looked a little like Gregory Peck's.

As the detective was getting into his car, he slipped a little on some black ice. Sandra giggled. Her father, who was just reaching the top of the stairs, glanced at her sharply. Like she wasn't supposed to laugh. She glared at him and went into her room, careful to slam the door.

She sat down at her computer and typed "Gregory Peck" in one of the search engines. A Web site created by someone named Jo-jo popped up. Pictures of the actor were surrounded by a border of roses.

"What a cutie," she whispered to herself. She clicked on an audio clip from one of his movies, but her computer froze and started to crash.

"Dammit to hell and back with a stick," she said. She loved making new sayings out of the bad words she knew. Her second favorite thing to say was "thanks ever so." She had picked that up from an old Marilyn Monroe movie her friend Lacey had rented. When Sandra's mother had told her that she was being shipped off to Colorado, she'd smiled sweetly and, with all the fake sugar she could muster, said, "Thanks ever so." She'd gotten slapped for that one.

She glanced at the phone on her desk. Her parents had cut off her phone and e-mail after the "second incident," as they called it. But they had forgotten about the cell phone in her purse. Her boyfriend had texted her seven times since yesterday—seven times. She was using her *Cosmo* trick—keep him guessing—and hadn't called him back. She was still getting used to the word *boyfriend.* She said it softly several times into the mirror.

Her suitcase was sprawled across her bed but she hadn't packed anything yet. She was still considering.

At first she had refused to pack, yelling baby things at her parents like, "You can't make me," and, "I'd rather die first." In the end, she'd given in after her mother started pulling out all her oversize T-shirts and baggy jeans. She was going to Colorado, not to Siberia.

But now she was having trouble packing. Lacey had been trying to convince her that her boyfriend—Sandra smiled at the word—would come to whisk her away, like in the end of *It Happened One Night.* A knight in shining armor and all that. But Sandra wasn't so sure. She thought that it would make more sense for them to play it cool, pretend that it was over, and then, when everyone least suspected it, fly off to Mexico.

She had to pack for either eventuality.

She walked over to her calendar hanging on the wall. Each day—for the past twenty-four days—had an *X* on it. Her mother had once asked her what the *X*'s were for. Sandra had lied, saying that she was marking off the days she had been dieting. She mother hadn't asked any more about it. Sandra had been careful since then to keep her mother out of her room.

If her mother had checked, she would have realized that the *X*'s started on the day of the first incident. Sandra counted the *X*'s again. For twenty-four days she had had a boyfriend.

The first incident had started like one of those stories you read in *Cosmo*'s agony column. Miss Baca had caught her with a silver flask—bought with birthday money from her grandma—full of vodka. She had been sent to the principal's office and they had called the cops. That was the first time she had met her boyfriend. Her lover. She giggled at the word.

She considered packing the calendar, but there was a chance that her aunt would be nosy and go through her suitcase once she got to Colorado. She made an exaggerated sigh—a "Greta Garbo lament," Lacey called it—and looked back at her empty suitcase.

Lucy got to work just in time for the editor's meeting at three o'clock, but she paid little attention. She was thinking about Melissa Baca. When she got back to her desk, she paged Tommy Martinez. He called her back fifteen minutes later.

"Hey, boss. I got your message. What's up?" he asked.

"Tommy, I need a favor. It's important."

She heard the wariness in his voice when he said, "Sure, boss."

She took a deep breath. "Tommy, I need to know the names of the sources who told you Melissa Baca was doing drugs."

He hesitated. For too long.

"Tommy, I know it's not usually how I do things, but I have to know." He still didn't answer. Lucy's run-in with Hector Morales last night had started her thinking. What if he was telling the truth? What if Melissa Baca hadn't done drugs? By the answers Hector gave to Gil's questions, she could tell the Gil had gotten bad info from someone. But from whom? And if Gil had gotten bad info, maybe the newspaper had, too.

"I promise you that I won't breathe a word of it to anyone

if I can help it, but there is the possibility that Melissa didn't do drugs. If we've misrepresented the facts to the reader . . ."

"We didn't misrepresent anything. The syringe was found in her car and our sources confirmed she was using drugs."

"I think our sources were wrong."

"No way. Not possible. These guys know what they're talking about. And we know drugs were found in her car."

"Tommy," she said firmly, "I will not argue this with you."

In the end, he told her the names of his sources—Santa Fe Police Officers Manny Cordova and Ron Baca and Lieutenant Tim Pollack of the state police. Tommy added that Pollack was the one who had leaked the autopsy to them.

Lucy was looking up triangulating cell-phone towers on the Internet when her managing editor gestured at her to come into his office. He said. "You said you wanted to talk to me?"

She had asked to speak with John Lopez right after her conversation with Tommy Martinez. At the time, she'd been pretty clear about what she wanted to say, but now she wasn't so sure. She started with, "I think we may have been wrong in the Melissa Baca story that was in Wednesday's paper."

Lopez always looked so concerned. "How so?"

"We said Melissa was a drug user, but I don't think she was."

"What makes you think that?" Even though she wanted to, Lucy couldn't mention what Hector Morales had said. She had promised Gil.

"Well, on a hunch, I asked Tommy Martinez who the sources were that said Melissa's Baca did drugs. He said one of them was Melissa's brother," she said.

"That's interesting." More of the concerned look.

"I think so. I mean, it's really weird that a brother would offer up that kind of information. Normally, he'd be the one screaming if we printed something like that. It makes me think that maybe he's involved in her murder."

"What do you want to do about it?"

"Well, it'd be great if we could say he was the one who gave us the tip, but we can't, because it was off the record. I think the best we can do is print a story that casts some doubt on the drug angle."

"Are the police no longer saying drugs were involved in Melissa's death?"

Lucy faltered. "No."

"Do you have any hard evidence that our sources were lying?"

"No, but it's very strange."

Lopez nodded. They sat without talking, Lopez just staring at her, as if waiting for her to have an epiphany.

"Why do you think you're really talking to me about this?" he asked. His psychiatrist-sounding voice was perfectly modulated. It was inquisitive, yet not threatening or judgmental. The man had missed his calling.

She stumbled, saying, "I don't know. . . ."

"Do you think maybe it's because you're feeling guilty?" She didn't answer. He continued. "Do you think that maybe if you'd asked Tommy Martinez who his sources were to begin with, that you would have handled this differently? That maybe you would have questioned the information about the drugs initially?"

That was the truth, of course. If she'd been like the other editors, she would have asked Tommy who his sources were. She would have known that Melissa's brother was the leak from the beginning. And she would have wondered why. She wouldn't have let the information about the drugs get into the paper. Now everyone in Santa Fe thought Melissa Baca had been an addict. And there was no taking that back. Ever. And it was her fault.

Lopez watched her, considering, before he said, "If the

police ever officially say that Melissa Baca didn't do drugs, we'll write a story about it. But, until that happens, we do nothing."

Mrs. Paine jumped up from the table, almost knocking it over, when she saw Gil come in. Her coffee was still swishing in its cup as they shook hands. Her skin was soft, but her nails were bitten down to the quick. The nail of her ring finger was shredded so low that it was spotted with blood.

Gil recalled an instructor at the police academy who used to categorize all the people he interviewed as animals. "Elephants never kill anyone, but watch out for those badgers," he would say. Mrs. Paine reminded Gil of a ferret. She looked like she was on something. Her small, dark eyes looked unfocused and her upper lip was sweaty. She wiped it with a napkin. She adjusted the scarf and the gold chain around her neck.

She had called him, saying that her husband had told her about Gil's visit and that she wanted to clear up a few things. They were at a coffee shop where a Chinese restaurant had been a month ago. Mrs. Paine didn't look like she needed coffee.

She said that her first name was Joyce, then said nothing else. She just sat there, tearing at the rim of her paper coffee cup, reducing it to small pieces.

"How did you find out about the photos?" Gil prompted.

"Oh, I . . ." She stopped and waved a hand in front of her face, then said, "I found them when I was cleaning up Sandra's room"

"Do you know who took the photos?"

"We didn't ask her. But believe me when I say it wasn't anyone we know."

"How can you be sure?"

"My husband ripped up the photos we found and tossed them out, so we don't have them anymore. The ones Miss Baca found must be extras." It wasn't exactly an answer to his question.

"Do you have any guesses as to who the man might be?"

"No. I've thought about it, wondered what I could have done to . . ." She stopped. "I don't know." Her way of answering his questions was interesting. It seemed that she was having a hard time following the conversation.

"Do you think Sandra was forced into taking the photos?"

Mrs. Paine laughed. "Sandra has never been forced into anything in her life. She wanted to take the photos, believe me. They were probably her idea."

"You have no idea who the man is? I think it's a little odd that you never asked her his name."

"I learned a long time ago that I can't make Sandra do anything, so I've given up trying. If I had asked, she would have laughed in my face."

Gil wasn't so sure. "How is your husband's relationship with Sandra?"

"My husband couldn't have molested her. He's never home. I don't see how it's possible." It surprised Gil that she'd brought up the molestation on her own. It was a strange thing to say.

"Have you ever seen anything that would make you think your husband molested her?"

"Of course not. Never. My husband loves her," she said calmly, without much emotion. Disinterested. She looked off into the distance. He wondered if she had some mental illness.

"How do you get along with Sandra?" he asked.

"She's very headstrong. She always has been, even as a baby. She doesn't tell me things. I'm not her confidante," she said.

"Does she tell your husband things?"

The same laugh. "God, no. He wouldn't even know what to do if she spoke more than two words to him. I think he'd die of fright." Gil noticed that she'd insulted her husband as easily as Dr. Paine had insulted her.

"Where is Sandra now?" he asked.

"In Denver at her aunt's."

"Can I talk to her?"

"I'd have to ask my attorney."

Maxine Baca sat with Veronica Cordova in the kitchen. Veronica was making rice and beans, which Maxine had told her she didn't want. Her friend was talking about Manny and how he was so upset over Melissa's death. Maxine was tired of hearing about Melissa. She wished that Veronica would stop talking.

"Remember when Melissa was born? You were so happy," Veronica said. "All you wanted to do was stay in your hospital room and hold your beautiful baby girl."

After Melissa was born, the doctors kept wanting Maxine to eat. But she wouldn't. She wouldn't make that mistake again. Not until her baby was baptized. Maxine had wanted to have Melissa's baptism right away, but Ernesto said no. He said that if Maxine wanted to starve herself because of some ritual, that was fine, but he wanted Melissa baptized in a church. But Ernesto didn't understand. Maxine had the priest come by the hospital and he baptized Melissa while some of the nurses watched. When Ernesto came to visit, Maxine told him about the baptism. He called her a name and went home.

But she couldn't go home. The doctors said that she was bleeding inside. At first, Maxine thought that God was punishing her for not remembering Daniel. So she got down on her knees in the hospital room and prayed the rosary for him, to prove to the Lord that Daniel would always be everything to her. But she prayed the rosary for three days, and the doctors found more things wrong with her. She had to have a blood transfusion and they gave her some drugs. Ernesto wouldn't come to the hospital. He said he had to work. Veronica came and brought Ron with her, but he wouldn't come into the room. Maxine kept asking God why she couldn't go home, but God wouldn't answer her. The priest came back and Maxine confessed her sins. But the next day, the doctors said that she was getting worse.

Then Maxine's mother came to visit. Her mother took Melissa out of Maxine's arms while she was nursing. Her mother kept kissing Melissa on both cheeks and her mouth, saying that it was to keep the baby smell away so that the evil that stole babies couldn't find Melissa. Her mother stayed past visiting hours and yelled at the nurses when they asked her to leave. She finally left after midnight, saying that she would come back the next day to visit. Before she left, she pinched Melissa under the arm. She said it was for good luck. Melissa started crying.

The next morning, Maxine left the hospital without telling anyone and walked the four miles home, carrying Melissa. She knew why her mother had come to see her. And she knew why God in his mercy had been making her sick. He had wanted her to stay in the hospital to protect her and Melissa from Maxine's mother.

Maxine knew that her mother was coming to take Melissa, just like Maxine's grandmother had taken Maxine's baby sister.

When Maxine was about five, she and her sisters had been home alone one day. Her mother had taken her brother with her while she got her hair done. Maxine's older sister, who was seven, was left in charge of Maxine and the baby. Their mother had been gone for only a few minutes when the front door slammed open and their grandmother walked in, carrying a suitcase. Maxine and her sister ran into the kitchen, afraid of *Abuela* and her pinching fingers. They heard her throwing things into the suitcase in the baby's room. Then *Abuela* was in the kitchen, carrying the baby and the suitcase in one arm. Maxine was hanging on to her sister and both were in the corner, crying. *Abuela* reached down and pinched Maxine hard under her arm and said, "If you weren't so fat, you would go with me, too." Then *Abuela* and the baby left.

Maxine knew that her mother would come for Melissa the

same way *Abuela* had for her sister. This was God's test. God, in his wisdom, was making sure that Maxine would sacrifice anything for her daughter. With Daniel, she had been tempted and had given in to the sin of gluttony. With Melissa, God was tempting her with the sin of sloth.

Maxine never left Melissa alone. After Maxine walked home from the hospital, she locked the front door of her house and closed the curtains to make her mother think she wasn't at home. Ernesto and Ron weren't allowed to turn the lights on at night in the living room or their bedrooms. The only light that could be turned on was in the kitchen, because it faced the back of the house. Ron slept mostly at Manny Cordova's house. Ernesto changed to the night patrol. Maxine didn't answer the phone and stopped going to church, instead saying her own Mass at her shrine to Daniel, with Melissa sleeping on the floor next to her. She would pray for God to protect Melissa and ask Our Lady to keep her mother away. Maxine moved her bed back into the nursery, holding Melissa all night and singing her songs. Then, one day when Melissa was fifteen months old, the Lord took Maxine's mother. The doctors said that it was a heart attack and Maxine said a novena to Our Lady in thanksgiving. No one had come to steal her baby. Maxine knew that she had passed God's test. She hadn't given in to the sin. God was going to allow her to keep Melissa.

The next day, Maxine opened the curtains and called Ron at Manny's house to have him come home for dinner. She made posole and chile rellenos. But Ernesto didn't come home for dinner. He stayed on the night shift until he was killed.

Maxine had seen her baby sister for the first time since they were children at Ernesto's funeral seven years ago. Her sister had come dressed in a fancy black skirt and blouse. She'd said that she was the superintendent of a school in Albuquerque and had been a French and history teacher before that. She had married an engineer and had three children.

One was teaching at New Mexico State University. They lived in a house with a swimming pool. She'd told Maxine, "The day *Abuela* took me was the best day of my life."

Joyce Paine gave Gil the name of one of Sandra's friends—Lacey Gould. Mrs. Paine didn't know the address but gave him directions and a map drawn on a coffeehouse napkin. The Gould house was in the foothills of the Sangre de Cristos. He rang the doorbell but didn't hear any chimes inside, so he knocked. A man with a long beard answered the door in slippers. Mr. Gould asked him inside before Gil had a chance to say who he was. In the foyer were stacks of boxes.

Gil introduced himself and asked, "Are you moving?"

"Oh, no. We moved in here about a year ago. We're just taking out time getting unpacked." The boxes would have driven Susan crazy.

In the living room were more boxes. The bay windows looked out on a piñon forest. A big dog, maybe a Ridgeback, took up most of the couch. Oblivious, Mr. Gould sat down in the only other seat. Gil was left standing.

"You're here about Miss Baca. Poor girl. My wife and I liked her very much. She was one of Lacey's favorite teachers." Mr. Gould had an accent that Gil couldn't figure out.

"Is Lacey here? I have a few questions for her."

"She may be." He yelled, "Lacey," several times without getting up. Someone ran down the stairs "Yeah, Dad?"

Lacey Gould looked at Gil curiously as she swatted the Ridgeback off the couch, saying, "Move, Beck." She folded her bare feet under her, her gray, wrinkled T-shirt blending in with the sofa.

"What's going on, Dad?" she asked, but before he could answer she said to Gil, "I know who you are. You're the cop checking out Miss Baca's murder."

"I am. How'd you know?"

Lacey shrugged, twisting a necklace with a blue bead on it around her finger.

"How well did you know Miss Baca?" Gil asked.

"I didn't really know her. But I liked her. She was nice."

"How well do you know Sandra Paine?"

Lacey glanced at her father. "Let's go up to my room."

She ran up the steps, with Gil and the Ridgeback following. Gil had to do a zigzag to avoid the boxes in the hallway.

Lacey seemed to be the only member of the Gould family who had unpacked. Her bed was made with tie-dyed sheets. The walls and ceiling were covered with old movie posters. It made the room claustrophobic.

"Beck, get out," she said, slamming the door on the dog. She plopped onto the bed and stared up at a poster of Cary Grant in *North by Northwest.*

Gil wandered the room, looking at the posters. "So what's your favorite old movie?" he asked.

"Give me a year."

"Nineteen thirty-five."

"Drama or musical?"

"Musical."

"Too easy. *Top Hat.*"

Gil picked up a postcard of a brooding Gary Cooper from 1930. "Does Sandra watch old movies with you?" he asked.

"Sometimes. She's learning."

"Are you and Sandra close?"

"I'm her best friend." She said it matter-of-factly.

"Why do you think I'm here?" he asked. Gil was hoping that they could talk in generalities; he didn't want to get into a conversation about the Polaroids.

"You want to know about the pictures Sandra and her boyfriend took."

"How do you know that?"

She answered with another shrug.

"What do you know about it?" he asked, still trying to keep it vague.

"That she met him about a month ago and it's been lovely." Lacey sighed heavily.

"Do you know the boyfriend's name?"

She rolled over on her bed and started picking at a thread on the tie-dyed sheet. "He made her promise not to tell. She could have told me, but we thought it would be cheating. I know all about what they did together," Lacey offered. This was the topic that Gil wanted to avoid unless one of her parents was around.

"Would you be willing to talk with me about this in front of your father?"

"Yeah, right. Not in a million."

He cracked open the bedroom door, but she took no notice. Now, anyone walking by could see into the room. "What did they do together?"

"Everything. There was this article in some magazine that Sandra reads about A Hundred Ways to Give Your Man Oral Sex or whatever and Sandra had done all of them."

Gil winced and changed the line of his questioning.

"Do you know where they spent most of their time together?"

"At his place, mostly."

"Do you know where that was?"

Another shrug.

"So it wasn't her dad?"

"That's disgusting. Have sex with your dad? Eww." She made a face and shook her head. "It was totally not her dad. Blech. She would have told me."

"How about a friend of her dad's?"

Lacey looked thoughtful. "I think it was some guy she met recently."

"Was it Mr. Hammond?"

"That teacher from school?" Lacey thought for a second. "I don't think so. I've never seen them together. And Sandra once said she thought having sex with him would be too much like studying. Like he would make you take a quiz after it." Lacey giggled.

"Did she ever tell you what the man looked like?" Lacey didn't answer. He said, "You must have played Twenty Questions or something. If I were you, I'd want to know all about him."

Her father started yelling, "Lacey, we've gotta go," from downstairs before she could answer Gil. She grabbed her gym bag and said, "Tae kwon do," as she ran out of the room. She stopped short at the doorway. "Sandra's right. You do look like Gregory Peck." He heard her banging down the steps before he could ask her how Sandra could have known what he looked like.

Lucy tapped her knee against the filing cabinet next to her desk as she edited a story about water rates. She was using the DELETE key a lot; the reporter was in the habit of using the word *that* as often as possible. She was having a hard time paying attention to the story. The newsroom, always as noisy as a shopping mall on the day after Thanksgiving, was distracting. The photo editor, who was leading an elementary-school tour, kept glaring at the copy desk, where three of the editors were involved in a conversation about group sex.

She answered her phone as if she were on autopilot.

"Hi, Lucy." She recognized the voice but pretended that she didn't. She started tapping her fingers on her desk.

"Who is this?"

"It's Detective Montoya. You called me?"

She flipped open a folder on her desk and took out an official OMI report. "Yeah. I didn't know if you had seen the toxicology report on Melissa Baca." She was using it as an excuse.

She wanted to talk to him, to somehow figure out a way to tell him who the confidential sources were. But it was impossible. She couldn't reveal the names. That would break a thousand journalistic rules. And she could end up in court.

"No, I hadn't. What are the results?" Gil asked.

She read from the report, " 'Subject shows no questionable or illegal substances in the bloodstream.' "

"She had nothing in her system?"

"Nope. Not a drop of anything. I'll fax you the report."

"Great. Thanks."

Lucy had thought carefully about what she was going to say next. "I also wanted to let you know about the sources who leaked it to the newspaper that Melissa Baca did drugs. . . ."

Gil started to interrupt, but she stopped him. "I can't tell you their names, of course, but I did want to let you know that those sources, who we believed were reliable at the time, are now suspect."

"Is the information the sources gave you suspect or are they personally suspect?" God, he was smart, Lucy thought.

"I would say the sources are in a position to know, but their motives are suspect."

Gil asked slowly, "Why are you telling me this?"

She knew how it must seem to him. To him, there was no reason for her to have brought it up. There was no code that said she had to admit it when the newspaper screwed up, or, more correctly, when she screwed up. But she had to do something. She couldn't tell him the names, but maybe she could get him thinking. She had chosen her words carefully, memorizing them. She'd used the word *suspect* on purpose, knowing that Ron Baca might be considered a suspect. Maybe Gil would think about her word choice. Wonder about it.

"I just wanted you to think about it, Gil," she said.

"Thanks, I appreciate it." He hesitated for a minute before he said, "Are you okay?"

"Yeah, fine. Why do you ask?"

"You're not as upbeat as usual. You haven't tried to make fun of me at all."

She smiled and said in her Scarlett O'Hara voice, "Oh, Gil, you do care. You just make my heart go a pitter-pat."

He laughed and said, "That's better," then hung up.

Lucy smiled to herself. She had gotten him to laugh. Again. She was getting good at this. And he was getting good at making her feel better. Her good mood ended as soon as she saw Tommy Martinez walk in the door, reminding her of her failure.

She still didn't get why Officers Ron Baca and Manny Cordova had leaked the information to the newspaper. The only person who made sense was Lieutenant Pollack—he always leaked info. He was easy to figure out—it was all about glory.

Gil sat in his car in front of the elementary school, trying to catch a glimpse of his daughters. Susan had a dentist appointment, so Gil was picking up the girls. He thought he spotted Therese's dark head in the crowd, but it went into a Honda in front of him.

There. He saw Joy. Talking to a boy. Therese was at her side, tugging on her sister's coat. Gil tried to get a better look at the boy through the crowd of children. Gil got out of the car to try a different angle, but by then the boy was gone and Joy and Therese were on their way to the car. Gil waved at them and the girls smiled back. He watched them buckle up in the backseat before he started to move through the after-school traffic.

He wanted to ask who the boy was. "How was school?"

He got a, "Great, Daddy," from Therese and a strange, "Wonderful," from Joy that wasn't sarcastic. What had happened to the preteen hostility?

"What did you guys do?"

Therese gave a list of things, starting with homeroom, while Joy stared out the window. When Therese was finished, he said, "What about you, Joy? Anything interesting happen?"

"Nothing really special." Still that strange lilt to her voice.

"Who was that boy I saw you talking to?" Gil tried to say it casually.

"Oh, come on, Dad. Please," she said, back in her usual annoyed tone.

"I was just wondering."

He watched in the rearview mirror as Joy shook her head. But she was smiling slightly. Gil gave up and asked Therese about her classroom's pet newt.

Susan was waiting for them when they got home. She kissed his cheek as he tried to brush the hair out of her eyes, but she beat him to it, pushing the dark strands behind her ear.

Gil watched the girls jabber at Susan, telling her things that they hadn't told him. Joy laughed as she told Susan about band recital, in which the tuba player, on a dare, had gotten his hand stuck in his instrument.

Gil checked his watch. He needed to get back to the office.

In all the years they'd been married, Susan had never asked him about his work. He sometimes wondered if the girls even knew what he did for a living. But that was all right. The least he could do was to save them from the horrors he saw every day. His job as husband and dad was to keep them safe not only physically but from the knowledge of what human beings were capable of doing to one another. But somehow the Melissa Baca case was different. Gil realized that he wanted Susan to ask him about it; he couldn't discuss it with any of the other officers, since Manny Cordova was involved.

"The Melissa Baca case is really interesting," he said to Susan. He was careful not to saying *killing* in front of the girls.

"Oh, really?" Susan said as she mixed up some chocolate milk for Joy.

"Yeah, I'm working with the state police on it, so it makes it even more complicated."

"I didn't know that." Susan handed the glass to Joy and started one for Therese.

Gil felt awkward. He was forcing the conversation. He sighed and gave up.

Ten minutes later, he was back at work.

CHAPTER THIRTEEN

Friday Night

Gil tried to call Lacey Gould when he got back to the police station, but she was at a slumber party for the night. He was hanging up the phone when he felt someone standing next to him. It was a police secretary who Gil thought had a crush on Manny Cordova. She shifted her stance when Gil asked if he could help her, then she walked into one of the empty offices, expecting Gil to follow.

They stood there, both waiting for something, until Gil repeated, "Can I help you?"

"I heard you were questioning Manny and I thought I should tell you that he didn't do anything." It came out in a rush.

"You mean Officer Cordova?" Gil asked. She turned pink. Gil hadn't said it to embarrass her, just to clarify her feelings.

"I'm sorry, yes, Officer Cordova. He didn't do anything."

Gil thought that her name was Cindy. He didn't know her last name. "What makes you think he wasn't involved?"

"He just couldn't have been." Her voice was desperate. "He's not like that. You know him."

"You know I can't really talk about this . . ." Gil said.

"Well, you should be talking to the brother of that dead girl."

"What makes you say that?"

She was smug. This was her ace in the hole. "Because I saw him talking to his sister the day she died."

"You saw Ron Baca talking with Melissa? Where was this and when?"

"It was at McDonald's. The one on Cerrillos Road. I was over there getting some fries when I saw them at a table. It must have been something like four thirty P.M."

"What were they doing?"

"They were talking and looking at pictures. You know, like Polaroids."

That's where Melissa had been for the missing hour—she'd been showing her brother the photos of Sandra Paine.

But Ron Baca's fingerprints weren't on the photos. Gil had run the fingerprints against all databases, including law enforcement. But Gil didn't think the secretary was lying. It would be easy enough to check with the McDonald's employees. Ron Baca would be hard to forget in his police uniform.

"Does that help Manny—I mean, Officer Cordova?" she asked.

"That's interesting."

Lucy looked up to see who had spoken. It was the newspaper's secretary, staying late to finish up some paperwork. She was typing in the agendas for the local government agencies, which were listed in the newspaper every Sunday.

"Stacy," Lucy said, "you've got to stop talking to yourself."

"Come over here and look at this," Stacy said. She handed Lucy a piece of paper. It was the agenda for the Citizens' Police Advisory Review Committee, whose name was too long and governmental. The committee met only a few times a year to hear the public's complaints about Santa Fe's police service. The idea was that people who were mistreated by the police would be less intimidated if they could air their concerns to a bunch of regular Joes instead of having to file formal grievances at the police station. The committee was fairly new and having a hard time getting started. The complaints usually amounted to nothing more than, "When the officer pulled me over, he was rude."

"What am I looking for, Stacy?" Lucy asked as she read over the agenda.

"Down there. On number five."

The fifth item on the agenda listed only a name—Melissa Baca—and then her occupation—teacher at the Burroway Academy. There was no other information. Very strange. So Melissa Baca had been planning to go in front of the police advisory committee. To complain about a cop?

"When does the committee meet next?" Lucy asked.

"On Monday."

"Oh, Tommy . . ." Lucy called to him, in an exaggeratedly sweet voice.

"I hate it when you use that tone. This can't be good news," he said as he walked over.

She handed him the agenda, pointing to Melissa's name.

"Damn," was all he said. Lucy knew what the problem was: it was almost ten P.M. For the second time in a week, they'd have to scramble to get anything for tomorrow's newspaper.

While Tommy was making phone calls, she finished editing an article about road construction on the interstate. It was the last story she had to read for the night. Unless Tommy found out what Melissa Baca's name was doing on that agenda.

There was already a Melissa Baca story for tomorrow's newspaper. Tommy had written it, and Lucy had looked it over and sent it to the copy desk for its final edit more than two hours ago. The story was slated for the local section, not the front page. It was a short story, only ten inches. Lucy had wanted the story on the front page. The first paragraph read: "Melissa Baca, a seventh-grade teacher whose body was discovered below the Taos Gorge Bridge Tuesday, did not have drugs in her system, according to a report by the Office of the Medical Investigator. However, the state police said they still consider drugs a factor in her death despite the toxicology results." Lucy had thought that maybe, if the story was on the front page, the readers would question whether Melissa Baca really had done drugs. But John Lopez had voted Lucy down; there were too many other breaking-news stories that deserved the five front-page slots. And Lopez knew the real reason why Lucy wanted it on the front page: she wanted to absolve herself. It was her chance at redemption, her way to make up for yet another error in judgment. If only she had asked Tommy about his confidential sources. If only she hadn't talked about Scanner Lady in a room full of cops. If only.

Lucy went over to the copy desk to tell the assistant copy-desk chief that the road-construction story was ready to be edited. The editor said, "About time," before calling it up on her screen. Lucy was watching her edit the story when Tommy came over.

"We've got a problem, boss," he said. "The chairman of the police advisory committee says he's never heard of Melissa Baca. He said the secretary who makes the agenda might know something about it. I called her three times, but she didn't answer and there was no answering machine."

"What do the state police say?" Lucy asked.

"I paged Lieutenant Pollack twice, but he hasn't called back. I even called his house and left a message." Pollack was their snitch, so he would call back. Eventually.

"Anybody else at the state police we can try?"

"I called some officers I know who are part of the investigation, but they gave me that 'the only person who can comment is Pollack' crap. I guess since we ran our story with the anonymous sources in it, the state police are cracking down on any officer who talks to the press besides Pollack."

"Which is pretty damn funny, considering the circumstances," Lucy said. Pollack was the leak, after all. Tommy looked nervous that she had alluded to it in the open newsroom.

"Any other ideas?" she asked him.

"Not a one."

Lucy thought about calling Gil, but hesitated. She didn't want to take advantage of their friendship. Is that what it was? A friendship? She didn't know. But she was pretty sure that he would think less of her for calling him. Not that he would tell her anything anyway. He wasn't that kind of cop.

"Okay, Tommy, let's give it a little more time. Maybe somebody will call you back. And keep trying that secretary. While you're waiting for calls, write up what you have and add it to the Melissa Baca story."

The assistant copy-desk chief, who had been listening to their conversation, asked, "You're calling the Baca story back?"

"Yeah. We'll just add to it."

"Do you want to move it to the front page?" the editor asked.

Lucy thought for a second. She was being handed exactly what she had argued for with Lopez. But, truth be told, the story still didn't warrant the front page. If they could say why Melissa had been about to go to the police advisory committee, maybe Lucy could justify moving it. She looked at the clock. It was almost ten thirty P.M. It was becoming extremely unlikely that they were going to get any calls back.

They could sit on the information, wait until they had time to check it out, and then run the story in the next day's newspaper. But the *Santa Fe Times* got the agendas just like the *Capital Tribune* did. Somebody might have been typing those agendas in and, just as Stacy had, noticed Melissa Baca's name. It was too chancy.

"No. The story stays in the local section," Lucy said. She wished that Lopez were there to witness her sacrifice.

"Why don't you call up those confidential police sources

who told you about the drugs and ask them about it?" the editor offered.

Tommy said, "Yeah, right" before walking away. Lucy just shook her head.

Gil was on his way home when he made a detour to Mrs. Baca's. He didn't plan on going inside. He was just driving by on the off chance that Ron might be back from the Pecos. Gil had called Mrs. Baca earlier to check on her but had gotten the answering machine. She hadn't called back.

When he pulled up in front of the Baca house, all the lights, inside and outside, were on and the front door was wide open. Gil got out of his car, flipping the snap on his holster but not switching off the gun's safety. He considered calling for backup, but the situation didn't warrant it. Not yet. He went up to the house, calling for Mrs. Baca.

He found her in Melissa's room, throwing clothes into boxes. The walls were bare; the picture of Melissa with her father was gone.

"Mrs. Baca, what's going on?" Gil asked.

"These things need to be put away."

Gil was starting to get mad at her relatives—it was like what people always said about the police: *Never around when you need one.*

"Mrs. Baca, let's wait until tomorrow to do that."

She looked up at him, considering, "Why?"

"It's late."

She seemed to accept that. She got up and fixed Melissa's bedcovers, turned off the light, and closed the door.

In the hallway, she turned to look at him. "What are you doing here, Detective Montoya?" It was the first normal thing she had said to him in days.

"I'm looking for Ron." She nodded.

Gil got an idea. “Mrs. Baca, did Ron call Monday night to tell you he was coming over to fix the washing machine?”

“Oh, yes. He called about an hour or so before he showed up.”

“Did Melissa answer the phone when he called?”

Mrs. Baca thought, then said, “She talked to him for a few minutes, then handed the phone to me.”

“Do you know what they talked about?” Gil thought that maybe Melissa had told him to meet her in Oñate Park to talk more about the Sandra Paine photos.

“I was in the kitchen. I couldn’t hear them.”

She was starting to fade. He didn’t want to leave her until she was safely in bed. He started going around the house, turning off lights. They got to her room. He looked around. It wasn’t very big; in fact, it was much smaller than Melissa’s room. Gil wondered why Melissa had had the master bedroom while Mrs. Baca stayed in a child’s bedroom. One entire wall of Mrs. Baca’s bedroom was taken up in a shrine with a large crucifix over it. An altar table had candles on it with an assortment of pictures—all of the same person in various stages of life. As a baby, as a boy, and then as a man. Gil guessed that it was Daniel. And he wondered where the shrine to her husband was.

He had Mrs. Baca lie down fully clothed in her tiny twin-size bed. He turned the light in her room off and cracked her door, leaving the hallway light on. Just as he did for his girls. To keep the boogeyman away. He didn’t want to leave Mrs. Baca like this. He thought about calling Mrs. Cordova, but it was late. In the end, he wandered around the house, peeking in on Mrs. Baca until he was sure that she was asleep.

He went out and sat in his car, watching the house, not sure what else to do. He called his mother. She answered on the fourth ring.

“Mom, I’m not going to be able to make it over there tonight. I’ve got some work to finish up.”

"Whatever you think is best, *hito,*" she said. "Your work comes first."

They hung up and he slouched down in the seat, knowing that he was going to be there for a while.

Lucy opened her front door quietly for the sake of her neighbors, then tripped on a stray shoe and fell to the floor with a loud crash. Damn. Hell. Great entrance. And she wasn't even drunk. For a change.

The copy editors had invited her out again and she'd gone with them to the bar. She'd quietly sipped a Sprite while they got louder and louder on their beer. She had wanted to drink. Badly. There were a thousand things she wanted to forget. Time might heal all wounds, but alcohol makes you forget you have wounds. But she was strong. Hear me roar. She had worked out at the gym today and not had any alcohol. Being this healthy was bound to be bad for you.

She had been careful to sit a few seats away from the sports reporter she had kissed two nights ago. She was nice to him. Said "hi" and "how are you?" with true sincerity. But she didn't want him to get the impression that she was overly interested. He kept giving her goofy drunken stares. *Lord, help me.* After an hour, she pretended to go to the bathroom and slipped out of the bar.

She picked herself up off the floor of her apartment and flipped on her answering machine. First message from Mom. Second one from Mom. Third one from Gerald Trujillo: "Lucy, I missed you at the fire station this afternoon." She erased the rest of the message without listening to it. She sighed and plopped onto the couch.

She stretched her arms over her head to release some of the tension in her shoulders. She needed to talk to Gerald. To really talk to him. She needed to ease her guilt.

She turned the television on and started watching an old *Cosby Show.*

The phone rang. She looked at her watch. Just after two A.M. Who would be calling this late? She let the answering machine pick it up. It was the sports reporter she had been indecent with. Damn. "Hey, Lucy, you left the bar tonight without saying good-bye." She went to bed without listening to the rest of the message.

CHAPTER FOURTEEN
Saturday Morning

Lucy tried to roll over in her sleep, but the movement made her back muscles cut with pain, jarring her awake. She had overdone it with the weights yesterday, a few too many reps—and too little previous gym time. She knew that her mother would say it was from stress: *Lucy, you always hold your anger in your shoulders.*

Sitting up stiffly, she looked at the clock—six thirty A.M. She groaned. It was her freaking day off, and she was awake and in pain before the sun was up. She tried to turn her neck from side to side to stretch it, but her shoulders wouldn't give. She now had aspirin but no heating pad or ice packs.

She tried to swing out of bed without hurting herself. She pulled on a button-up shirt without putting on a bra, afraid that trying to hook the contraption might strain something. She tried to put on a pair of jeans but couldn't bend over. She decided to wear the sweatpants—aka pajamas—that she had on. She then slipped on her tennis shoes without tying them.

She drove to Walgreens, the only twenty-four-hour store in Santa Fe, and cruised the aisles looking for pain-relief stuff. She was loading up with ice packs and Epsom salts when she noticed a toothbrush sitting in the vitamin rack.

She sighed and walked past the toothbrush, her aching back giving her an excuse to ignore her obsession for a day.

But a second later she was back, picking up the toothbrush and detouring to the soap, shaving cream, and toothpaste aisle. The toothbrush deserved to go home. She walked up and down the aisle, staring at the shelves. Why weren't the toothbrushes in this aisle? She walked the aisle again. Toothbrushes had to be in this aisle—it defied all shelf-stocking logic that they weren't. Toothbrushes go next to toothpaste. Everyone knows that.

She looked for ten minutes more before finally giving up. She was too sore to keep up the search. She decided to buy the toothbrush—she couldn't bring herself to throw it on any old shelf, and it was about time she got a new one anyway.

She was in the checkout line when she glanced over at a rack next to the register. Next to the batteries, in the impulse-buy area, was a display of toothbrushes.

When had the purchase of a toothbrush become an impulse buy? Who says as they stand in line with Pepsi and Doritos, "Gee, it's been months since I brushed my teeth. Maybe I should get one." Lucy slipped the toothbrush onto the rack, making sure that no one was looking. But there was no one else in the store.

She was back at home, toweling off from an Epsom salts bath, when the phone rang. It was Major Garcia.

"When we interviewed Mrs. Schoen the other day, she said that Mrs. Burke used to keep a log of the scanner calls she heard," Garcia began. "The original inventory from the house didn't show any log, so we searched it again, but no luck." He was chewing on something and getting harder to understand. He swallowed and said, "I don't suppose you saw a log near the scanner when you were first there? It was just an ordinary notebook."

Lucy thought. She had been intent on Mrs. Burke's body. She had no idea if there'd been a notebook nearby. She said so to Garcia.

"All right. The son is sending up a videotape of his daughter's birthday. Mrs. Burke's voice is on there. We should have that today or tomorrow at the latest. I'll call you when I get it so you can ID her voice. And another thing—at this point I'm going to involve the police investigating Melissa Baca's murder, just to let them know that our two investigations might be connected. It seems suspicious that the only thing stolen was a notebook."

He hung up before Lucy could say anything more. She stood naked in her bathroom. In a quick few sentences, Garcia had given her what she had been desperate for. Validation. With a capital V. Another human being actually believed she wasn't crazy. But Garcia's words didn't affect her as she had expected. She'd thought she would feel happy. But instead, there was only cool determination.

Gil rubbed his eyes as he sat at his desk. He'd had only a few hours' sleep since leaving Mrs. Baca's last night. He had watched her house until he was hunched over from lack of sleep and then had driven home.

He had called his mother an hour ago but there had been no answer. She must still be at church, he thought.

Now, he was checking old reports to see if Melissa Baca had ever filed a complaint against the boyfriend who had slapped her, which, according to Judy Maes, had happened three years ago. He already knew that there was nothing. The first thing he had done after Melissa's death was to check her record. She had never been arrested or filed a restraining order against anyone. There wasn't even a parking ticket. Now, he was rechecking.

He also was looking at statutory-rape offenders to see if any of the men might have come in contact with Sandra Paine—someone like a teacher or a friend of her father.

At least those were the reasons he had given the officers who had asked why he was in the office just after sunrise.

He checked his watch again—seven A.M. He still had an hour until the morning shift came in. He was really checking the arrest records of Officers Ron Baca and Manny Cordova, something he couldn't do in a room full of officers. He had spent the first hour just trying to get organized. He had looked over Ron Baca's reports but found nothing unusual.

He was just getting started on checking Manny Cordova's reports when someone called his name. He quickly blanked out the computer screen before looking up.

Officer Joe Phillips tossed a *Capital Tribune* onto Gil's desk.

"I thought you might be interested in that story," Phillips said, pointing to an article.

Gil started to read it. As he'd expected, it was about the toxicology results on Melissa Baca. When he got to the fifth paragraph, he realized why Phillips was showing him the paper: "According to an agenda released by the Citizens' Police Advisory Review Committee, Melissa Baca was scheduled to go in front of the committee on Monday." The story didn't say why Melissa had been going to the meeting.

Gil thanked Phillips and went in search of Mrs. Sanchez, the police-station receptionist who compiled the agenda for the police advisory committee.

He found her making copies, the Xerox machine humming loudly. Her gray hair was pulled back in a bun and she had on her usual brown skirt and blouse. On weekends she was part of the Motor Maids, a national group of women motorcycle riders. Last year, Mrs. Sanchez had ridden to Palm Coast, Florida, on her Honda Gold Wing for the Motor Maids national convention. Gil had a hard time thinking of Mrs. Sanchez as a leather-clad biker. He suspected that was on purpose. Gil wondered if she played the part of the grandmother at work so that her biker hobby would come as more of a shock. Her voice always had a strange pitch to it, as if she was quietly laughing at everyone.

"Detective Montoya," she said, greeting him. The copies were flying quickly off the machine and into the holding tray.

"Mrs. Sanchez, did you put together the agenda for next week's Citizens' Police Advisory Review Committee?" he asked.

"Was there a typo?"

"No. I had a question about one of the items. Number five on the agenda."

"Yes. The young woman who wanted to complain to the committee about a police officer." Gil wondered how Mrs. Sanchez had remembered that without looking it up.

"Can you tell me about it?"

Mrs. Sanchez stopped the copy machine and looked at Gil over the rims of her glasses. "The young woman, a Miss Baca, I believe . . ." She stopped, considering for a second before saying, "Ahh, yes. Now I see where you're going with this. I can't believe I didn't make the connection before. But Baca is such a common last name in Santa Fe. I assume my Miss Baca is the same Miss Baca who died this week? Interesting."

Mrs. Sanchez continued, not expecting Gil to comment. "Miss Baca called last Friday to say she had a complaint to make against a police officer. I told her about the advisory committee, and she asked me to put her on the agenda. We didn't discuss who the officer was or the circumstances of her complaint." If Gil had actually become a lawyer, he would have wanted a witness like Mrs. Sanchez—precise and articulate.

"Did she say anything else?"

"She did not. That's it. I mailed out the agendas as usual."

"Including the ones to the newspapers," he said. It wasn't a question.

"Of course." She realized the problem and looked at Gil accusingly. "Of course, at the time I mailed out the agendas to the newspapers, Miss Baca was still very much alive."

"There's an article about it today in the *Capital Tribune.*"

"That's why they were calling me last night. I swear, they

called every five minutes. It was well after ten P.M. I saw their name on the caller ID and didn't answer. I decided if they wanted to talk to me, they could do it during business hours."

Gil called Pollack at the state police to tell him about the article and what Mrs. Sanchez had said.

"Yeah. I got a thousand messages from the *Capital Tribune* last night," Pollack said. "I had already given them their daily briefing so I didn't call them back. I figured they were just being pushy. I guess you can tell I've only been the PIO for a few months. I'm not too bright sometimes. At least that's what my boss told me when he called me an hour ago, yelling."

"I'm going to head over to Mrs. Baca's to see if she knew what Melissa was going to say to the advisory committee."

"Actually, you better come over here. I'm not really sure what this means, but Officer Manny Cordova turned himself in to us a few minutes ago."

Gil watched Manny Cordova through the two-way mirror in the interrogation room. Cordova sat alone, drinking a Coke and reading an old *People* magazine.

"What did he say when he showed up here?" Gil asked Pollack.

"Nothing really. He said his lawyer told him to turn himself in but not to say anything. The lawyer is on his way here, but got stuck in some snowstorm in Farmington."

"How long will it take him to get here?"

"Well, it's a four-hour drive normally. In a snowstorm, I'd say closer to five or six. I think the weirdest thing is that it's gonna snow. I thought the forecast was clear."

Pollack went on about the weather but Gil had stopped listening. He wondered if Manny was the police officer Melissa had been planning to lodge a complaint against.

"Actually, I'm glad you're here," Gil heard Pollack say. "Someone has to call your boss and tell him that one of his officers turned himself in to us. And don't ask me how, but the press already knows.

"Oh, and something else. The sheriff's office called and said they might have an investigation connected to ours, but they don't seem to think there's much to it. You know that old lady who died out in the county? A Mrs. Burke? They're seeing if there was some association to Melissa Baca. We haven't combined the cases yet. For now, they keep their dead body, we keep ours, until we can prove the two are connected."

Pollack gave Gil the details of the case, calling Lucy "some newspaper editor" and calling Mrs. Burke "some tipster." Gil smiled. Lucy had finally managed to get someone to listen.

Pollack started snapping his fingers and said, "And just so you know, we checked some more on Ron Baca's alibi. It seems a next-door neighbor was outside working on his car most of the night. The neighbor saw Ron Baca go into his mom's house around eight P.M. and leave after eleven P.M. The neighbor says he was outside all night and would have seen Ron Baca if he had left the house at all. I guess the guy was trying to change the oil, which is a five-minute job, so he must suck at it."

So Mrs. Baca had told the truth when she said that Ron had been fixing the washing machine. But that still didn't explain why Ron hadn't told anyone that Melissa had shown him the photos of Sandra Paine. Ron was not a sloppy police officer. Maybe Melissa's death had made him forget about it? But Gil doubted it. Maybe Melissa had asked Ron not to mention it? Maybe.

Gil called Chief Kline, who didn't say much about Manny Cordova. Kline was just about to hang up when Gil said, "Sir, I really feel that it's time for me to stop being a part of this investigation. Manny Cordova is a fellow officer. This is strictly state police territory. I believe it's a conflict of interest for me to continue to be involved."

Kline didn't answer, but asked to speak to Pollack. Gil

handed the lieutenant the phone. The two men talked for a few minutes. Pollack said, "I'll tell him," and hung up.

He started jingling the change in his pocket as he turned to Gil. "Sorry, buddy, you're in for the long haul."

Pollack's phone rang. Gil went over to survey the snack machine. The Doritos might start to look good after a few hours of waiting for Manny's lawyer to show up.

He felt someone clasp him on the shoulder. Pollack.

"I've got a job for you, buddy. That was Judy Maes on the phone. She says she needs to talk to us. I think you're perfect for the job."

Judy Maes lived on Alameda Street, her adobe house sporting a nice view of the now-dry Santa Fe River. He waited for her to answer the door. A four-inch-high santo of St. Anthony sat in a niche next to the door. The santo was beautifully carved, a tiny cardinal perched on its hand. Gil picked it up and looked on the bottom, where R. MAES was carved. Judy opened the door, greeting Gil and noticing the santo he was still holding.

"Rudy Maes is my father," she said as she let him into the living room. "He normally doesn't do santos. He did that one when he was eighteen."

Rudy Maes was a sculptor. Gil had once handled a case in which an art collector had hired a man to steal some Maes pieces. But he didn't count on the huge sculptures being so heavy. The next morning, when the gallery opened, the owner found the man still trying to move a granite piece called *In My Eyes*.

"Do you do any art?" Gil asked as they sat down.

Judy laughed. "Good lord, no. Just stick figures."

Maes had on red lipstick, but it didn't hide how tired she looked.

"Do you have any idea when they're going to release Melissa's body?" she asked.

"In a few days," Gil said.

"It may be a weird thing to say, but I could really use the funeral. It's so hard to deal with this all without seeing her body, you know?"

Gil doubted that it would be an open-casket funeral. When Melissa was thrown off the bridge, she had landed face-first. He didn't tell that to Judy.

"So, you said you had something to tell us?" Gil prompted.

"I remembered who the boyfriend was who hit Melissa. I racked my brain after you left. I finally looked in my diary. I knew I had written about it. It was some asshole named Manny Cordova."

Gil nodded. He had expected that answer. But it didn't give him any pleasure. He had hoped it wouldn't be a fellow cop. He wished it could have been Hammond.

"Did you ever meet Manny?" Gil asked.

"No. They only went out for a few weeks before he hit her. And that was a couple of summers ago."

"What did they get in a fight about?"

"They were in her car, and she was driving, and he got it into his head that she was too close to the wheel. They got into a fight about it. He decided to push her seat back while she's driving. She freaks out and pulls over and yells at him. He slaps her."

"Did he ever hit her again?"

"She never gave him the chance. She made him get out of the car and left him there." Judy smiled. "Good for Melissa. That girl's got balls. Anyway, she never saw him again. But she said he kept calling."

"Was he stalking her?"

"Probably not in the way you're thinking—I mean, not according to the legal definition—but ask any woman, and they'd say he was stalking her."

"Was he threatening her?"

"See, that's what I mean. He never threatened her and

didn't follow her to the grocery store or anything like that. He was just weird. He would call and try to small-talk her. She would make it clear that she didn't want him talking to her, so he'd hang up. And a month or so later he'd do it all over again. He was a pest. A weird pest. I think he finally stopped it a year or so ago."

"Did she know that he's now a police officer?"

"That asshole is a police officer? You've got to be kidding. Melissa would have had a real problem with that." Which was what Gil was thinking.

Manny had told Gil that he had seen Melissa recently. What would Melissa do if she saw the man who hit her three years ago in a police uniform? She would call Mrs. Sanchez and put her name on the agenda for the police advisory committee, planning to register a formal complaint against him.

"Did she ever mention to her brother that Manny slapped her? Ron could have helped her with him," Gil asked.

"Ron? I doubt it."

"Didn't they get along?"

"That's an understatement. They played happy family for their mom, but otherwise steered clear of each other."

"Was there ever any violence?"

"Only really low-key stuff, kind of threatening stuff on his part. Like this one time when Melissa was six, he put her in the fold-up couch, closed it up, put the cushions back on the couch, and left her there. Her mother found her a few hours later."

"Sounds like the typical brother-sister relationship."

Judy shook her head. "But Melissa was six and Ron was twenty. He was an adult. An adult doing that to a child is just cruel."

She got up, obviously bothered by the conversation, and paced along a Chinese rug. She continued. "He was always doing stuff like that. He once put her in the dryer when she was three. He told her it would be like some kind of roller-coaster ride. She was in there for five minutes before the door came open. He didn't even take her out—she fell out. He just sat there and watched. She could have died."

CHAPTER FIFTEEN

Saturday Afternoon

As Gil was saying good-bye to Judy Maes, his cell phone rang. It was Officer Joe Phillips. "Hi, Gil. I have someone who wants to see you in the interrogation room. Says he has something on the Baca killing."

"Who is it?" Gil asked.

"Hector Morales."

Five minutes later, Gil was back at the police station, looking for Phillips. Gil found him picking through a salad, eating only the croutons.

"Hey, Joe. What did you pick Morales up for?" Gil asked.

"For beating up his girlfriend." Phillips smiled coldly as he popped a crouton into his mouth. "It seems Morales's two-year-old son was sick, so the girlfriend put the kid into bed with her. The kid pukes his guts out all over the bed. Morales gets home and finds the girlfriend changing the sheets. He gets the wrong idea and beats the shit out of her."

"How bad is she?"

"Bad. She's at St. V's. They think her jaw is broken."

"How many times have you arrested Morales for aggravated battery against her before? This is, what, his fourth time? She won't press charges again and he'll be out tomorrow."

"Not this time." Phillips's smile got bigger.

"What happened?"

"It was the neighbor who called it in when she heard all the yelling. Valdez is the first cop on scene, and she sees Morales hit his girlfriend through the open door. Valdez goes in and orders Morales to stop. Morales doesn't see the uniform, he only sees another woman. So he hits Valdez in the stomach and kicks her."

"Is she all right?"

"She's fine. She had her armor on, so Morales banged up his knuckles pretty good, the poor baby." Phillips was grinning widely now. "We finally got him on agg battery, agg assault against a police officer, resisting arrest, and disturbing the peace. We're going to have the DA think up a couple of new charges later today."

Gil followed Phillips to the interrogation room. Inside sat a disheveled and handcuffed Hector Morales, who looked high and smelled drunk. Gil guessed that he was on cocaine.

Morales started talking as soon as he saw Gil. "Hey, man, I knew you wouldn't let me down. I knew you'd help me."

"Hector, let's get one thing straight: I'm not here to help you. Do you know something about Melissa's murder?"

"Yeah, man. I think I do, but you gotta get these assholes to let me go. I'm innocent. I didn't hit no cop." Phillips, standing in the corner, snorted his disbelief.

"Hector, just tell me what you know."

"Hell no, man. I ain't telling you anything until you get them to let me go."

Gil, still standing, leaned forward, bracing himself against the table. "You hit a police officer, Hector."

"The cops drove me to it. They set me up. I hit that bitch cop after she came into my home for no reason. She violated my rights."

Gil stared at Morales. This wasn't getting him anywhere. "Why don't you just tell me what you know about Melissa's killing, and I'll see what I can do." Gil made it sound as noncommittal as he could.

"Okay, man. So, this is it. I sold Baca some heroin a couple of times a few months ago."

Gil was confused. "You told me Melissa Baca didn't do drugs."

"Not her, man. The other one."

"Her brother?" If Ron Baca was on drugs, that would explain a lot.

"Not him. The other one. The other bitch. You know which one I mean."

Gil didn't know what Morales was talking about. Melissa had no sisters. She had several aunts, but he didn't know their names. Did Morales mean Judy Maes? "Can you describe her to me?"

"You goddamn asshole cops," Morales said, spit collecting at the corners of his mouth. Phillips started toward Morales, but Gil put out an arm to stop him. Morales kept yelling. "You know which one I mean. Stop screwing with me, man." Morales was rocking back and forth. He must have been starting to come down from his high.

Gil let Morales calm down for a minute before he asked again, "Can you describe her to me?"

Morales didn't answer. He was starting to sway in his seat, his glassy eyes fixed on the tabletop. Gil started pacing, then stopped cold as the thought came to him. "Hector, do you mean Mrs. Baca, Melissa's mother? Maxine Baca?"

Morales smiled. "That's the bitch."

Lucy tried to go back to sleep after her bath, but after an hour or two of trying, she gave up. Her shoulders felt better, but she knew that the only way to get rid of the pain was to stop avoiding the problem that was bugging her—Gerald Trujillo. She pulled her hair back in a ponytail and decided to forgo the makeup. She didn't need to look good to beg for forgiveness and tell him that she was quitting the medic-training program.

She scanned radio stations as she drove, too nervous to settle on one song. She took a couple of deep breaths as she pulled up to the fire station. She had no clue what she was going to say. The only speech she could think of started and ended with "hello." She opened her glove compartment and rummaged around. She tossed out a windshield wiper and some old insurance papers before she found her EMS pager.

She got out of the car and squinted at the sun as it was making a halfhearted attempt to warm up the January air.

Gerald was in the ambulance bay, sitting at an old desk covered with dust and speckled with grease. As she came in, he looked up but didn't speak.

Lucy took a deep breath. "I'm sorry I didn't show up yesterday. I know I'm a flake."

Gerald looked at her, measuring. She continued. "I thought you might want this back." She held out the pager to him, but he didn't take it. She shifted on her feet. He didn't even look mad.

She sighed and decided just to come out with it. "Gerald, how come you're the only person who can't see that I suck at being a medic?"

"You remember Earl Rivera?" he said, annoyingly calm.

Lucy was confused. "Yeah. The guy from the car accident on Wednesday. What about him?"

"I saw you with his wife. No one else would go near her because she wouldn't stop screaming, but you went right up to her."

"I just wanted her to shut up. She was giving me a headache."

"You can joke about this all you want, but you were the only one with enough guts to try to comfort her. You really helped her. You have a way with people. You care, and they can tell. That's all that being a medic is." Lucy stared at an oil stain on the garage floor, embarrassed. She had never been good at accepting compliments. Gerald got up from his chair and took a few steps toward the office before he stopped and said, "You just refuse to be a grown-up."

"Wait a second. That's a little harsh. Just because I can't do the work . . ."

"It's not that you can't do it. The blood doesn't scare you. The patients don't scare you. You were one of the best students in my class when you paid attention. It's that you refuse to try. If you tried and failed, that would be one thing, but you won't even try. I have no respect for that." He walked into the office and closed the door.

"What? You won't even talk to me about it?" she yelled at the closed door. He didn't answer. She sighed. Exasperated. She was trying to do the right thing. She was trying to quit. Wasn't that best for everyone? What did he want from her? She could throw open the office door and confront him. But, to be honest, she was much better at being passive-aggressive. A confrontation would require energy. Passive-aggression just required her to be snarky. And she could be really snarky.

"Fine, Gerald, I'll keep the damn pager," she yelled at the closed door. "Here, look, I'll even turn it on." The pager made a weird beeping noise as she flipped the switch. He didn't answer.

Gil had watched as Officer Phillips broke the bad news to Hector Morales: "In your statement, Mr. Morales, you admitted to a felony—selling heroin—so therefore any deal struck with Detective Montoya is null and void. I also must inform you that we will be filing drug-trafficking charges against you based on that information."

Morales had told them that Mrs. Baca bought heroin from him a few times a year. "Drug addiction runs in the family," was all Phillips said to Gil as they left the interrogation room.

Gil got into his car and tried to wrap his head around what

Morales had said. Did it make sense? Had Gil seen anything to suggest that Mrs. Baca did drugs?

Northern New Mexico is the heroin capital of the United States. And nothing done by any government agency had ever done much to cut away at its power. In tiny towns across the area, almost every family had lost members to drug overdoses. Some entire families had been addicted for four or five generations.

It wasn't unheard of in villages like Española for the mother to be in charge of doling out the heroin for the family. He had heard story after story about addicts who'd been given their first shots by their mothers. It was common to hear addicted mothers say that since their children were going to do drugs either way, they might as well learn how to do it right. The mothers considered it part of their familial duty.

Gil pulled up in front of the Baca house and knocked on the door. Mrs. Baca opened the door in her bathrobe. She looked like she had been sleeping. The house was hot. He took off his jacket and went in search of the thermostat. It was set on ninety. He turned it down to seventy and followed Mrs. Baca into Melissa's room. The bedcovers were messed up; Mrs. Baca must have changed beds during the night.

Gil was starting to lose his patience with her. While her pain was palpable, he couldn't help but wonder if it was an act. Was all this confusion and helplessness just a cover-up?

"Why didn't you tell me about the heroin?" he asked almost coldly. She said nothing. "Mrs. Baca, you have to be straight with me. I have to tell the state police about this," he said, trying to keep from sounding frustrated.

Gil considered the possibility that Mrs. Baca had played a part in Melissa's killing. Mrs. Baca was the only one who had said that Melissa left the house at eight P.M. the night she was killed. Melissa could easily have found out about Maxine's drug use. Could Maxine have strangled Melissa after they argued about it? It was possible. This whole time he had been looking at Mrs. Baca as an alibi for Ron, but Ron was also an alibi for her. Pollack had interviewed the neighbor, who said that he'd seen Ron and his car but never mentioned seeing Maxine. The only person who could vouch for Maxine's whereabouts was Ron. Was he trying to protect his mother by staying out of town?

Maxine started straightening the covers on Melissa's bed. She was fixing the pillows when she said, "I did it so I would know what it had been like for him."

"Like for who?"

Maxine continued. "He was *mi hito.* He was everything to me, and I let him die. . . ." She trailed off. Gil understood—it was about Daniel.

"How often do you do drugs?" Gil asked.

She didn't answer him. She stood still for a second, swaying, then walked past him, through the kitchen and out the back door. Gil quickly followed. She walked into the backyard, past a swing set and a small shed, to the corner of the property marked by a fence. She stopped at a small hill of sandy dirt and dropped to her knees. She started digging, the frozen dirt not giving easily under her bare hands. As Gil stepped toward her to pull her away, he saw a syringe sticking out of the newly dug earth.

Gil called the crime-scene techs out to the Bacas' backyard. They unearthed a few dozen syringes, a half-dozen spoons, and hundreds of small plastic bags of heroin. Gil kept trying to get Mrs. Baca out of the cold, but she refused to go inside. She sat watching them with a strange look on her face.

Pollack showed up a few minutes later. He pulled Gil aside, saying, "Does she trust you?"

"I guess."

"Good. Then you can go *Magnum, P.I.* on her." Gil translated this to mean that he should be the one to interview Mrs. Baca.

Gil had an officer go inside to get Mrs. Baca a blanket. Gil waited until she was wrapped in it, still watching the excavation, before he started.

"You've been buying heroin since after Daniel died? That was more than twenty years ago?"

Maxine nodded.

"And you never took the drugs?"

"No . . . I . . . I . . . It was because of my sin that he died."

"What sin was that?" She didn't answer him and instead started to recite the Hail Mary. Gil spoke over her prayer. "Did Ron know?"

She stopped and said, "Yes. He tells me the best place to buy it. Sometimes he comes with me."

A strange mother-and-son activity, thought Gil. "Did Melissa know about it?"

Mrs. Baca didn't answer right away. Gil waited, watching the crime tech catalog the items. A few moments later, she said, "I don't think so."

"But you can't say for sure?"

"No. I . . . No." She started saying the Hail Mary again. Gil watched her for a few minutes, not sure what to do for her.

Gil walked over to Pollack to update him. At first, Pollack wanted to bring her in on drug-possession charges to question her more forcefully. He seemed to think that Mrs. Baca was hiding something. But Gil quickly talked him out of it. They had no proof that Mrs. Baca had ever used any of the heroin, and the media would want to know why they had arrested a sixty-four-year-old woman whose daughter had just died.

Gil didn't mention to Pollack that Mrs. Baca was mentally ill. He was sure of that now. It had been hard to tell whether she was just a grieving mother, but he wondered how normal she had been before Melissa was killed.

He got permission from Pollack to call the crisis hotline to get Mrs. Baca some help. The woman on the phone said that they would send out a counselor within the hour. Gil needed to find Ron, but he didn't want to leave Mrs. Baca.

If Melissa had found out that her brother was helping their mother buy drugs, she might have confronted him. Maybe Melissa hadn't been going to file a complaint with the Citizens' Police Advisory Review Committee about Manny. Maybe it had been about Ron. If she had reported her brother, he would have been fired. Maybe it had always been about Ron.

Gil didn't know Ron Baca well, but he had looked over Ron's arrest records. Gil knew that the way an officer writes a report can tell a lot about him. Ron was an average officer. Not clever. Not unintelligent. Just unremarkable. His reports were short on details and long on missed opportunities. In one recent report, Ron had made note of a car that he had stopped for weaving in traffic. By the time dispatch came back to tell Ron that the car was stolen, he had already let them go. And then didn't try to catch them. As Ron said in the report, "unable to ascertain location of vehicle."

Gil had also gone over Ron's personnel file, with Chief Kline's permission. There were no complaints about excessive force, but there also were no commendations for bravery. He hadn't taken any classes that might lead to advancement or boost his investigative skills. He didn't go above and beyond. His performance reviews were short and monotonous. Year after year, supervisors had urged Ron to take the initiative. But year after year, no change. His inability to impress meant that he had gone as far as he ever would in the department. He would never rise above his position as sergeant. A quick handwritten note on one of the reviews read, "victimization?" Gil didn't know who had written it, but he knew what it meant. It fit what he knew about Ron.

Nothing was Ron's fault. Gil remembered the stolen-car incident. Gil had overheard Joe Phillips ask Ron what had happened. Ron's response, in all seriousness, was, "It wasn't my fault the car was stolen. What was I supposed to do?" Ron didn't even realize why that answer revealed all his flaws. When backed into a corner, he would blame everyone else for his getting there, even if he'd walked into the corner himself.

Gil knew that Ron Baca hadn't killed his sister. His alibi was solid. The neighbors had seen him go into his mother's house at the same time that Melissa was being killed in Oñate Park. Ron might have had a motive if Melissa was going to complain about him to the police advisory committee, but he still had no opportunity. And there was still Manny Cordova, waiting back at the state police station.

Mrs. Baca was shivering now as she prayed, but Gil still couldn't persuade her to come inside. As the crime-scene techs worked, Gil pulled Adam Granger, the lead tech, aside. Gil had known Granger, who was also the tech in charge of Melissa's case, for years. Their daughters were on the same soccer team.

"I don't suppose there was dirt on the syringe found in Melissa's car?" Gil asked him.

Granger kicked a clump of dried mud. "I was just wondering the same thing. I'll go to the lab right now and check on it."

Pollack came up to Gil and asked, "Do you think she knows anything else?"

Gil stared at Mrs. Baca for a minute before saying, "No."

"Well, in that case, we got a bunch of loose ends that we need to tie up," Pollack said. "Where do you want to start? I'm thinking about the brother. . . ."

"Actually, I'd rather track down the principal and get his take on the pictures," Gil said. He was worried about Sandra Paine, despite what her parents had said. For him, the endangered living took precedence over the dead. He wanted to find out who had abused her, and, knowing that the parents wouldn't help, he hoped Strunk would.

Pollack nodded. "Yeah, and tell him one of his students is banging an adult. That might get his attention."

Pollack said that he'd keep an eye on Mrs. Baca until the counselor showed up.

Strunk's home was in the foothills, down a long driveway. The house must have been about ten thousand square feet. It was finished with adobe-colored stucco and had a big, arched entranceway. It couldn't have been more than a few years old. In Santa Fe's market—where the average price of a home is $282,000—it had probably cost at least $2 million.

As Gill pulled up to the house, he saw Ken Strunk standing outside. He got out of his car, and Strunk shook his hand warmly as the two of them stood in the driveway, where Strunk had obviously been cleaning out his car. The trunk and all the doors were open. A bucket of water and a few wet rags dripped on the pavement next to the gray Lincoln Town Car. A wet/dry vacuum sat nearby.

"Detective Montoya. I received your messages. Sorry I haven't gotten back to you. My wife and I drove to see her mother in Las Cruces Wednesday night, and we just got back in town." He gestured at his car. "I never realized how much stuff you find between the seats after a long road trip."

"Was it a planned trip?" Gil asked, mostly to make small talk.

"Actually, no." Strunk hesitated. It took him a moment to add, "I probably shouldn't tell you this, but we went because the school's board of governors thought it would discourage the media's interest in our school. It was a public relations move. The hope was that things would have died down by the time I got back. But clearly that's not the case if you're here." Strunk put down his wet cloth. "So, what can I help you with, Detective?"

"Did Melissa ever mention anything to you about a student of hers named Sandra Paine?"

"Yes. About a month ago, Sandra was caught drinking vodka on school grounds."

"How was Melissa involved?"

"She's the one that turned Sandra in."

"What did you do?"

"We called Sandra's parents. They insisted we call the police. The parents wanted to scare her straight, that sort of thing. So two officers came and brought her down to the police station. There were no charges filed."

"Do you remember the officers' names?"

"I don't know, off the top of my head, but I keep my school files here at the house for security reasons. I made a note of it in her file. We can go check."

They walked though the garage and into a study done in the same muted tones as Strunk's office at school.

"Detective, do you mind if I ask why you're asking about Sandra? She's an intelligent girl but has an inconsistent home life."

"Do you know her well?"

"Actually, we only met that one time when she was brought to my office. Is she in more trouble?"

Gil answered his question with a question: "Did Melissa ever mention anything else to you about Sandra?"

Strunk smiled. "I get the feeling you're not going to tell me why you're asking. Okay, Detective, I'll try to control my burning curiosity. Did Melissa ever mention Sandra?" Strunk thought for a moment. "No, just that one time."

Strunk pulled a manila folder out of a tall wooden filing cabinet. "Here it is. It was about a month ago. The students had just gotten back from Christmas break. And the officers who came were . . ." He hesitated. "I only have last names but it looks like Officers Valdez and Cordova."

Sandra Paine lay on her bed, waiting for her mother to come home to drive her to Santa Fe's airport so they could ship her off to Denver. They still hadn't told her how long she would be exiled for. She gave them a week before they caved and took her back. All she had to do was call her father "Daddy" and talk to her mother incessantly about college.

She picked up her cell phone and for the fourteenth time—she had been counting—played the last message from her boyfriend. "Sandra, I need to talk to you right away. . . ." The message cut off after that. She played it again. She loved listening to his voice. He had left the message yesterday, but she hadn't called him back. That had been Lacey's idea. "Sandra, men only want women they can't have, so play aloof," Lacey had said. "Don't talk to him. Make him really sweat." They decided that she would call him from Colorado but only leave a message. They called it "denying him access." As Lacey had said, "He'll be pining away."

Sandra started biting her nails. She wished she still had the Polaroids they'd taken together. They would make her miss him less. She especially liked the ones she had taken of him. But her father had confiscated those in the "second incident." That had been a week ago and it was completely her mother's fault.

Her mom had come home crazed from some party disaster she had been in charge of and decided that Sandra's room needed to be inspected. The inspections usually meant rumpling through Sandra's closet until her mother broke down crying and left. But this time Mommie Dearest had been deranged. She threw things out of drawers and sent stuffed animals flying while Sandra watched. She found some of the Polaroids taped under the bottom shelf of Sandra's entertainment center. But she didn't find the other ones, taped under the TV.

Mom slapped Sandra hard but said nothing, then went to her room, turned off the lights, and closed the door. Her father came home a few hours later. Sandra heard them yelling at each other. She wasn't worried. After the "first incident," a month ago, when she got busted with the vodka, she had been grounded for three weeks. Two days later she was at the mall, shopping for shoes with Lacey.

The parents came in to give her the verdict a few minutes later. Her father opened her door without knocking and said, "What did you do with him?"

"Like I'm going to tell you," Sandra said.

"You are going to tell me, young lady."

Sandra ignored him and, with a sly smile, turned her back on them and started typing on her computer.

"Sandra, why won't you tell Daddy what he wants to know?" her mother asked. God, but she was annoying.

"Because it's none of his business." Sandra started typing faster.

That's when they told her that they were sending her to her aunt's in Denver. That got her attention. She cried and threatened, but they didn't give in. Her mother sat in the corner and said little. She wasn't normally that quiet.

"You are going, and that's all there is to it," her father said, sounding old, not angry.

"Thank you ever so," Sandra said. A second later, her mother slapped her. That was more like her mom. As soon as they left her room, Sandra pulled the rest of the photos from their hiding place. She was going to put them in her school locker in case Mommy decided on another inspection.

But once at school, she'd just had to show them to Lacey. That's what she'd been doing when Miss Baca caught them.

Sandra stopped biting her nails when she heard her mother's Explorer drive up. She ran downstairs with her suitcase, suddenly excited to be going on a trip.

Gil said good-bye to Principal Strunk, leaving the way he'd come in. As soon as he reached the driveway, he opened his cell phone and called the station. He needed confirmation quickly that Manny Cordova had been Sandra Paine's arresting officer. It now made sense that Ron Baca had never told anyone about the photos of Sandra Paine that Melissa had shown him the day she died: Manny Cordova—a fellow officer and friend of the family—had taken them.

Gil told the records officer who answered what he wanted to know and was put on hold. He started pacing the driveway, almost tripping over his shoelace. He sat down in the driver's seat of Strunk's Town Car—all its doors were still open from being cleaned—to tie his shoe. He fiddled with the blinker as he waited, then leaned back in the seat to look up. There was a Jiffy Lube oil-change sticker on Strunk's windshield. Gil did the math to distract himself. He figured out that Strunk had had his oil changed on Monday.

The records officer clicked back on the line, telling Gil that she couldn't check right now because the computers were down but she'd try to find the hard copy, which might take fifteen to twenty minutes. Gil thanked her and called Pollack. Gil got his machine and left a detailed message.

As Gil was about to get into his car to leave, another Lincoln pulled up, this one maroon. A blond woman stepped out of it, carrying a shopping bag from a natural-food store. Her hair was in some kind of upsweep and her brown shawl was starting to slide from her shoulder. Gil guessed her to be about forty and wondered if she had had a facelift. He introduced himself.

"Ah, you must be here about Melissa Baca, that poor girl." Mrs. Strunk smiled tightly, showing perfect teeth, almost too white.

"Had you ever met her?" Gil asked. She didn't protest as he took the shopping bag from her; she seemed to expect it. Now he would have to go back into the Strunks' house.

"I greeted her when she first came to town." She had an East Coast accent and her husband's big-word way of talking.

"Had you seen her since?"

"No," was all she said as she closed her car door and started walking up the driveway. Gil changed the subject to something more innocent: "So how was the drive to Las Cruces?"

"The weather was perfect, for a change. I swear, every time I try to go somewhere in this state the weather gets atrocious. Last time I went to Albuquerque it snowed the whole way."

"How is your mother?" Gil asked,

"She's fine, although all she could do was complain that my car seats are too soft for her bad back." Mrs. Strunk laughed softly.

"I thought your car is the maroon one?"

"It is. I think next time we'll fly."

Gil wondered why Mr. Strunk had tried to give him the impression that they had taken his car to Las Cruces.

Lucy slammed on the brakes as a shrill chirping came from under the passenger seat. Since storming out of the fire station, she had been running errands—paying her utility bill (late); trying to find a baking sheet to replace one she'd burned—and was now on her way to the Plaza to get a pork tamale for lunch.

She pulled over and frantically threw her tennis shoes and old McDonald's bags into the backseat, trying to find the noise. She found the source under a sock. Her EMS pager. A dispatcher's voice came up: a seventy-nine-year-old female was feeling sick. The dispatcher gave the address. Lucy had a general idea of where it was. She took the next side street and turned her car around, speeding off to the address. She was still mad enough at Gerald to want to prove him wrong. But was she trying to prove that she was a grown-up or that she sucked as an EMT? And how do you prove that you suck as an EMT? She hoped she wouldn't have to kill someone.

Gerald was already there when she pulled up. He and another male EMT were standing in front of the mobile home, shifting from side to side to keep warm in the wind. He didn't look surprised to see her. Whatever. The mobile home was white with blue trim. A double-wide that looked like it was built in the 1980s.

"The woman's name is Lily Hitts," Gerald said without greeting her. "She's inside the bedroom but won't let us men come in until she's dressed."

"Okay," Lucy said, unsure of what he wanted her to say.

"So, I need you to go in and talk to her. We could just go in anyway, but I don't want to agitate her." Gerald looked at Lucy and smiled. Was this a test to see if she would balk? Was that a mean smile? Well, she wouldn't balk.

"Fine," Lucy said roughly as she headed into the house. She took a couple of deep breaths. She could do this.

She started calling out, "Ma'am, ma'am, I'm a medic." It reminded her of when she and Gerald had first gone into Patsy Burke's house. She heard an answer from the back of the mobile home. Lucy made her way past overstuffed furniture and shelves of dolls, which the woman collected. *She must be the sole supporter of the Franklin Mint.*

The woman lay on the bed overflowing with more dolls; their unanimated faces creeped Lucy out. The woman was in a long-sleeved nightgown, trying to draw it over her head. Lucy murmured, "Let me help you with that."

The left side of Lily Hitts's face was drooping, and she looked out of it. Lucy needed Gerald inside. Now.

"You know what, Lily? I think we're going to need some help." Lily looked panicked. Lucy continued in a soothing voice. "It's okay. The guys outside are friends of mine. I'll make sure you look decent."

Lucy yelled for Gerald to come in. A second later, Gerald and the other EMT came in. The EMT took Lily's vitals while Lucy tried to keep her calm and Gerald hooked up a heart monitor. Lily kept trying to get out of her nightgown and into a skirt and a blouse. Lucy gently kept her still. She didn't even listen as Gerald and the EMT talked to each other, doing what needed to be done, while Lucy tried to keep Lily's attention. Lucy tried to think of questions to ask. But all she could think of were the creepy dolls, so she asked about them. Lily was able to tell her that she had been collecting dolls for fifty years, but within a sentence or two she stopped talking and could only hold Lucy's hand tightly. Gerald was suddenly at her side with the gurney. They moved Lily onto the stretcher, with Lucy making comforting noises the whole time. They got her out of the mobile home and into the ambulance. Lily never let go of Lucy's hand.

"Good job," was all Gerald said with a smile as he hopped into the ambulance. Still, Lucy smiled back, her anger at Gerald easing a little. Maybe she could do this medic thing after all. She got back into her car and smiled with pride. Then stopped. She had no right to be proud of herself. None at all. So she had helped one old lady. That didn't make up for the other one, who had died.

Ten minutes later, Lucy was parked in front of Patsy Burke's house. The crime-scene tape was gone, probably taken by the wind. She tried to imagine Patsy Burke's life—listening to the scanner, calling the paper. But all she could think of was her body slumped backward over the chair, her body contorted in death. Lucy shook her head to make the image leave. She tried to remember the Patsy Burke who was in the pictures that lined the walls—smiling, joyful, alive.

But Lucy couldn't remember what Patsy Burke looked like. Had she had full gray hair or salt-and-pepper? Had her eyes been blue or brown? It bothered Lucy that she couldn't remember. Patsy Burke deserved to be remembered. It was Lucy's duty to remember. She owed her that much. In truth, she owed her so much more.

Lucy drove to the *Capital Tribune* office even though it was her day off. She knew how she could find out if Mrs. Burke's eyes had been brown.

Gil set the groceries on the counter, eager to get out of the Strunks' and find Pollack. Gil glanced through the kitchen door into the living room, where Ken Strunk was sitting on a couch. Strunk jumped up quickly and rushed into the kitchen with an exaggerated, "I could have helped you with the groceries, dear. Detective Montoya needs to get going." But Gil had seen the couch—a light blue one with dark blue swirls—an exact match with the one Sandra Paine had been photographed on.

He tried to hide his surprise, forcing his face to be impassive, knowing that Strunk was watching him closely. He walked nonchalantly into the living room, which was decorated in pastels and watercolors. The couch matched the room perfectly.

"This is an interesting couch," was all he said.

Mrs. Strunk piped up with, "Yes. It's one-of-a-kind. I had it made to match the picture behind it."

Gil glanced at the picture. It looked like something Therese might have drawn with her crayons. It had pink lines and green circles.

Gil pulled out his cell phone and said, "I think the state police are going to want to question you in more detail."

"Are you sure that's necessary?" Strunk glanced at his watch. "We have dinner plans soon."

"Officer," Mrs. Strunk said, copying her husband's tone, "I believe we have given you enough time. The other police can stop by later. We have our lives to get back to." She stood up, as if ready to escort him to the door.

"Actually, let's wait for them," Gil said.

Ken Strunk wasn't a good enough actor to look confused. Gil called Pollack, who answered this time. Gil quietly talked into the phone so that the Strunks couldn't overhear.

He told Pollack, "I need you at the principal's house," then rattled off the address. Pollack didn't ask why, only, "How fast do you want us there?"

"Now," Gil said, before clicking his phone shut. He turned back to the Strunks and said, "Mr. Strunk, have you been on any long trips in your car lately?"

Ken Strunk looked disinterested and exasperated. "I told you we went to Las Cruces."

"But not in your car. You went in your wife's car."

Mrs. Strunk looked bewildered. Ken Strunk answered quietly, "No. I haven't been anywhere."

"Just to work and back, no trips to the store or anything?"

Mrs. Strunk answered quickly, "I do all the shopping. He's only been to work." She seemed eager to say it, as if it would help.

"You know," Gil said, "while we're waiting, let's get a better look at your car."

He motioned both of them outside and had Strunk give him the keys. Gil peered into the open trunk, which had been vacuumed. No flecks of blood or a blanket used to wrap a body in. Gil went to the front of the car and reached in to turn on the ignition, careful not to touch anything else. He wished he had on a pair of latex gloves. The odometer lit up on the electronic dashboard. According to the oil-change sticker, Strunk needed to get his oil changed at 39,535 miles. Gil did the math in his head. This meant that on Monday, when he'd gotten the oil changed, his car would have had 36,535 miles on it. The odometer now read 36,765.

"Mr. Strunk, how many miles would you say it is from home to work?"

"About five, one way."

"So, you drove about thirty miles total this week. You were in Las Cruces since Wednesday night, so your car has just been sitting here since then, is that right?" A state police car pulled up; they must have done ninety miles per hour to get there so quickly. Gil watched Pollack get out of the car as he asked Strunk, "Can you explain then why there's an extra two hundred miles on your car?"

The exact number of miles it would take to drive to the Taos Gorge Bridge and back.

Maxine Baca heard the police drive away. She was left alone with the counselor, who kept wanting her to talk about the drugs. Instead, Maxine studied her hands, which were folded on the kitchen table, where she sat.

After Melissa was born, Maxine had thought that everything would be all right. She had served her penace. But her Anger Sickness hadn't gone away. After a year, it was still with her, making her lose her hearing and feel pins and needles in her hands. The doctor said it was an imbalance left over from Melissa's birth and all the blood Maxine had lost. But Maxine knew that something else was wrong. She saw the *curandera* in Española again, who made a circle around her three times with red carnations. Maxine went home with a hankerchief full of leaves from an orange tree and slept with them under her pillow. The next day she took the leaves back to the *curandera,* who told her what was wrong: Daniel was calling to Maxine. Maxine and the *curandera* spent weeks trying to reach him. Every day they would sit for hours on the floor until Maxine's legs hurt. She would have to give Melissa a drink of NyQuil to make her sleep so that they could perform the ritual. Finally, after a month, Daniel spoke to them. He told her that he needed his drugs or he would get sick.

The next morning, Maxine asked Ernesto where people sold their drugs. He asked her why she wanted to know, and she told him. He looked at her, but didn't ask her more about it. She drove over to the place Ernesto had told her about. She wasn't scared. She wore the gold crucifix she'd gotten for First Communion for protection from the evil. A white woman whose hands shook handed Maxine some heroin for thirty dollars. Maxine watched a thin girl heat the drug in a metal spoon and inject herself with it.

Maxine went to the cemetery and took the heroin to Daniel's grave. She carefully dug a hole on top of his grave and put the heroin in it with some holy water. She said a prayer over him to Our Lord and placed some flowers in the hole, too. She went back every few weeks to buy more drugs with some of the grocery money and buried those near his grave. But last year, the cemetery had put grass over all the graves. She had tried to dig through the grass, but one of the cemetery workers had yelled at her. She didn't know what to do. She couldn't go to Española and ask the *curandera* what to do because the *curandera* had died. Maxine decided to bury the drugs in the backyard near where Daniel used to play. She would pray to him every time to tell him where to find them.

The counselor was saying something, but Maxine ignored her. She started praying the rosary in her mind, since she didn't have her beads. She started the Carrying of the Cross, imagining herself holding the heavy cross on her back, the wood scratching her skin. She was walking slowly up a hill and the cross was getting heavy. The Roman soldiers were pushing Simon of Cyrene toward her, to have him take the cross. She pushed him away as hard as she could. But when he looked up, he had Melissa's face, with cuts on her cheeks. Maxine stopped her prayers and opened her eyes. The counselor was on her cell phone.

Maxine made the sign of the cross, closed her eyes again, and said the Our Father, starting the Crucifixion.

She said a Hail Mary and thought of herself on the cross. Her hands started to shoot with pain from the nails the guards were pounding in. She turned to look at one of the guards, but it was Melissa, with her face covered in blood. Suddenly, Melissa was the one on the cross and the guards were nailing her to it. Maxine was far away, watching Melissa. Her daughter was screaming to her for help. She opened her eyes and crossed herself three times, wondering again what God was trying to tell her.

Gil stood in the Strunks' driveway, waiting for the state police to return with a search warrant for the house and car. They had decided to also get a warrant for Mrs. Strunk's car. Ken Strunk had stopped talking after the state police came and called his attorney. As Pollack had said, "He's lawyered up."

Pollack jingled the change in his pocket as he walked over to Gil.

"This is looking interesting," he said with enthusiasm, eyeing Ken Strunk's car while he said it. Mr. and Mrs. Strunk were sitting in the back of a state police car across the street. They weren't technically under arrest yet.

One of the officers called over to Pollack, saying that the Strunks wanted to see him. Pollack went to the patrol car, opened the back door to talk to the couple, and crouched down.

He trotted back to Gil a few minutes later, chuckling. "Those people have some balls. They're stupid balls, but still balls. Mrs. Strunk wanted to know if she would be outta jail by tomorrow because," Pollack changed his voice to a falsetto, "she's expected at a function with the mayor." Pollack laughed. "I think she thought that would impress us. I'm impressed. Are you impressed?" Pollack stopped dead for a second and smiled. "I got an idea."

He walked to the patrol car and spoke quietly to the officer, then came back to Gil and said, "Let's have some fun."

The officer escorted Mrs. Strunk out of the car and over to Pollack and Gil.

"Mrs. Strunk," Pollack said in a tone that sounded exaggeratedly polite to Gil. "It occurred to me that you must be freezing in that car and that you might be more comfortable if we waited inside the house." Mrs. Strunk glanced toward her husband. Pollack said, "He'll be fine out here."

She hesitated. Pollack said in the same tone, "You know, Mrs. Strunk, you're not a suspect. We would just like to talk to you." He added with a whisper and a smile, "But we're really just using that as an excuse to get out of the cold." Still she hesitated, then she nodded and the three went inside.

They sat at the kitchen table, and Pollack, all smiles, offered to make coffee.

"So, how long have you and your husband been married?" Gil asked.

Mrs. Strunk seemed to examine the question for tricks before she answered. "Four years."

Gil could almost hear Pollack smiling behind him. That might be good news. If it had been twenty years, she might have been in too much denial to help them. If it had been only one, she might still be too infatuated with her new husband to betray him. But four was perfect. After four years, the shiny-new marriage would have given way to the everyday marriage. And everyday marriages are prone to cracks and leakage. Mrs. Stunk might have noticed the cracks but ignored them for the sake of the marriage. It was their job to shine a bright light on those cracks.

"If you'll pardon me for asking," Pollack said, with the same false decorum, "but were you ever married before?"

Mrs. Strunk answered more quickly this time. "Yes. For ten years. I have a son who goes to UCLA." Pollack made noises like he was impressed.

"And Mr. Strunk—does he have children?" Gil asked.

"He was married to this awful woman for thirteen years, but they never had children."

"How'd you and Ken meet?" Pollack asked.

"We were at this gallery opening on Canyon Road, the Hewitt Gallery." Pollack nodded like he knew it, but Gil was sure he didn't. "The hostess introduced us."

"How long was it before you two got married?" Pollack asked.

"We both decided that since we were older, a long courtship wasn't necessary, so it was just a matter of months. Why waste time? We weren't children." She was starting to warm up to the conversation, not checking her words for flaws before she spoke.

"Did you meet his family before the wedding? Go on long vacations together to get to know each other?" Pollack asked, sounding casual.

She faltered. "No, not really. I just . . ." She stopped, then started. "I thought there'd be time for that after the wedding."

Pollack said, "I can understand that. Of course." He put the filter into the coffeemaker before saying, "You know, when you're married kinda quick like that, there are bound to be some surprises."

"Well, the normal things. Adjusting to home life together, trying to get our schedules to mesh."

"This whole business must come as a shock," Pollack said slowly.

"Yes," she said quietly. "I'm not sure what to make of it."

"Did you have any idea that this was all going on?" Pollack asked.

"I'm not really sure what *this* is," she said with some heat. "What can you tell me?"

"Well," Pollack said, "we think it's possible Mr. Strunk was seeing one of his students."

Mrs. Strunk said with resignation, "I wondered if it was something like that."

"What made you think so?" Gil asked.

"Oh, little things. He's been acting strange for a month. He was secretive yet had a new kind of energy. He spent more time out of the house and seemed anxious that I get increasingly involved in my work. I'm on several committees for non-profit groups." She sighed. "It seemed he wanted me gone all the time." She didn't seem too distraught, only disappointed. Maybe a little relieved to have an answer to her husband's behavior.

"How have things been this week?" Gil asked.

"More of the same. He got an odd phone call on Monday that he took in his study. He never takes calls in his study, even work calls. He purposely lets me overhear those. He said he wanted me to know what was going on with his work, that it would keep us close."

"What did you think the call was about?"

"I don't know. I answered the phone. It was an Hispanic man." She quickly looked at Gil as if she had offended him. "I mean, he sounded like he had a local accent, a typical Northern New Mexico accent." She stopped, embarrassed. Gil wasn't. It was a fair description.

"What time was this call?" Pollack asked.

"Just after eight thirty P.M.."

"And did your husband do anything after he got the call?" Pollack asked.

"He went out."

"Do you know where he went?" Gil asked. She shook her head. "How long was he gone?"

"Until after midnight. And he wouldn't come to bed. He just sat up the rest of the night. That's when I knew there was another woman."

An officer came in to tell Pollack that the search warrant had arrived, and Pollack excused himself and went outside.

"How about Tuesday night? Where was he then?" Gil asked. He wondered if Strunk was somehow connected to Scanner Lady's murder as well.

Mrs. Strunk looked down at her hands. "Well, after he was so distant on Monday, I decided we needed to see my therapist."

"What time did you go there?" Gil asked, as Pollack came back and sat down quietly.

She got more embarrassed. "Ken won't go see Dr. Shepard, so I invited her over for dinner to kind of ease us into the discussion. It didn't go very well. Dr. Shepard was here when Ken came home from work, about five thirty P.M. We had dinner about an hour later. Ken felt very defensive. Dr. Shepard left about nine P.M."

"And then?"

"We got into a disagreement."

"You mean a fight? When did you finally go to bed?"

She shook her head. "I had to . . ." She paused. "When I get agitated, I sometimes can't breathe very well, so we went to the hospital. We didn't leave there until after three A.M.."

"You have panic attacks?"

Mrs. Strunk nodded. "I have to be careful. If someone even raises their voice to me, it can start up."

The time frame meant that Strunk couldn't have killed Lucy's Scanner Lady.

Gil got up and found some coffee mugs made of glass. They seemed impractical: why have a coffee mug that won't hold the heat? Gil pretended to busy himself pouring the coffee, but he was really trying to figure out how Manny Cordova was involved. Had he and Strunk worked together to kill Melissa? Maybe Manny knew that Strunk had killed Melissa and was blackmailing him? The two of them could have met when Manny went to the school to arrest Sandra Paine. Maybe Manny was blackmailing Strunk about his relationship with Sandra?

Pollack must have been thinking along the same lines. "Mrs. Strunk, is it possible that your husband was being blackmailed?"

"I don't see how. He doesn't really have any money. Everything is in my name, the house, the cars, our portfolio. It was to make sure his ex-wife never got it. The bank account is mine; we don't have a joint one."

"What if he needed cash?" Pollack asked.

"Well, he used to have a credit card, but I took that away from him months ago. Ken had to declare bankruptcy after his divorce. When we first got married, he had real problems saving his money. We have this system in place to help him control his spending habits."

"What if he needed to get a large amount of cash?" Gil asked. Then he realized that to the Strunks, a large amount of cash would be in the hundreds of thousands, and added, "Or even a little bit of money. Say, a thousand dollars at a time?"

She thought about this and shook her head. "I really don't see how. He doesn't have access to his own salary. He's on a budget."

"Do you mean an allowance?" Pollack asked.

She looked down and smoothed the tablecloth. "I guess that's more accurate. He has to explain to me what the money is for before I give him any cash. I know how this sounds, Officers, but Ken wanted to get his spending back on track. He was determined to do it."

"Does he own anything of value?" Gil asked. Maybe Strunk had sold something to pay off a blackmailer.

"Everything we own is mine. He sold off all his things when he went bankrupt. We talked about him buying some pieces of art as an investment, but that was a few years down the line, when he had proved himself."

Gil sipped his coffee. Manny Cordova couldn't have been blackmailing Ken Strunk since Strunk had no access to money. But how were Strunk and Manny connected to Melissa's murder?

Gil watched Mrs. Strunk stare at her coffee, wondering if she knew that every forced therapy session and every talk about an allowance backed her husband, step by step, into a corner. All of Ken Strunk's life was under her complete control. He was inadequate at home; Sandra Paine was his way to regain some power. A twelve-year-old has no expectations, only devotion. Strunk might have been happy to see Melissa killed if it meant that he could keep Sandra.

Gil watched Manny Cordova through the two-way glass. Cordova was surrounded by people—his lawyer, a district attorney, Pollack, and a state police officer Gil didn't recognize. He looked scared.

The search of the Strunks' home had been almost over when the call came that Cordova's lawyer had finally made it through the storm. Pollack had wanted to go lights and sirens back to the state police station, but Gil had talked him out of it.

On his side of the window, Gil was joined by three state police officers, another DA, and Chief Kline, who watched impassively through the glass as the two lawyers jockeyed. Cordova's lawyer wanted a deal. The DA wanted to hear what Manny had to say. Their fight made Gil happy that he'd dropped out of law school.

Ten minutes later, it was all sorted out. Manny Cordova would tell what he knew, and for his testimony the DA would drop some of the charges.

"Tell us what happened, Manny," was how Pollack started.

"Last week, on Thursday, I was at the mall when I ran into Melissa Baca. She and I dated a few years ago. She . . ." He stopped and rubbed his eyes. When he continued, his voice was tired. "I had just gotten off work, so I was in uniform. She stopped me and we got into an argument."

"What were you fighting about? The time you beat her up?" the female DA said scornfully.

"I didn't beat her up." Manny's voice went up an octave. "I sort of just lightly slapped her. Just once. Not a hard slap. That's it. I didn't mean to. I was just trying to show her that I was angry. . . ."

"Weren't you angry when you met her at the mall? Did you

hit her again?" the DA asked. Pollack was staring at her, hard, but she was ignoring him. The DA was new; Gil had never met her before. He didn't even know her name. She had long brown hair and was about thirty. Her gray suit seemed not to fit her.

Cordova's voice shook when he said, "Ma'am, I never . . ." Manny's lawyer reached out a hand to calm him. Manny took a rough breath. "I love Melissa. I've always loved her. Maybe you can't see that, but I did."

The DA snorted.

Pollack clearly had had enough of her questioning. He said, "Officer Cordova, please, if you could just continue with your story."

Manny looked sideways at the DA before saying, "When she saw me in my uniform she got upset. She said she was going to report me. She said it was wrong for a police officer with a history of violence to be out serving the public, or something like that." Gil nodded. That sounded like Melissa Baca. She would do the right thing and tell the police advisory committee that Officer Manny Cordova had hit her three years ago.

Manny continued. "I tried to talk her out of it, but she wouldn't listen. I tried calling her and stopping by the house, but she wouldn't see me. On Monday, I saw her driving down Cerrillos Road, so I pulled her over at Oñate Park."

"You used your police vehicle in the commission of a crime?" the DA asked. She sounded like she was trying to think up new charges.

Pollack, ignoring her, said, "About what time was this, Officer Cordova?"

"About eight fifteen P.M. She got out of her car and we started talking. I tried talking her out of turning me in. I tried to tell her she was overreacting, but she wouldn't listen. . . ." His jaw was clenched; his hands, not knowing where to go, went everywhere as he talked.

"So you hit her?" the DA asked.

Manny nodded. He wiped his eyes with his fingers and stared at the tears. "She fell backward and . . . and . . . I . . ."

"You choked her?" Pollack asked with a gentleness that surprised Gil.

Manny nodded again, not bothering to wipe away the tears anymore. They fell on his shirt, making dark spots. When he spoke, his voice was hard to understand. "She just stopped moving. I didn't know what to do. She was just lying there and I didn't know what to do. She wouldn't move. . . ."

Pollack quietly prompted Manny. "What did you do next?"

Manny took a long breath. "I called Ron Baca. I knew he would be able to figure it out. He told me to call some guy named Ken Strunk and tell him that if he didn't help me, Ron would bring him up on statutory-rape charges."

"What did Strunk say?" Pollack asked over the voice of the DA, who was saying something about birds of a feather.

"Strunk didn't really want anything to do with it, but I told him there were pictures to prove he molested some girl and that if he helped us, we'd give them back to him," Manny said. His tears were starting to dry up.

"Did you see the pictures?" Pollack asked.

"No. Melissa showed them to Ron and told him that Strunk was dating one of her students. I guess she wanted Strunk arrested or something. When I called Strunk, I just repeated what Ron told me to."

"What happened next?" Pollack asked.

"That Strunk guy shows up fifteen minutes later, I guess about eight forty-five P.M., maybe a little bit earlier. We put Melissa . . ." Manny hesitated. "We put her in the trunk of his car. Ron told him to toss her off the bridge in Taos to make it look like a drug deal. And it got her out of our police district."

"And you went back on patrol?" Pollack asked.

"Yeah. I went to an alarm check."

"And Ron was at his mom's house fixing the washing machine when you called him?" A nod from Manny. "Whose idea was it to lie to Detective Montoya about seeing Melissa buy drugs the day she died?"

"Ron's. We did it to throw you guys off the track. He said it would be okay because we'd be getting Hector Morales off the streets. And we told the newspaper that she did drugs." The anonymous sources Lucy had tried to tell Gil about.

"Did you talk to Ron Baca again the night Melissa died?" Pollack asked. Gil was pretty sure he knew where Pollack was headed with the question.

"Don't you mean was murdered?" the DA said.

Manny answered Pollack. "I called Ron on his cell phone. I wanted to turn myself in to the state police and call the OMI, but he talked me out of it."

"What did he say?"

"He said he didn't think I should ruin my career over something that wasn't my fault."

"What time was the phone call?"

"About eleven thirty P.M. or so." Pollack looked directly at Gil through the two-way mirror. Gil knew what he was thinking: Cordova's call to Ron Baca on Monday night was the cell-phone call that Scanner Lady had overheard. Lucy was right.

"Manny, were you on patrol Tuesday night?"

"Yeah. A rookie was doing a ride-along with me." Which meant that he was with someone all night, making it impossible for him to have killed Scanner Lady.

"Manny," Pollack said, "why do you think Ron helped you get rid of Melissa's body?"

Without hesitating, Manny said, "Because Ron's a good friend. He's like my brother."

Taking a break from the questioning, Pollack and Gil stood in the parking lot of the state police station. Pollack had wanted to get as far away as possible from the DA. When they left the interview room, Gil had heard Pollack say to the DA,

"He's still a police officer," overlapped by the DA saying, "He's a cold-blooded killer."

Now, in the parking lot, Gil watched Pollack pace. Pollack was smarter than Gil had given him credit for. Much smarter. Pollack had purposely not asked Manny about Patsy Burke's killing. If he had, the defense would have known that there were more charges to be added against Manny, and they would have ended his confession.

Plus, their case for Mrs. Burke's murder was weak. The sheriff's deputies had recovered very little physical evidence at the crime scene. If they told Manny Cordova's lawyer about it now, before they had a chance to question Ken Strunk or Ron Baca, they would ruin their chances of making the case.

"We have got to find Ron Baca. It was him, wasn't it?" Pollack asked. Gil nodded. He knew what Pollack was talking about: Ron Baca had killed Patsy Burke. There was no one else left. Manny had been paired with a rookie cop Tuesday night. Strunk had been at the hospital with his wife. That left Ron.

"But how the hell did Ron know that Mrs. Burke was what's-her-name—this Scanner Lady that editor told you about? How did he know that Mrs. Burke was the one who overheard their cell-phone call? He couldn't have known her name. Dammit. How did he know to kill her?" Pollack said, kicking at a gum wrapper on the ground. "But I'm starting to think Ron Baca is a goddamn genius. He gets Cordova to call Strunk and gets Strunk to toss Melissa's body, and the whole time Ron's playing fix-it man at his mom's. This guy is good. He had no real involvement. We can't really prove a goddamn thing. All we have is that maybe he planted the drugs in Melissa's car."

Adam Granger had called back while they were interviewing Manny Cordova to confirm that the dirt on the syringe in Melissa's car could have come from the Bacas' backyard. Gil figured that Ron had planted the syringe and heroin in Melissa's car after leaving his mother's house. But Granger admitted that the dirt had very few unusual characteristics, so it could have come from more than a dozen places in Santa Fe—something any good defense lawyer would point out. Or Melissa could have simply dropped the needle in her yard before putting it in her car.

Pollack continued his rant. "If we're really lucky, we can get Ron Baca on accessory for Melissa's murder. But as it stands, with the evidence we have right now, we're looking at conspiracy. A goddamn conspiracy charge. He gets out in time for the Super Bowl next year—hell, he may not even do time—and Manny Cordova gets to rot behind bars."

"How many guys do you have out looking for Ron Baca?" Gil asked.

"Pretty much everybody we could scrape up."

"How about a search warrant on Ron's trailer and his car?"

"We're working on it." Pollack started snapping again. "You know, I get why Cordova did it. I get why Strunk did it. I just don't get Ron Baca. I mean, he helped his sister's killer clean up. He must really be a helpful kinda guy. How does Manny's conversation with him go: 'Hey, Ron, I'm really sorry, dude, I killed your sister. Can you give me a hand?' "

Gil thought he might ask Mrs. Baca to explain it.

Lucy flipped through stacks of pictures in the photo department at the *Capital Tribune.* She had been searching for ten minutes but still hadn't come across the photo of Scanner Lady that Mrs. Schoen had dropped off. The newsroom was deserted. It was late Saturday afternoon. No one would be in for hours yet. It had taken her a while to get used to a newsroom that basically shut down on the weekend, but Santa Fe was a small town. The newspaper didn't need to have a staff twenty-four/seven.

She finally found the photo five minutes later in a mailbox marked TO BE ARCHIVED. The picture showed Patsy Burke sitting at a kitchen table with three other women, playing what looked like a card game. Oh, that's right. Mrs. Schoen had said they had a bridge team. Mrs. Schoen sat across from Patsy Burke, smiling into the camera. Lucy went into the darkroom and got out a photo-magnifying glass. She peered at the face of Patsy Burke. Lucy had remembered right. Scanner Lady's eyes were brown. Her hair was full gray. Lucy frowned. She had thought that Mrs. Burke's hair was darker. Maybe she had dyed it recently. Lucy flipped the photo over to see if the date was written on the back. It wasn't—but the names of the other players were. It took a second for the names to jar Lucy's memory. When they did, she almost had to keep herself from yelling out.

She felt the need to batter her head against something. She had been the worst type of racist—someone who believes she's not a bigot but still completely buys into the ethnic stereotypes. She had assumed that the bridge club Mrs. Schoen mentioned was made up of all Anglo women. Hispanic women don't play bridge, right? Her and her stupid southern mentality. *Idiot, idiot, idiot.*

Lucy glanced again at the picture on the desk. A smiling Patsy Burke sat across from her bridge partner, a smiling Claire Schoen. And seated between them were two women Lucy had never met, but she knew their names. An unsmiling Veronica Cordova sat across from her partner, a smiling Maxine Baca.

As Lucy dialed Claire Schoen's number, she knew that she should have been calling the sheriff's office or Detective Montoya. But that meant having to endure long conversations with them and the hope that they would call her back and tell her what Mrs. Schoen had said. It meant waiting. She couldn't wait. Mrs. Schoen picked up on the third ring and Lucy asked her about the bridge club.

"Well, yes, I told you we were widows. I'm almost positive I said we were a bunch of police wives. All of our husbands were police officers. I said we were blue widows, right? I'm sure I did. That's what we call ourselves, you know. It's a dumb name, if you ask me, but all the other ladies liked it. Patsy wanted to get some kind of T-shirts made with that on it, navy blue with white lettering. I wanted turquoise because we were in Santa Fe."

"Have you ever played over at Mrs. Cordova's or Mrs. Baca's house?"

"Oh, yes, all the time. I feel so bad for Maxine, she just lost her daughter, Melissa, bless her heart."

"Did you ever meet Mrs. Cordova's or Mrs. Baca's sons?"

"Well, I met Manny Cordova. A police officer like his father was. And I met one of Maxine's boys, I don't remember his name, but he's a police officer, too, if you can believe it. You would think those women would have more sense than to let their boys be cops when their husbands got killed on the job."

"Was it common knowledge that Mrs. Burke listened to a police scanner?"

"Oh yes. Veronica's boy, Manny, used to tease her about it all the time. He'd say things like, 'You know, Mrs. Burke, every time I talk on my radio, I'll be thinking of you listening to me.' " Mrs. Schoen laughed. "That boy. What a clown."

"And everyone knew she called the newspapers?"

"Pat told anybody who would listen about it. She wouldn't shut up. She would go on and on when one of her stories was in the *Santa Fe Times*."

"But she also called the *Capital Tribune,* right?"

"I don't know. I know she had a subscription to the *Santa Fe Times.* She liked their classifieds."

While Pollack went back to finish interviewing Manny Cordova, Gil went to Mrs. Baca's. The police records officer called back as Gil was driving—Sandra Paine's arresting officers had been Kristen Valdez and Eduardo Cordova, a fifteen-year veteran of the force and no relation to Manny Cordova. One more loose end tied up.

Gil pulled up to the Baca house. There were four cars in

the driveway. More company that Mrs. Baca didn't want. An unknown relative let him in the front door without asking who he was. There were a few people in the living room. Veronica Cordova appeared at his side.

"Detective Montoya, I need to talk to you," she said. "I've been waiting for you. The police have *mi hito* and won't tell me why. They just keep saying, 'We'll call you when we know something.' "

"Mrs. Cordova, there's nothing I can do. It's a state police investigation."

"But you know what's going on?" Her voice was quiet and full of tension. She kept glancing around the room to make sure no one could hear them. "You have to tell me. He didn't do anything. You know him. You know he'd never do anything. He's a good boy."

"Mrs. Cordova, I can't discuss it. The state police will call you when they know more. You should go home."

He went to Mrs. Baca's room. She was on the bed and looked like she was asleep, but Gil knew that she wasn't. Her breathing wasn't right.

He called her name. She didn't move.

He walked over to the shrine to Daniel. He counted fifteen pictures of Daniel; the last one showed him at about age eighteen. Someone had added a framed picture of Melissa to the shrine since Gil had last been there. It was the one that Gil had seen of Melissa with her father. Now all the dead people in the Baca family had their pictures on the shrine.

He turned back to Mrs. Baca.

"Mrs. Baca, I need to know about Ron and Melissa."

She mumbled something. Gil had to crouch down to hear her.

"Mrs. Baca, I didn't hear you. I need to know about Ron and Melissa."

He heard her more clearly this time when she said, "Melissa and who?"

"Melissa and Ron." Mrs. Baca didn't answer. He said more loudly, "Ron, your son." She still didn't answer.

Someone said from the doorway, "What do you want to know?" He looked up at Veronica Cordova. She was more composed now.

"I want to know about Ron. How did he and Melissa get along?"

"I'll tell you if you get the state police to let me see my son."

"Mrs. Cordova, I can't promise anything. . . ."

"Just ask them. I just want you to ask them if I can see him."

Gil nodded. He would ask Pollack, but he knew what the answer would be.

Mrs. Cordova sighed. "I've known Ron all his life, and I can tell you how he was with Melissa. They hardly ever talked to each other."

"How did Ron get along with Daniel?"

"He didn't. The two of them fought like you wouldn't believe. They would get into fistfights out in the street."

"What did they fight over?"

"Everything since the day they were born. I truly thought those boys would kill each other someday. When they were done, I would clean them up so Maxine wouldn't see. I hate to speak ill of the dead," she crossed herself twice and whispered, "but Daniel started the fights. He once pushed Ron through a window because he didn't like how Ron was eating."

Her voice went back to normal as she said, "After Daniel died, things got better. Ron stayed at our house mostly and shared Manny's room. Maxine wasn't . . . Maxine wasn't able to take care of him."

"How long did Ron stay with you?"

"Almost two years. He would try to go home every once in a while, but Maxine would forget to make him meals, so then he would come back. After Melissa was born, Maxine tried to take care of him, but she couldn't handle a new baby and a teenager, so he came back here." Mrs. Cordova seemed not to be watching her words around Mrs. Baca.

"How did he act around Melissa?"

"I never really saw them together. He was fourteen when she was born. He had moved out on his own by the time he was eighteen. He always said . . ." Mrs. Cordova stopped and looked over at Mrs. Baca, on the bed.

"What did he always say, Mrs. Cordova?" Gil asked quietly.

She sighed. "Ron always said that Manny was his real brother . . . and . . ." She stopped again. Gil waited for her to finish. She said in a whisper, "He said that Melissa stole his mother and made her crazy."

Mrs. Baca moved on the bed; she sat up and stared at them. "I want you out of here. Get out," she said in a daze.

Mrs. Cordova started to go to her friend, saying, "Maxine, it's all right. . . ." But Mrs. Baca pushed her away. Mrs. Baca got to her feet and went to the shrine. She picked up her rosary beads and knelt, steadying herself on the altar. Mrs. Cordova knelt beside her. Gil looked at their two gray heads bent in prayer and wondered what would happen when Mrs. Baca found out that Manny Cordova had killed her daughter.

Gil went to Melissa's room and took his cell phone out of his pocket, intending to call Pollack to keep his promise to Mrs. Cordova. But just as he was about to punch in the number, his phone rang.

Lucy sat at her desk at work, tapping her foot against the floor, waiting for Gil to answer. He finally did, on the fourth ring.

"Hi, Gil. It's Lucy. I hope you don't mind, but I sweet-talked a police officer at the station into giving me your cell number."

"Not a problem. What's up?"

"Actually, a couple of things. I heard you're searching the principal's house?" Gil didn't answer right away. He was amazed that she knew about it already. He needed to stop being surprised so easily. It was all over the police scanner at work. She had been listening to the cops chatter about it while waiting for Gil to answer his phone.

She knew what Gil's silence meant. "Before you say it, this is all off the record, completely. Let me explain why I'm asking. Scanner Lady used to keep a log of all the calls she heard. Now that log is missing. The sheriff's department is thinking that the killer took the log, and I was just wondering if you knew to look for it at the principal's house."

"I didn't know about it, but I'm not in charge of the search. I'm sure the sheriff's department told the state police about it, but I'll check," Gil said, then added, "But Principal Strunk didn't kill Mrs. Burke. He was with his wife all night on Tuesday."

"Actually, I didn't think it was him, either. I think it was Ron Baca or Manny Cordova."

She explained to Gil about the bridge-club photo and talking to Mrs. Schoen.

Gil listened silently, then he said, "You told this—"

"Yes, I told all this to the sheriff's department. I called them right before I called you. You're getting predictable, Montoya. I think the mystery in our relationship is starting to fade," she said with a laugh.

She could almost hear his smile before he said, "Manny Cordova confessed to killing Melissa. They got into a fight at the park, and he started choking her—"

"The usual."

"And . . ." He stopped. "You know, the state police are going to have a press conference about this tomorrow morning. I'd feel more comfortable if you heard all this from them."

"Goddammit, Gil." Now she was pissed. She let her anger get the better of her. "Has a single word you've told me gotten into the paper? *Has it?* I've been nothing but straight with you. Are you ever going to trust me?"

"I think we should just stick to discussing the facts of the case in which you were directly involved," Gil said, his voice never breaking from its monotone.

"Fine. Whatever." He was such a cop. His skin probably felt like a polyester uniform. "So what can you tell me about Patsy Burke's murder? Please make sure to speak clearly so my tape recorder catches it all."

He ignored her sarcasm. "We're fairly certain Ron Baca killed Mrs. Burke. Manny Cordova had another officer with him all night Tuesday, so he couldn't have done it. But Officer Cordova did admit that he made a cell-phone call to Ron on Monday night right about the time Mrs. Burke said she heard it."

Lucy had thought that when she finally had concrete confirmation that she wasn't crazy—that she had been right in believing Scanner Lady's death was connected to Melissa Baca's—something would happen inside her. But nothing did. She felt empty, sodden.

"Manny Cordova was standing right next to you and me at the station when we talked about Scanner Lady and the cell-phone call she overheard," Gil said.

"Which one was Manny?"

"He was sitting on the desk next to mine. He's kinda stocky; short, like you."

"I'm not short. I'll have you know I'm the tallest person in my pygmy tribe," she said with no humor in her voice, more to annoy him than as a joke. She was still mad.

Gil didn't take the bait. "Manny Cordova and Ron Baca both knew that Patsy Burke was Scanner Lady."

"I seem to be the only person who didn't know. . . ."

Gil continued. "So, Manny Cordova tells Ron Baca that Patsy Burke overheard their cell-phone call—"

"And Ron kills Patsy Burke because maybe it's only a matter of time before she recognizes his voice. Maybe he's afraid she'll mention it to his mom at one of the bridge-club get-togethers. He takes the log from her house, probably burns it,"

Lucy said. It was so much supposition. So much guesswork. "But, of course, you realize what the problem is, Gil?"

"Yeah, I know. Ron killed her, and we can't prove it. At least not yet. But now we know that he knew Patsy Burke. It's a start. And if he confesses . . ."

"He won't. He's been so smart. He just shuts up and all they can get him on is accessory for Melissa's murder, right? And he never gets convicted for Patsy Burke's murder. How many years is that?"

"Actually, we're not sure we can get Ron on accessory. We might only be able to manage a conspiracy charge. That's a fourth-degree felony. I think the standard time is eighteen months; but he's a cop with no priors, so I'd say he gets probation."

Maxine stood in the doorway of Melissa's bedroom. Detective Montoya's back was to her as he talked on the phone. "Ron killed her, but we can never prove it." The rest of the conversation hadn't made any sense to her. She had heard only Detective Montoya's half of it. "Ron killed her, but we can never prove it."

She gripped the doorjamb. She seemed to be moving, floating. She held on tighter.

Someone was talking to her, but she couldn't let go. The voice got louder and someone touched her elbow. They took her arm, and she let go of the doorjamb; she knew she would float away. The person guided her down the hallway and put her in a chair.

Maxine heard Detective Montoya in the kitchen, filling a glass with water. She smoothed the armrests of the chair and wondered where the keys to her car were.

CHAPTER SIXTEEN

Saturday Night

Ron Baca flipped through the notebook, looking for calls he had gone to. There was one about a woman getting slapped by her granddaughter. He had been to that one. Mrs. Burke only wrote down calls about kids and old people.

The writing in the notebook was that old-lady writing, like his mother's. It was hard to read. He flipped the notebook shut. He would dump it tomorrow.

He got a Coke from the fridge and peered out the corner of the kitchen window. It was starting to get dark. He could leave soon and go check on his mom. He'd take only back roads.

On Monday, he would show up back at work. By then the state police would have busted Hector Morales or some other drug dealer for Melissa's killing. He was only a little worried that Manny hadn't called to check in. He was probably still on patrol and sticking to the rules: no calling from cell phones. That was how they had gotten into this mess. Well, part of it, anyway.

At one point, he had thought about having Manny take Melissa's jewelry off her so that they could plant it at Hector Morales's house. But too many things could have gone wrong.

He wondered again where Melissa had hidden the Polaroids of Sandra Paine. When he was supposed to be fixing the dishwasher, he had looked through everything in Melissa's bedroom twice. He'd never found them. But even if they were found, it wouldn't be a huge problem—for him, anyway. At most the photos might lead the police to Strunk. But no one knew that Melissa had shown the photos to him. His fingerprints weren't on them. He had been careful not to touch the pictures when she showed them to him at McDonald's. At the time, he had been doing it to preserve evidence. He'd planned to bring it up to his boss the next morning. He had tried to talk Melissa into giving him the photos, but she wouldn't turn them over until she had a promise that the girl would be put into some kind of therapy. That had been so like Melissa.

He picked up Mrs. Burke's notebook and went with it into the kitchen, trying to decide how to get rid of it. Mrs. Burke had recognized him as Maxine's son and invited him inside, never asking him why he'd come to her back door. He had only wanted to talk to her, maybe scare her a little so that she wouldn't tell his mom about his cell-phone call with Manny. Afterward, he'd thought about taking her TV and VCR, to make it look more like a robbery. But the problem was getting rid of it. He had taken her log of scanner calls, just to be on the safe side. He hadn't realized until he got home that Mrs. Burke hadn't written down his cell-phone call to Manny that she'd overheard.

He was itching to get out of the trailer and go find his mom. She really needed him. He was the only one left.

The police scanner on the kitchen table started to beep. Santa Fe dispatch was paging out one of the volunteer fire-and-rescue crews. Somewhere on US 84/285 there had been an accident. He listened as the volunteers called in.

A noise outside made him jump. Someone was on the front steps. He reached for his Smith & Wesson.

Gil watched Mrs. Baca go into the mobile home before he could stop her.

He had left her sitting in her living room while he had gone in search of a glass of water, hoping that it would snap her out of her stupor. By the time he'd gotten back to the living room with the water, she had left. He had gone out the front door, thinking that she might be getting some air, just in time to see her pull away in her car. He had twisted his ankle on the curb as he ran to his car to catch up with her.

He followed her through town, with his ankle aching every time he pushed on the brake or the gas pedal, wondering if he should stop her. He decided that the best thing was to find out where she was going. She was driving slowly, as if she wasn't used to being behind the wheel. He followed her for about five minutes as they went down side streets, away from the busy roads.

Gil was about a block behind her when she pulled into a mobile-home park and up to an old trailer. It wasn't Ron's trailer. This mobile home had weeds growing snugly next to it. Gil checked the address in his map book. It sounded familiar. Then he realized—it was Daniel's. The family must have kept it. Mrs. Baca had known where Ron was the whole time.

Gil tried to get out of his car to stop Mrs. Baca from going inside, but his ankle gave way under him. He was close enough to hear the trailer door shut behind her.

He was on the radio, calling for backup, when he heard two loud pops inside.

He ran down the street, gun in his hand, holding his body-armor vest and trying not to put any weight on his ankle. As he stopped in front of the trailer, he heard the police radio—dispatch was sending out three backup units. But the sound hadn't come from his own radio. It had come from the trailer. Gil strained his ears. He heard the muffled sounds of a police scanner somewhere inside the mobile home. Now Ron knew that they were coming. But it didn't change things. Gil still had to get inside.

As Gil put on his vest, he looked around the corner and

slowly made his way to the front door. He glanced along the side of the trailer, looking for a back door. There was one, but it had no steps leading down. A person would have to jump about four feet to get to the ground. Gil decided that he would have one of the incoming officers stationed there as he moved to the front of the trailer. Gil wanted to get into position while he waited for his backup and make sure that Mrs. Baca was all right.

Gil reached the front door and, crouching low and to the side, turned the knob. It was unlocked. He pushed the door open with his foot, expecting Ron to shoot or at least to make a run for it, but nothing happened. No noise inside. He looked behind him and to the sides of the trailer, wondering if Ron had gone out a window.

"Ron," Gil called inside. "It's Gil Montoya. I'm here to help."

No answer.

"Ron, I just want to make sure your mom's okay."

No answer.

"Mrs. Baca, can you hear me?"

Nothing.

"Mrs. Baca, if you can hear me, please make a noise."

Silence.

He called out a few more times, but it was quiet. He heard the police scanner inside, but nothing else. The silence made him even more edgy.

There wasn't a clear line of sight to the interior. All Gil could see through the open door was a brown-paneled hallway wall three feet away. He guessed that the living room was down the hallway to the right and a bedroom to the left, like the standard layout of a mobile home. He would have had to lean his head through the door to get a look in either direction. But Gil expected that Ron would be armed.

He would need another officer to provide cover to get through that door. One-man entry was against regulations. All he could do was wait. The way he was crouched was killing his ankle. He tried to focus on the door, to take his mind off the pain.

A patrol car pulled up. He signaled the officer—he didn't see who it was—to go around the trailer. Another officer appeared. He motioned her to him.

"We're going inside," he said to the officer. He thought her last name might be Lopez. She nodded, looking calm.

They went into the trailer, his adrenaline rush making the living room a blur of brown furniture. He could see into the open kitchen. On the linoleum floor was a growing puddle of blood. It was coming from Ron Baca, who was facedown on the tile with his Smith & Wesson still in his hand.

Mrs. Baca sat in a vinyl kitchen chair, her hands in her lap. An old police-issued revolver on the table next to her. She watched the blood as it oozed across the floor, fascinated.

"Mrs. Baca?" Gil asked. His gun still out. "Mrs. Baca, what happened?"

"He killed my baby," she said, still looking at the blood. "I heard what you said. You said he killed my baby."

Gil went to the table and pushed the gun away from her. He heard Lopez calling on her radio for an ambulance.

Lieutenant Pollack—the newspaper's one-and-only snitch—had called Lucy to ask if she would mind talking to him about Patsy Burke's death. As Pollack had said it, "We have combined the investigations of Melissa Baca and Patsy Burke."

It was getting dark, almost five thirty P.M., as she drove to the state police department.

Meeting Pollack would be interesting. She had this image in her head of a used-car salesman in a police uniform or a washed-up high-school football star. The kind of guy who needed glory; the kind of guy who got off on seeing his words in the newspaper.

She was two blocks from the police department when the EMT pager in her glove compartment went off, making her jump at the noise and swear out loud. Hadn't she turned that thing off? She frantically opened the glove compartment, throwing Taco Bell napkins everywhere. Where was it?

She found the pager and was trying to turn it off—where was the stupid switch?—when the dispatcher loudly gave the address of the call: only a few blocks away. Lucy took a deep breath. She should go to the call. Actually, she had to go to the call. She would prove to Gerald that she was a responsible adult if it killed her.

Lucy looked at her watch. Pollack had been up in the air about what time he wanted to talk to her, "Just sometime tonight" was the way he put it. He could wait a little while longer.

She was already shaking when she pulled up to the old mobile home behind the other emergency vehicles. *Take a deep breath,* she thought. *You were trained to do this. Sort of.*

She met Gerald Trujillo on the way in. He gave her his summary of the situation: "The patient is a seventy-six-year-old female named Phyllis Parker with respiratory problems," he said without animation. "She's perfectly fine, but we need to check her out."

"Cool," was all Lucy said. He could at least have smiled at her and said hello.

Inside, other paramedics were bent over an old woman in a La-Z-Boy. They were asking her questions, but she stubbornly wouldn't answer.

One of the medics was yelling, "Look, we just need some answers so we can help you better."

"Lucy, why don't you get a blood pressure," Gerald said. Hell. Was he trying to punish her?

She rooted around in the paramedic's medical bag, looking for a blood-pressure cuff and stethoscope. After a few seconds of watching her futile search, Gerald opened the front compartment of the bag and handed her the equipment. Damn.

She was trying. Honestly. She moved toward the woman to put the BP cuff on her, knowing full well that she had no clue what she was doing.

"Get the hell away from me," the woman said sharply to Lucy. "Not you. I want one of them to do it." The woman gestured toward the male paramedics.

Lucy stepped back, stunned. It took a second for her to realize what the old woman had said. For the first time, Lucy looked around the room. It was dingy and cluttered. The dark-paneled walls made it look cryptlike. The garbage can in the kitchen was overflowing and a dog was yapping behind a closed door. In the corner were stacks of *Capital Tribunes.* Next to a half-filled ashtray on an end table was a police scanner.

"Lucy," she heard Gerald say from somewhere across the room. "Lucy," he said again. Why was he yelling? She turned and saw that he was standing right next to her. "Earth to Lucy. Let's focus here," he said. She took a deep breath to steady herself. She gave Gerald the stethoscope and blood-pressure cuff, her hand shaking. He noticed, but he didn't comment. He probably just thought she was freezing up again. She took a few long, hard breaths as she watched him fasten the Velcro on the BP cuff around the woman's flabby upper arm.

Lucy stepped back toward the old woman and said, "Hi. You might remember me from the *Capital Tribune.* I'm Lucy Newroe. And you must be Scanner Lady."

It was almost six thirty P.M. by the time they had transported Scanner Lady to St. Vincent for treatment of chronic emphysema and bronchitis. Mrs. Parker wouldn't talk after Lucy told her that she was an editor at the *Capital Tribune.* But Lucy didn't need to hear her speak again. She was sure. She knew that voice.

During the ride to the hospital, Lucy busied herself with

putting away equipment in the ambulance so that she wouldn't have to think. If she thought, she might explode. Or more likely implode. She felt nothing. And she wanted to stay that way for as long as possible. She needed a drink. Hell, she needed a keg.

Lucy was in the hospital hallway, putting clean sheets on the gurney—making a bed, finally something she knew how to do—when she heard someone call her name. She looked up to see Gil limping toward her.

"Gil," she said, "what are you doing here? I was just going to call you." She watched him walk for a second before saying, "You're limping."

"I rode in with the paramedics. We brought Ron Baca in."

"Great, you found him. What happened? Did you beat him up?" She smiled as she tucked the sheet under the gurney's mattress.

"He's dead. His mother shot him."

"Oh my God," Lucy said. She stared at nothing on the tea-colored wall. Patsy Burke's killer was dead. But Patsy Burke wasn't her Scanner Lady. Patsy Burke was someone else's Scanner Lady. Lucy closed her eyes for a moment. She couldn't think about it. She couldn't.

"Is Mrs. Baca all right?" she asked.

Gil didn't answer; he just shook his head. They stood for a few moments more before he asked, "What are you doing here?"

"I brought in a patient," Lucy said. She felt the need to protect him from the truth. She would suffer for both of them.

Gil stared at her, his look unreadable, before saying, "Mrs. Baca overheard us on the phone when we talked before. She thought that when I said Ron had killed Mrs. Burke, I meant he had killed Melissa. She misunderstood. She thought her son killed her daughter. That's why she shot him."

Lucy moved to him and touched his arm. "Oh, Gil."

He reached out and brushed her hair out of her eyes.

They stood silently for a moment before she spoke. "It wasn't your fault, you know."

"It wasn't your fault either," he said intently.

"If only I believed that." She turned and walked down the hallway, pushing the gurney to the ambulance bay doors. Outside, the dark sky was low with clouds.

Gil was opening the front door of his house when he heard someone in the kitchen say, "I was just getting ready to go to bed." Susan sat at the table in her nightgown, her calculator and a few bills cluttering the tabletop.

Gil sat heavily in the chair opposite hers. She opened the refrigerator, grabbed a beer, and set it down in front of him. "You look like you could use one," she said.

Gil took a swig. "What are you doing up?"

"Waiting for you," she said, punching a few numbers on the calculator. "Your mom called and wondered when you were coming over. I told her that you couldn't make it tonight. I figured you were too busy at work."

"Thanks," he said. He watched Susan as she went back to clicking at her calculator. "The Melissa Baca case is over," he said, realizing that he was hoping she would ask him about it.

"Good. You could use a break. You should see if you can get Monday off."

He stood up, planning to take the beer with him as he changed into his pajamas, but he stopped at the door. "We should take the girls to Bandelier Park tomorrow. It's been a long time since we've been there."

"Joy was just there a few days ago, and besides, the girls and I are going clothes shopping."

"I think we should do something together as a family." He tried to make it sound unimportant.

Susan looked at him curiously before saying, "Okay. I'll make some sandwiches."

Gil took his beer off to bed.

It was almost eight thirty P.M. when Lucy made it to the state police station. After leaving Gil standing in the hospital hallway, she'd gone and sat in the ambulance. Gerald had found her there. They'd ridden back to her car in silence.

Now she sat in the state police station, waiting. She didn't know what she would tell Pollack. She couldn't possibly tell him the truth. The truth would leave her too exposed. She would have to lie. She just didn't know what she would lie about. Anything. Everything.

She got up and paced in front of the blue metal chairs in the hallway where she'd been told to wait. She couldn't do this. She wouldn't. Someone else could tell her story. She was done.

She walked out of the police station, got into her car, and went home. She opened her front door and, without turning on the lights, went into her bedroom. She dropped into bed, fully clothed.

Sleep came fast, but it was laced with strange dreams about barking dogs that turned into babies who could talk. She eventually gave up, annoyed. Not knowing what else to do, and scared to be left with her thoughts, she dressed again and got back into her car.

As she took the highway out of Santa Fe, it started to snow lightly, the clouds obscuring the view of the mountains in the early light. Snow. She was too tired to be scared of driving in it.

She knew that she should call Pollack, to tell him why she had flaked out. She knew that she should call the newspaper, to let them know that the Melissa Baca case had been solved. She glanced at her cell phone on the passenger seat. She picked it up and switched it off, tossing it into the backseat. She heard it clunk its way down to the floor. The state police would hold a press conference about it in a few hours. The newspaper could find out then.

No one would care that Mrs. Burke's murder would never be solved. The state police would close the case in a day or two and never officially announce that Ron Baca had been the killer. "He's dead," they would say. "What purpose does it serve to charge him with Mrs. Burke's murder?"

Lucy took the turnoff to Chimayó and pulled up in front of the santuario. There was only one other car in the parking lot. Tourists don't do cold, snowy, Sunday mornings. The church looked hollow and somber. She noticed for the first time that all the windows had security bars on the outside, a twentieth-century theft deterrent on a 1700s church. A hard reminder of how the village of Chimayó had become a camp for black-tar-heroin dealers. She walked into the dimly lit church, past the pews. The church was darker than usual because of the clouds outside. The badly painted white walls did little to brighten it. She felt like the carved black vigas on the ceiling were reaching for her head. She quickly went to the front of the church. She didn't genuflect or bow in front of the altar as she passed it, not knowing how to do it, convinced that she would trip if she tried.

She squeezed through a low door and stopped. She was in a room crammed full of leg braces and crutches, discarded by those who had been healed. Statues of Jesus and saints she couldn't name were everywhere.

She went through a smaller door, into the tiny back room with the holy dirt. Weak light streamed through a small window. A crucifix wrapped in blue satin had been placed in a glass box with a kneeler in front of it.

Squatting in front of a hole in the ground, she scooped up a handful of the sandy dirt, letting some of it slip though her fingers and fall back into the hole. She stared at the dirt in her hands for a moment before she began to rub it all over herself—

in her hair and on her face and her clothes. Bowing her head, she felt the dirt run down her back. She closed her eyes but nothing would come. Praying was not something she knew how to do. "Oh, hell," she said out loud, to no one. She laughed at herself, the sound muted by the old adobe walls. Then she started to cry, the tears skimming down her dirty cheeks.

ACKNOWLEDGMENTS

I would like to thank Anne Hillerman, Jean Schaumberg, the Tony Hillerman mystery writing contest, Peter Joseph, Thomas Dunne Books, and everyone at St. Martin's Press, for giving me the opportunity to bring my work to print.

I also wish to thank Kristen Davenport, Pat West-Barker, Annice Barber, and Angela Barber for always believing in me despite all evidence to the contrary; and the women and men of Agua Fria Fire and Rescue, the Santa Fe County Fire Department, the Santa Fe County Sheriff's Office, the city of Santa Fe Fire Department, and the city of Santa Fe Police Department, for putting their lives on the line every day to save ours.

Finally, to the editing staff at the *Santa Fe New Mexican* newspaper, I apologize profusely for the previous run-on sentence, which included the incorrect usage of a semicolon and the general mangling of AP style. You taught me better than that.